Record of Lodoss War
The Grey Witch

A hundred chosen heroes dared
challenge the deadly labyrinth. Most fell
within, their corpses gone cold—and yet
their light illuminated the abyss. Seven
heroes dared challenge the Demon God.
Six survived, and the world was saved.

Parn

Our hero. A young man from the village of Zaxon who believes in justice above all else. He worked as a mercenary, but after a disastrous battle decided to go on a journey of self-improvement. He inherited his sword and armor from his father.

RECORD OF
DRAMATIS

Deedlit

A high elf warrior who controls sprites and elementals. At 160 years old, she is the youngest of her tribe. Despairing at the slow decline of her people, she left her forest home to explore the world beyond. Dislikes dwarves.

Etoh

A priest of the Supreme God Pharis and Parn's childhood friend. Calm and serene yet strong-willed. He and Parn left to fight goblins near their home, but things took a turn for the worse...

LODOSS WAR
PERSONAE

Woodchuck

A middle-aged thief.
After a job in his
youth went wrong,
he was sentenced
to prison for over
twenty years.
He tends to joke,
but underneath
his jesting he is
actually a very
proud person.

Slayn

A wizard who
studied at the
Wizard Academy
in Allan before
moving to Zaxon
as a teacher. He
is always calm
and composed.
Searching for "his
star." Ghim is an
old friend.

Ghim

A craftsman from a dwarven settlement
north of the village of Tarba. Resilient
and reserved, he enjoys a good meal
and can hold his liquor. He left home in
search of a friend's daughter. Old friends
with Slayn.

Parn slowly stepped inside, already in a low, respectful bow—but when he raised his head, he couldn't believe his eyes. "K-Karla..." he groaned, trailing off into shocked silence.

RECORD OF
LODOSS WAR
The Grey Witch

RECORD OF LODOSS WAR: THE GREY WITCH
GOLD EDITION HARDCOVER

© Ryo Mizuno, Group SNE 1988, 2013
Illustrations by Yutaka Izubuchi

First published in Japan in 2013 by
KADOKAWA CORPORATION, Tokyo.
English translation rights arranged with
KADOKAWA CORPORATION, Tokyo.

TRANSLATION: Lillian Olsen
ADAPTATION: Rebecca Scoble
INTERIOR LAYOUT & DESIGN: Clay Gardner
COVER DESIGN: Nicky Lim
PROOFREADERS: Jade Gardner, J.P. Sullivan
LIGHT NOVEL EDITOR: Jenn Grunigen
PRODUCTION ASSISTANT: CK Russell
PRODUCTION MANAGER: Lissa Pattillo
EDITOR-IN-CHIEF: Adam Arnold
PUBLISHER: Jason DeAngelis
Seven Seas Entertainment

ISBN: 978-1-626925-70-0
PRINTED IN CANADA
FIRST PRINTING: NOVEMBER 2017
10 9 8 7 6 5 4 3 2 1

RECORD OF
LODOSS WAR
The Grey Witch

WRITTEN BY
Ryo Mizuno

ORIGINAL CONCEPT BY
Hitoshi Yasuda

ILLUSTRATIONS BY
Yutaka Izubuchi

Seven Seas Entertainment

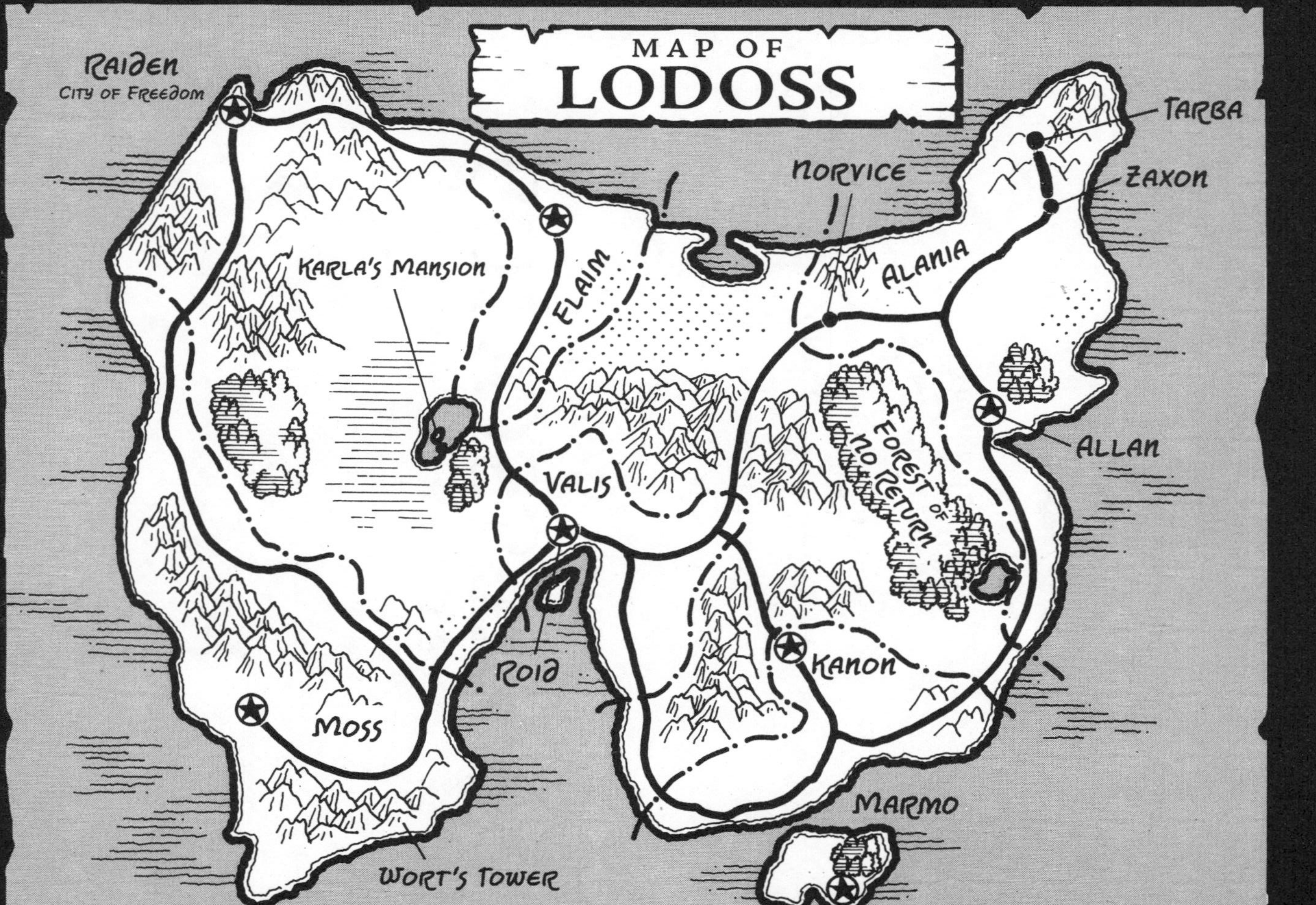
MAP OF
LODOSS
Raiden
City of Freedom
Karla's Mansion
Flaim
Valis
Roid
Moss
Wort's Tower
Norvice
Alania
Tarba
Zaxon
Allan
Forest of No Return
Kanon
Marmo

Table of Contents

CHAPTER I

The Adventurers

1

THE WHITE MARBLE WALLS OF THE GREAT TEMPLE OF Marfa shone brightly in the spring sunshine, welcome after the long winter. New grass peeked from the patches of snow that still lingered on the ground, and yellow wildflowers had started to bloom along the road from the temple to the village center.

The temple stood on the edge of Tarba village, northernmost point of Lodoss. A few hundred villagers led simple lives on the plains between the peaks of the White Dragon Mountains, home to the ice spirits that pushed spring later than in the southern regions. In a few days, though, the snow blocking the passes would melt, and young couples from all over the island would come to receive blessings from the goddess Marfa for happy marriages.

For Neese, the high priestess, the busy season was just beginning. She and her guest sat together at a small table in her private quarters. Neese was perched on a simple wooden chair and dressed in pure white robes embroidered with the sacred emblem of Marfa, the goddess of all creation. Her long, black hair had turned to grey, and deep wrinkles etched her fifty years' experience into her face, but her posture and bearing radiated vitality.

"You're leaving on a journey?" she asked her visitor with rare uncertainty.

"I am," he replied gruffly from his seat across from her. He was stocky and half as tall as an average man, with a disproportionately large head and a neatly trimmed grey beard—a dwarf, one of the fae folk of the earth. His skin was tanned from the glare of the sun reflecting off the snow, and his amber-colored eyes showed fierce determination.

"Why?" Neese asked, rising from her chair and kneeling beside the dwarf to look into his eyes. She lay her hands on his shoulders.

"No reason. I want to, that's all," he said in typical blunt fashion.

Neese knew the dwarves well. It was said that their hearts were made of iron—and that their stubborn streak was what gave these seemingly clumsy fae folk such incredible skills as craftsmen. This particular dwarf was a fine artisan who could transform rough gemstones into brilliant jewels, precious metal into glittering ornaments.

She knew the dwarves, and she knew this dwarf in particular. Once Ghim had decided on something, he would never change his mind.

"If this is about Leylia, it isn't necessary. I gave up on her long ago." she said, but her pained expression betrayed her.

If she ever felt her age, it was when she thought of her daughter. Leylia had disappeared seven years previous—signs of a struggle had been found at the temple, evidence that she'd fought an intruder and been taken away.

Neese had been gone at the time, called to heal Ghim after an accident in the dwarven mines left him gravely injured. Leylia's absence broke Neese's heart, but the old dwarf's guilt might have been even greater. Ever since the incident, Ghim came to the shrine to help out every chance he could.

Ghim didn't answer. Dwarves never lied—they simply fell silent.

"It wasn't your fault, Ghim. How can you feel responsible for the timing of that attack? Not even the gods can know the future completely—how can we mortals expect to know more?" Neese offered a smile, but Ghim didn't break his stony silence. "I've asked the goddess Marfa about her many times—where she is and whether she's alive or dead…" She paused, thinking back to the response she'd received every time.

"What did Marfa say?" Ghim ventured.

"It wasn't an answer, really. More of a riddle. She said that Leylia is alive, but doesn't exist."

"Alive, but doesn't exist?" Ghim cocked his head in puzzlement and watched Neese's doleful expression. He'd met her way back when she first arrived at the temple—beautiful and wise, radiating inner strength and kindness. She had collected an impressive array of titles: she was a Saint, one of the Six Heroes who defeated the Demon King during the Demon Wars, the Earth Mother Goddess's beloved daughter, and the Dragon Tamer, to name a few. But despite all that, there was no arrogance to her, and she dealt with everyone equally. She loved to see the dwarven workshops, and she often visited the Iron Kingdom, the dwarven settlement closest to Tarba. Even the grumpiest dwarf couldn't help but smile when talking to her.

But her radiance had clouded since Leylia went missing.

Of course he knew that her disappearance wasn't his fault. But he also knew that he had to go look for her. He owed Neese so much. He would never be at peace while she was suffering.

The thought was always in the back of his mind, but he also knew there was no point in searching aimlessly. But circumstances had recently changed—he had a clue, now. Someone from the settlement had just returned from a journey and reported that he'd seen a woman who looked just like Leylia—only ten days earlier in the town of Allan, not far from Tarba. Ghim didn't hesitate for a moment before making up his mind.

"I'm not a thinking dwarf, but I trust my strength. I can't solve your riddle, but dragging your prodigal daughter back home shouldn't be a difficult task."

Neese felt her eyes mist over. The dwarf was always so gruff and serious, but inside his iron heart, deep passion stirred. All dwarves revered the truth and thought nothing of risking their lives for a cause.

She sat silently for a while, almost starting to speak several times before trailing off into silence. Finally, she shook her head.

She closed her eyes and clasped Ghim's hand in hers. "Thank you. Please bring Leylia home."

Ghim's eyes crinkled in delight. "Just leave it to me. I promise I'll bring her back. The Goddess's strange riddle will be solved by then, I'm sure," he said with vigor.

Neese gently hugged the dwarf's solid frame with her thin arms. "When are you leaving?"

"I'll stop by the settlement, then leave at once from there."

"The journey will be dangerous. Not like it was in my youth, but all the same—be careful." Neese's travels had been during a time of great death and destruction, when demons sealed in the Deepest Labyrinth had been released to wreak havoc throughout the land. She'd been revered as a Hero—one of the six who had saved the country—after the defeat of the Demon King, but that title meant nothing to her. She only cared that humanity was flourishing on Lodoss again.

"Thank you, Priestess of Marfa. And do me a favor, will you? Pray that I'll be able to solve this riddle and bring your daughter back. Praying's not my job."

"Where are you going?"

"To Zaxon, for now. There's only one road, after all, and I've got a friend called Slayn living there. I haven't figured out the rest yet. The path will lead me, I'm sure."

A few hours later, the dwarf craftsmen took his first steps down the road. Thick, grey clouds covered the sky above his destination to the south.

2

LODOSS WAS A REMOTE ISLAND A FORTNIGHT'S VOYAGE south of the Alecrast continent. The voyage was long and perilous enough that there was little sea traffic between the two landforms—only occasional merchant galley ships from Raiden, the free city northwest of Lodoss. Some people on the continent called Lodoss "The Cursed Island," and it was true that there were some ominous places there that lived up to that title: The Forest of No Return, The Storm and Fire Desert, and Marmo, The Island of Darkness. Underground labyrinths crawled with loathsome monsters, and the God of Darkness, Phalaris, had a dedicated following. The Demon Wars thirty years prior had terrorized the island, and it had taken an alliance of elves, dwarves, and humans to drive the demons back into their underground prison. The scars from the battle had healed and peace had returned, but tales from those days had forever stained the island's reputation.

The ordinary people of Lodoss, however, didn't think much about what outsiders thought of their island. Daily life held more than enough problems for anyone.

The island of Lodoss was divided into kingdoms. The most powerful was the Kingdom of Moss in the southwest, unified after the Demon Wars by Mycen, a Dragon-Knight-turned-King. The original countries had been fiercely independent and fought amongst themselves constantly, until foreign threats united them. Then the fractured kingdoms, each named for a different body part of a dragon, came together under Mycen, the king of Highland, the Dragon's Eye. Mycen's heir was a Dragon Knight named Jester, and he and the twelve Dragon Knights who served him were the central pillars of Moss. Thus, he came to be known as "Mycen, the Golden Dragon King." When Mycen passed away, Jester inherited his name, his title, and the golden dragon he used to ride.

At the center of the island lay Valis, the Holy Kingdom of Justice. It was ruled over by Fahn, one of the Six Heroes. Most people there worshipped the supreme god Pharis, so the Order of Pharis held power. Rule over Valis was not passed down through blood. Instead, the new king ascended to the throne after being nominated by the Order from among the Holy Knights and royal guardians of the kingdom. Religious commandments from the order were also made law.

North of Valis was Flaim, the desert kingdom, a nation that rose from the recent defeat of local barbarians. The desert people were brave, and their mercenary king and founder—Kashue— was widely respected. The land was harsh, but the young country was vibrant with hope.

Kanon, in the southeast, was ruled by a scholar king. It was known for its natural beauty and temperate climate.

To the south lay the feared Dark Island of Marmo, home to monsters and exiled criminals. For years, the land had been ruled only by chaos, until a warrior called Beld declared himself Emperor and brought the entire island under his rule. He'd spent most of his ten years of leadership ruthlessly crushing every rebellion that sprung up. In recent times, Marmo appeared peaceful—at least on the surface.

Alania, in the north, was a center of culture and history. The citizens took great pride in their stone buildings and the marble dwarven-built castle.

Within Alania, there was a small village nestled in the mountains of the peninsula north of Allan, the capital city. This village was called Zaxon, and its inhabitants led simple lives far from the culture and bustle of the capital.

That village was dealing with a serious problem...

"I told you—I'm going to *destroy* them!"

Good Reunions, the only pub in Zaxon, thundered with the pounding of an armored fist on a table, and wooden goblets spilled their contents everywhere.

A young man stood in the back of the crowded room. He wore plate mail and a longsword at his hip—a sword with a long grip to allow the wielder to hold it two-handed. He had a thick iron shield strapped to his back; all he needed was a helmet, and he'd look like a fine knight. But his breastplate bore no crest, only a large scrape across the chest.

"But Parn," Filmer, the village chief, replied, "you can't fix this by yourself. These are *goblins*—lots of them. I don't care how good a swordsman you are. You'll be outnumbered."

Parn glared back in disgust. He wasn't getting anywhere with this pack of cowards.

"That's why I'm asking for help! Like you said, I don't have a chance alone, or even with Etoh's help. But look around! If everyone here grabbed a weapon, we'd be invincible! Don't let a few goblins scare you—think about how it makes our village look not being able to handle this!" Parn scanned the crowd. The people at the tables all kept their heads down, avoiding his gaze.

A group of about twenty goblins had dug a cave in the hills close to Zaxon while isolated by the winter snow. Goblins were about the size of a human child, with reddish skin. Because of their skin tone, they were sometimes called "red ogres," but they were originally fae of the earth and soil. In the ancient wars of the immortals, they were summoned by the gods of darkness as their vanguard. The gods of both sides died at the end of the war, so the surviving goblins had no way to return to the fairies' realm—and no choice but to live primitive lives in the mountains and forests.

Humans and goblins could not live together—any contact between the two always ended in conflict. And while the goblins near Zaxon hadn't harmed the villagers in the three months since they'd arrived, it was only a matter of time—considering their evil reputation.

Parn had called on all the strong, healthy men of the village to help him mount a preemptive strike. They had more than thirty men, outnumbering the goblins. But as for their reaction…

"Nothing bad has happened yet. Maybe it never will. Why

risk our hides by provoking them? If we fail, they'll attack the village," someone muttered.

Parn looked at the man in dismay. It was Zamji, a hunter—Parn had been counting on his skill with a bow and arrow.

"Zamji, that's dangerous thinking." Parn replied. "You've heard the horror stories. You want to wait until that happens here? Defeating them *now* is our only option."

"But Parn…" This time it was Riot the woodcutter. Parn's spirits fell even lower—Riot was the strongest person in the village.

Others mumbled their objections—and not a single voice rose up to agree with him.

Parn smashed his fist into the table again. This time, the whole table flipped over with a thundering crash, alarming the pub's owner.

"Why don't you people *get* it?! My dad fought thirty bandits by himself. Don't you have a *tenth* of that courage?"

"We all know the story. Didn't your dad run into those bandits after he ditched his knight position? And he got himself killed, too," Moto, the owner of the general store, sneered. He and the pub's owner, Old Man Jet, were the town's gossip mongers.

Parn, whose face had been flushed with excitement, went pale.

"Wh-what did you say about my dad?!" Parn glared at the man with open hatred.

"I'm just repeating what I heard. If it's not true, then why was the crest of the Holy Knights scraped off your breastplate? Why did your mother have to leave Valis and settle out here in the country?"

Parn's hand went to his sword—the urge to charge Moto and chop his head off was almost overwhelming. But drawing his sword against a villager was clearly not the right thing to do.

"Fine," he muttered, and pulled his hand away from his weapon. "Etoh and I will handle it ourselves."

With that, he strode out, ramming the door into the wall as he left.

The villagers sat slumped in their seats until the metallic clanking faded away.

"They're not actually going to go alone, are they?" Riot whispered to Moto.

"He wouldn't be that reckless," Moto answered uncertainly. They all knew Parn. He would *absolutely* do foolish things in the name of justice.

The village chief listened to them talk for a while, then quietly announced the meeting over. He slipped out the door Parn had left open, toward the shack on the outskirts of the village.

3

PARN STORMED HOME AND VICIOUSLY KICKED OPEN the door. The floorboards creaked in protest as the metal studs of his sabatons made fresh divots in the wood.

"How'd it go, Parn?" a gentle voice asked from the back of the room.

"How do you *think* it went?!" Parn shouted at the smiling young man—Etoh the priest. Etoh wore a baggy, sun-bleached cotton robe with a blue sash at his waist. The silver amulet around his neck was the talisman of Pharis.

Etoh had been Parn's friend from childhood—his *only* friend, really. Both orphans, their similar circumstances brought them together despite their opposite personalities. Etoh was much more reserved and always thought carefully before he acted. But they shared the same steadfast resolve.

When he was ten, Etoh worked doing odd jobs for a mission-ary of Pharis. He was so impressed by the doctrine of justice and order that he decided to follow the missionary when he left, and was eventually accepted to study at Pharis Temple in Allan, the capitol. Once he completed his training and became an official priest, he returned to the village.

Etoh put his hand on his talisman and said a quick prayer to Pharis while he listened to Parn explode in anger.

"You can't blame them. They're not used to combat." Alania hadn't been at war for a hundred years—they were the only king-dom that had avoided major battles during the most recent war.

"But we can't handle a horde of goblins by ourselves," Parn re-plied. He sat heavily at the table and gulped water from the bag at his hip. It was warm and reeked of leather. With a sigh, he tossed the empty bag on the table, but he threw it too hard and it slid off the far edge. Etoh picked it up, folded it carefully, and placed it back on the table—like he'd done a thousand times before.

"We can't let the goblins roam free, either. We may be fine for now, but they'll be a threat someday." Etoh closed his eyes and raised his left hand as if preaching the words of Pharis. He didn't have his own temple, so any preaching he did was on the roadside or in the assembly hall. But he was an authentic priest nevertheless—he could cast holy spells, and even perform miracles like curing diseases or healing wounds. He was also trained in combat—conflicts between his Order and the kingdom meant that government guards wouldn't offer them protection, so they had their own Holy Knights for self-defense.

"Can we really do this alone? There are twenty of them—that's ten apiece." Master warriors might be able to slay ten goblins at once, even twenty or thirty. But Parn knew his skills weren't at that level yet.

"There might be a way..." Etoh muttered thoughtfully, and Parn knew better than to interrupt. When he was with Etoh, it wasn't his job to think—a warrior's job was to improve his skills and slay his enemies.

At last, Etoh turned to Parn. "I don't think it's a very good plan..."

Parn grinned. "You've got a plan?" he said. "Sounds good—let's do it!"

Slayn Starseeker's house lay north of Zaxon. He'd moved in two years prior and quickly endeared himself to the villagers by teaching reading and writing.

He was also famously eccentric. His small house was cluttered with books, and the shelves of his cupboards were laden with herbs and bottles of dried insects. He gazed at the stars at night, mumbling to himself. All in all, he simply just *stood out*. Because of that, most people were friendly to Slayn but kept him at a distance. He didn't get many visitors.

Except for that day—when he had *two*. Filmer, the village chief, was surprised to see that someone else was already there— and doubly so when he realized that the guest wasn't human, but a dwarf.

The dwarf awkwardly introduced himself as Ghim while Slayn served him a flagon of ale, and remained still and silent while Filmer reported to Slayn what had occurred at the meeting—that Parn and Etoh had gone after the goblins alone, and couldn't Slayn do something?

"Goblins?!" Ghim cried suddenly. "How many of the filthy burglars are there? I'll chop them to bits!" At that, he grabbed the huge, double-edged axe propped against the wall. In his head-to-toe chain mail and sturdy helmet, he was utterly prepared for war.

Filmer nearly jumped out of his skin at the outburst, but Slayn barely batted an eye. "Goblins and dwarves have been enemies since ancient times," Slayn explained in a solemn tone while Filmer tried to regain his composure.

"They're thieves," Ghim growled. "They hoard beautiful jewels, but they don't even know how to appreciate them. Since the days of old, we've chopped off as many goblin heads as there are stars in the sky, but they *still* infest this place."

"There are infinite stars," Slayn gently reminded Ghim. "Luckily, there are only about twenty goblins here. Though that might be too many for Parn and Etoh. Did they really go off by themselves?"

The chief nodded, and Slayn gripped his chin, thinking, *This isn't surprising for Parn, but Etoh usually has a better head on his shoulders.*

"Youth is the bane of reason," Slayn mumbled to himself. "All right," he continued louder, "We cannot abandon two promising young people to their fate. I'm sure we can figure out a way to deal with twenty of the goblins."

"I swear upon my beard," snorted the dwarf as he slung his axe over his back.

"You'll go?" Filmer asked, visibly relieved. "Thank you both."

"Don't mention it. This village is my home, too." Slayn stood and grabbed a wooden staff that had been left leaning haphazardly against a wall. One end of the staff was strangely crooked and covered in mysterious writing—a Philosopher's Staff, only permitted to wizards of the Wizard Academy, a guild in Allan. Wizards learned an ancient language to control mana, the origin of everything. Their chanted spells could unleash powerful magic.

When the villagers ignored Parn's request, Filmer had hoped Slayn would be able to help him. Meeting a goblin-hating dwarf at his house was an unexpected bonus.

"Knowing Parn, he's probably woefully unprepared. We'll have to hurry, or it'll be too late." Slayn picked up a thick book with the same ancient language stamped on the cover in gold leaf. Translated, the title read *Slayn Starseeker's Book of Spells.*

4

PARN AND ETOH PICKED THEIR WAY CAREFULLY DOWN the path through the woods, watching for any movement as they approached the hills where the goblins lived. The area was littered with boulders, providing cover for their approach.

Despite moving with caution, the duo was making their move in broad daylight. Goblins lived in darkness and abhorred sunlight, which meant they usually came out at night and slept through the day in their caves. Parn and Etoh relished the spring sunlight as they walked along.

The first part of Etoh's plan was simple: use ranged weapons to take out any lookouts, and take them by surprise. They'd keep the rocks at their backs to stop the goblins from getting behind them. The fact that the sun was out would weaken them further.

Parn was reluctant to attack from a distance but had begrudgingly agreed. The goblins were evil creatures, after all, and there were too many to make it a fair fight.

Having a plan put Parn at ease, as if knowing what they *wanted* to do meant they'd already succeeded. Etoh, the brains behind the attack, was still worried. He glanced at his friend as Parn crept forward, sword at the ready—and reached up and gripped his talisman, reciting a short prayer to himself.

When they reached the cave, Etoh sighed and looked to the heavens. The bad feeling gnawing at his gut had been right.

There, before them, were two ugly goblins. They were shaped like humans, but only half as tall as a grown man, and their bare limbs were thin and gnarled like weathered trees. They had no hair, and their bald heads made their already large eyes and ears seem even larger. Their noses were so flat that their nostrils looked like two gaping holes in the middle of their faces, and their mouths were slits with yellowed fangs and blood-red tongues peeking out. They wore filthy rags tied over their reddish skin, and crude daggers dangled on straw ropes around their waists. Each of them held a wooden shield in its left hand, and they stood hunched and blinking in the bright sunlight.

They hadn't noticed Parn and Etoh hiding among the rocks yet—they were milling around, aimless and bored.

"Looks like we'll have to improvise," Etoh whispered with a wry smile. They'd assumed there would only be one lookout, and between Parn's bow and Etoh's sling they would've had a good chance of taking a single enemy down in one hit. With two opponents, if either of them missed their mark, their plan would fail.

Etoh took his sling out of his pack and started clumsily gathering suitable rocks.

"I'll take the one on the right—you get the left," Parn muttered as he took the bow from his shoulder and tightened the string. He pulled out two oak and eagle feather arrows and nocked one to his bow, drawing it back as he did so. Etoh tucked a rock into his sling and started swinging.

At Etoh's signal, they both let their weapons fly.

"Gah!" the goblins squawked as they were hit—they both staggered, and one fell to the ground. Etoh's rock had hit the goblin square in the head and crushed its skull, but Parn's arrow missed its mark, burying itself deep in the goblin's right shoulder but leaving it alive.

"Hofurk!" the surviving goblin howled into the cave.

"*Blast!*" Parn shouted, quickly nocking the other arrow to his bow and making a shot. This time, he pierced the goblin's gut, and the creature fell to the ground gushing dark red blood.

"We have no choice—we'll have to kill them one by one." Parn jumped out from behind the rocks, followed closely by Etoh, their armor clanking as they moved. Parn drew his sword and pointed it toward the sky, the blade shining in the sunlight.

Etoh, determined to at least try his plan, pulled two vials of oil from his satchel and threw them into the cave. The glass shattered, splattering a slick liquid all over. But when he took out his flint to light it aflame, he realized it was too late—the hideous creatures were already leaping out of the cave. A few slipped on the oil and fell, and one hit its head on a rock and stopped moving, but the rest kept coming.

"Die!" Parn roared beside him.

"Parn! Put your back to the rocks so they can't get behind us!" Etoh yelled before Parn could leap into the fray. Etoh retreated; Parn hesitated a moment, but followed.

The goblins were already upon them. Each was armed with an axe or dagger, crude and rusted and disgusting. The blades were all coated with a thick, green liquid.

"Careful, the blades are poisoned!" Parn warned. With the rocks at their backs, they at least only had to deal with the goblins in front of them—but both of them still had to fight multiple foes at once. There was no escape—the only way out was the goblins' extermination, or their own deaths.

Parn wielded his sword and shield deftly, blocking one attack while stabbing at another foe. One goblin failed to block and fell, blood spurting from its shoulder. Parn finished it off with a thrust to its back. He may not have been a seasoned veteran, but he could keep up with goblins.

Etoh had been trained for combat at the Pharis Temple and was used to handling a mace and shield, along with holy spells of attack. In his lighter armor, he was quicker than Parn—he danced artfully around the goblin blows and swung his mace hard when he saw an opening.

The clang of metal on metal and the dull thud of striking flesh blended together. One by one, the goblins fell, but the survivors made no move to retreat—they stood their ground to protect their lair.

As the battle raged on, Etoh started to tire; his arms felt as if they were made of lead. Parn noticed him flagging and tried to shield him, swinging his sword in wide arcs to threaten the goblins attacking his friend. He was tiring too, but the sturdier man had stamina to spare.

They were through about half the horde—a dozen bodies were strewn around them, the smell of blood thick in the air. But the remaining goblins boldly clambered over the corpses. Perhaps their rage overcame their fear, or maybe they could sense the humans' fatigue; goblins were ferocious when they could smell victory.

"It's over..." Parn mumbled. His parries had slowed and

his feet dragged. Etoh was overwhelmed by a coughing fit and slumped against the rocks.

Parn knew what he had to do. He threw down his shield and, wielding his sword with both hands, let out a mighty roar to summon all the courage he had. Then he slammed into the two goblins poised to finish off the immobile Etoh and charged like a berserker into the other five that remained.

Will this death be honorable? he wondered. Dying in battle should have been a noble end for a warrior—and yet, his father's hopeless battle against bandits had been deemed dishonorable, forcing Parn and his mother to leave Valis altogether. Disease claimed his mother's life when he was ten, and ever since, Parn had helped in the fields and hunted in the woods to earn his keep. At sixteen, when he could finally fit into his father's armor, he went to Flaim to fight desert savages as a mercenary; he'd then returned home, taking jobs guarding the village or the occasional trade caravan, waiting for a chance to return to the battlefield. That was his dream—to be a knight, serving a king somewhere.

If this death isn't honorable, then what was my life for?

Suddenly, he felt white hot pain slice into his left shoulder. A goblin had gotten behind him—with gritted teeth, Parn turned and slew it. But that left him in an awkward position where his legs couldn't support the weight of his armor. Metal slammed against rock in a shower of sparks as he fell to one knee.

Another goblin pounced and stabbed him in the left thigh. It tried to yank out its knife, stuck deep in the muscle, and every jerk sent a new shock of pain through Parn's body.

Soon, though, the pain started to fade, and the world slowed like he was wading through molasses. The poison on the blades worked quickly. Parn struggled to stand, but his energy was gone. Even craning his neck to look for Etoh was too much effort.

All he could see was the cloudless blue sky. He suddenly felt oddly free. He dropped his sword and flung out his limbs. He could only stare blankly while a filthy goblin aimed its dagger straight at his throat—

And then an arrow punched through the goblin's chest.

It collapsed in a heap, almost seeming to deflate. Parn heard someone new speaking, though he couldn't understand the words. His vision began to fade, and he struggled to draw breath.

As the darkness overcame him, one final thought crossed his mind.

I get it now, Dad...

Then everything went black.

"Looks like we made it just in time." Slayn breathed a sigh of relief as Ghim took out the attacking goblin with a crossbow.

Three of the goblins noticed the new arrivals. They let out a wild screech and charged, but Slayn gave his staff a quick wave and began reciting, "Tranquil breeze that brings slumber..."

The charging goblins pitched forward as if the life had been sucked out of them. He'd cast the spell Slumber Cloud, which created a soporific haze in the air. Only two goblins remained.

Ghim switched from his crossbow to his battle axe and charged. In one blow, he cleaved the head from one goblin's body—it still had a shocked expression on its face as its head flew through the air. When the other one turned in panic to flee, the axe sliced into its side, tearing the goblin's body apart at the chest and sending its legs toppling sideways in a shower of blood.

"Finish off the sleeping ones, will you?" Slayn requested while he carefully scanned their surroundings. Nothing else moved. He turned his attention back to the goblins' lair—he focused briefly and recited a short spell, sending his perception deep into the cave. Advancing slowly, he searched ahead for any creatures left lurking.

Once he confirmed that the depths of the cave were clear, he stopped chanting and said, "We're safe now."

"I'm done, too. They're all dead," said Ghim as he remorselessly chopped off the last sleeping goblin's head.

Slayn nodded and made his way to Parn's side. Kneeling, he pressed his fingers to the young man's neck. His hand came away covered with blood.

He's alive, Slayn thought, *but this is bad.*

"I need some help over here!" he yelled to Ghim, "We need to get him home, *now*. He doesn't have much time left!"

5

SLAYN AND GHIM CARRIED PARN TO HIS HOUSE, PEELED off his armor, and laid him in bed—he had injuries on his head and leg, but the shoulder was the most serious. They brought Etoh, too. The priest was uninjured but had lost consciousness upon using magic beyond his ability—when he finally came to, he quickly closed Parn's wounds with healing magic, but by that point the goblin poison was already coursing through his body, and Etoh didn't know a detoxification spell. He and Slayn tried every treatment they could think of, but for several days nothing seemed to make much difference.

The third day after the battle left Parn wracked with a high fever and no recovery in sight. Etoh went to the creek countless times for snowmelt to cool Parn's feverish body—but they could only hope that the young man's strength and vitality would carry him through.

Parn's fever broke the following morning, finally allowing him to fall into a deep, peaceful slumber that lasted until evening. From that point on, he recovered quickly—though he was stuck in bed for three more days.

It was the tenth night after the goblin battle. Slayn sat in his house, reading his ancient books as usual, when someone knocked at the door.

"Oh, it's you two," he heard Ghim say from the doorway.

"Who is it?" Slayn asked as he walked over, only to see Parn and Etoh standing respectfully at the door. Ghim was offering the pair clumsy words of encouragement, which seemed to embarrass Parn—who answered with uncharacteristic restraint.

"You seem much better," Slayn said as he looked Parn over. The young man had lost some weight, but his complexion was healthy and his eyes had a youthful sparkle to them.

"Thank you for everything," Parn said, bobbing his head to Slayn.

"You should thank your friend. He went to great lengths to care for you. You may well have died otherwise." While he spoke, Slayn noticed that Parn was fidgeting. "But it seems that gratitude isn't the only reason you're here today. Come in. Pardon the clutter."

"Thanks," Parn replied. He and Etoh exchanged a glance and a nod as they entered.

True to Slayn's word, his small house was overflowing with books, equipment, and all kinds of materials used for magic. Four people was a tight squeeze, and without enough chairs, Etoh and Ghim ended up sitting on the bed.

Parn scanned the room. He seemed like he didn't know where to start, so Slayn gave him an encouraging nod.

"I... I want to go on a journey," Parn began haltingly. "I never wanted to live my whole life in this village anyway, and I completely humiliated myself against those goblins. And I wake up to people calling me a hero? Getting credit for something I didn't do just makes me feel miserable."

"It doesn't matter how it ended, you do deserve to be called a hero for what you did. You don't need to put yourself down," Slayn replied, though he knew Parn wouldn't accept what he said.

"There's so much evil on Lodoss," Parn continued. "Goblins— and so much worse. And I know I'm not strong enough yet to defeat that evil. But I still want to go—no, that's *why* I want to go. And Etoh agrees with me. It'll be much better to go together so we can watch each other's backs."

"So, you want to go on a quest to better yourselves?" Slayn asked. "It makes sense. But what is it you want from *me?*"

"We want you to come with us," Parn blurted out. "You're a wizard, and magic is a powerful tool against the kinds of things we'll be facing. I hear there are some monsters that you can't even hope to defeat without it! So…will you please join us?"

Ghim let out a hearty laugh. "It's a good idea, Slayn. And as for myself, well—I'm leaving on a journey of my own soon. Might as well travel with you all a ways. And with this magician and his tricks on board, we'll at least never want for food."

Slayn met Parn's gaze dead on. He recognized that unclouded, unwavering stare. Back when he'd been a student at the Wizard Academy in Allan, he had a friend—a mercenary with a strong sense of justice, just like Parn. The kind of man who'd stick his nose into any trouble he could find and always fought for what was right.

One day, he'd asked Slayn for his help taking down the Thieves' Guild. It was a dangerous task even with a magician on board, and Slayn had refused—and tried as hard as he could to dissuade his friend. He hadn't been able to change the man's mind in the end and had reluctantly lent him an enchanted invisibility ring.

Three days later, his friend had been stabbed in the chest with a poisoned dagger.

Later, rumors reached him that the leader of the Guild—a man known for his villainy—had been found dead. The Guild replaced him with a more orthodox leader who respected the thieves' code. His friend had made the city a better place. Nevertheless, Slayn still had regrets. He still wished he'd found a way to stop his friend that last night he saw him alive.

He would never forget the sincerity in his friend's eyes. And here, right in front of him, was a youth with the same gaze, setting off on a journey to face off against who-knows-what evils.

"Dangerous, isn't it...?" Slayn murmured.

"What was that?" Parn asked with a questioning look.

"I'm being forced to make the same decision twice." Slayn wondered if this was the work of Rahda, the god of knowledge. He knew that even if he persuaded Parn to stay, it wouldn't change anything—his youth, his sense of justice, and his inability to see when *retreat* was the best option would eventually get him killed.

But Slayn was different now. He was smarter and more knowledgeable, and he had much greater magic than he'd had when he lived in Allan. He might be able to protect this young man.

He closed his eyes and let stony silence fall over the room, then muttered hoarsely, "All right. I'll go with you." Slayn opened his eyes and glanced over at Ghim. "And Ghim is itching for an adventure for some reason."

"Hm..." Ghim grumbled and looked away.

"But nothing dangerous, please. I'm a timid man." Slayn turned to Parn, deadly serious. Ghim, however, let out a loud guffaw.

Etoh and Parn exchanged a look. They'd gotten what they'd hoped for—though they seemed completely bewildered by that fact.

CHAPTER
II

The Black Shadows in Alania

1

THE FOREST ENDED IN A LOW HILL, COVERED IN KNEE-high grass that rippled in the night breeze.

At the edge of the trees, a shadowy grey figure raised both hands; a strange voice cried out, carried by the wind. A red streak seared across the sky, the light growing as it travelled until it formed into a massive fireball—headed directly for the walls of the great castle at the top of the hill.

A blinding flash turned the black sky red, and a moment later an explosion thundered. The castle wall crumbled and erupted into flames, making the shadows of Kanon's imperial castle, Shining Hill, shimmer and dance.

Emperor Beld of the Marmo Empire watched with all the solemnity of a priest performing some divine ceremony. He sat astride a giant black stallion and wore blood-red armor and a black cape. He was an old man, over sixty, but despite his advanced age he still had the body and mind of a man in his prime—thanks to the power of the great sword at his hip.

Beld had defeated the Demon King to claim the coal-black blade, and since attaining it he'd used that long, broad sword to destroy countless lives. It seemed to tremble with pleasure whenever it met a new sacrifice.

Beld himself often saw a demon when he looked in the mirror.

A victorious cheer rang out from the hundred knights behind him as they watched the castle burn, but Beld's expression didn't change. He knew this was only the beginning. The wall may have crumbled, the fire might have caused chaos, but his men were outnumbered ten times over by the enemy soldiers still inside.

Beld advanced slowly out of the cover of the forest, then looked back at the elite troops waiting for his signal. He raised his right hand and swung it down swift as a flash.

The black-clad, armored knights galloped out of cover and rushed up the hill toward the castle, the thundering of their horses' hooves competing with their angry bellows and shouts.

Beld drew his sword. The black blade absorbed and trapped all light, intimidating even in the darkness of a moonless night. The evil energy emanating from it sat heavy in the air around them. He held the blade out parallel to the ground and prepared to spur his horse forward.

"Taking the field yourself, Your Majesty?" a voice asked from beside him.

Beld deftly wheeled his horse about to face the voice. The woman at his side appeared to be in her mid-twenties, with long, thick black hair tied back and a mysterious circlet on her forehead—several golden bands bundled together with a green jewel at its center and two red, eye-like gems mounted on either side.

The woman's name was Karla, but Beld knew nothing else about her. Nothing, except that she was a wildly powerful wizard, and she was on his side—which was all that mattered.

Wagnard, the court wizard, had warned him time and time again that her strange magical powers were dangerous.

That same dangerous magic had just shredded Shining Hill's walls like parchment.

Beld smiled fearlessly as he displayed his sword to Karla, swinging the huge blade with one hand.

"The sword craves more blood—human is its favorite."

"Does it?" she said. "Perhaps the same could be said of you. After all, a sword reflects its wielder—so they say."

"Indeed," Beld laughed, the sound barely distinguishable under the noise of battle. "You could say the same about magic—your flames show your destructive tendencies," he said with a gesture at the blazing castle.

"Perhaps..." Karla smiled frostily. "Well then, my job here in Kanon is done. I will depart shortly for Valis. Events have been set in motion, and I must prepare for the next move."

"You're busy," he replied. "I hear you're plotting something in

Alania as well."

"Yes, I have many plans in motion. They're all necessary if I'm to make you Overlord of Lodoss."

"I look forward to it." Beld pulled his steed's head around and kicked hard at its sides. The horse galloped like lightning up the slope toward the blazing castle.

Beld never doubted his victory.

2

THE CITY OF ALLAN, CAPITAL OF ALANIA, WAS ABOUT a ten days' journey south of Zaxon. The castle there, Stone Web, was the home of Alania's King Kadomos VII and his family. The city was known for its rich 400-year history and as the thriving cultural center of Lodoss. The buildings and roadways were all stone, built by the dwarves and unchanged since the days of old.

Parn and his companions had travelled to Allan at Ghim's request. Their original plan had been to leave the city and head west, pass through Norvis and The Storm and Fire Desert, and finally arrive in Valis from Flaim. But a sandstorm raged in the desert, forcing them to change their route—the only open path to Valis was through Kanon to the south.

Allan, a city usually known for its tranquility, was in the midst of a bustling festival when they arrived. The celebrations were being held in honor of the birth of King Kadomos VII's first child, a prince born just five days earlier. The streets were lined with food stalls, and there were crowds of people everywhere. The dazzling sun of early summer helped fuel the excitement. Strolling over the stone pavement, Parn and his companions enjoyed the sights.

"Looks like we came at the right time," Ghim grunted through mouthfuls of the chicken leg he'd just bought.

"We really did," agreed Parn.

"It's so auspicious that a prince was born. The future of the Alanian royal family is now secure." Etoh looked around with blessings bright in his eyes.

"Festivals are nice, but I'm tired from the journey. We should come back once we've found lodgings." Slayn, as usual, plodded along at the back of the pack. They'd been walking since morning without rest, so he was out of breath—it was hard for the older academic to keep up with young men like Parn and Etoh, or someone as tireless as Ghim.

"You're out of shape because you read too many books. You need to get more exercise," Ghim lectured, giving Slayn a look. Slayn hummed something noncommittal and hustled to catch up. "Although I *am* pretty hungry. All kidding aside, we should get some grub at an inn, or we'll all pass out from starvation long before the exhaustion hits us," Ghim continued through another mouthful of chicken.

Certain that it was his *third* chicken leg, Etoh shook his head in astonishment at Ghim's bottomless stomach. The dwarf only came up to Parn's chest, but he ate three times as much as the large man. Etoh wondered if the rumors were true—that a dwarf's round belly was entirely filled with digestive organs.

At Slayn's suggestion, the four quickly found lodging—an inn called the Crystal Forest, discreetly tucked into an alley off the main avenue. Despite the poetic name, the building was less than impressive—but for a poorly funded group in a city filled to the brim with festival-goers, it was the best they could get.

"Off to the festival!" Parn cried, gulping down the last of his food, and called for Etoh to come along. The priest stood up with a laugh and Ghim followed.

"What about you, Slayn?" Ghim asked the wizard, who had remained in his seat.

"Don't mind me, go see the sights. There's somewhere I have to go, but I'll be back by tonight."

"Eh, I don't have time to waste worrying over a wizard. You're going to that Academy, aren't you?"

Slayn nodded.

"We're off, then. But you should really take a break once in a while—otherwise you'll suffocate in all your books."

Slayn had begun his studies at the Wizard Academy in Allan when he was twelve. His mother was a low-raking Alanian noble, and when planning for the future of her little bookworm, she'd used her connections to get him admitted. Slayn had lived alone in the city for most of his life—until, after the loss of his friend, he'd feared retribution from the Thieves' Guild and fled.

It had been years since he'd last seen it, but the changeless city still felt the same. Walking up the hill to the Academy, a wave of nostalgia rushed over him. The Academy was on the outskirts of town, built on a hill overlooking the harbor—a majestic building constructed entirely out of black marble and as large as a small castle. Both it and the white steeples of Stone Web could be seen from anywhere in the city.

But the building he found himself in front of wasn't as he remembered. The outer walls looked dingy, as though they hadn't been cleaned in a long time—in the past, a magically summoned spirit had kept up on the whole place, from top to bottom. The front gate was different, too—tightly closed, and the usual Spartoi gatekeepers were nowhere to be seen. Slayn felt uneasy. What had happened here?

"Samalugan!" His voice shook from growing apprehension as he spoke the password to open the gate. With an unpleasant squeal of metal, the doors opened inward to allow him inside.

The inner courtyard was falling apart—weeds taller than Slayn obscured the path to the building, and the faint smell of animal feces hung in the air. Slayn's face contorted into a grimace. The Alania Wizard Academy had been renowned throughout Lodoss. It had turned out countless great wizards for over two hundred years. It was a place of magical innovation—and a rebirth, however small, of that lost civilization of magic, the ancient city of Kastuul.

"How could this have happened…?" Slayn asked the empty courtyard, a tremor in his voice.

Parn, Etoh, and Ghim walked hurriedly down the main avenue. It was the fourth day of the festival already, and the city seemed to have hit peak merriment. They saw troupes of street performers from all corners of Alania and heard minstrels singing seductive love songs. Parn, a country boy through and through, found all the new sights bewitching—especially the flamboyant clothing on the women. Ghim, as usual, went out of his way to sample all the exotic foods, and Etoh watched everything so cheerfully that Parn had to ask what he found so amusing.

Etoh's enjoyment of the festival was different from the others'—simply watching the happiness of the people around him brought joy to the priest. Total strangers slapping each other's backs like old friends, music everywhere, friendly drinking contests. Witnessing such things made a peaceful, virtuous world feel within reach.

But then…

"Is that a fight?" Ghim asked suddenly, gesturing toward a nearby alley.

"A fight?" Parn's gaze jerked to where Ghim pointed. There, he saw four scruffy men surrounding a slender figure with long blonde hair and grass-green clothing. "That's a woman!" he exclaimed, and dashed into the alley without another word. With a cry of shocked disapproval, Etoh ran after him.

"A woman?" Ghim muttered, following reluctantly. "True as that may be, she's *also* an elf…"

"You'll never catch me like that," Deedlit said as she danced effortlessly around the men who tried to grab her. She tripped one up, delivered a knife-hand strike at his solar plexus, and kicked him in the back when he doubled over. They kept coming, too blinded by anger to notice that they had no chance. She snickered to herself—how foolish for these slow humans to pick a fight with an elf.

"Idiots." Deedlit jumped up to evade the man charging at her like a bull, and dropped an elbow into his back as he passed.

When she looked up from her felled attacker, she noticed two more men running over. For the first time, a flicker of uneasiness crossed her mind—were they friends of these men? She slid over to the armor-clad one and swept a low roundhouse kick at his feet.

He leapt away in a dodge, surprised. "Hey, I'm on *your* side!" he shouted, spreading his arms wide to show that he meant no harm.

"On my side?" Deedlit asked, eyeing him suspiciously. Naïve eyes met hers. He looked young.

He seems okay, she decided, and threw him a wink.

Just then, one of the thugs regained his feet and lunged at her from behind. Deedlit tried to sidestep but took a hit in the back—the man took advantage and wrapped his arm around her in a stranglehold. A groan escaped her lips.

"Four grown men against a woman?!" the youth shouted, and in one motion he grabbed the man's hair, lifted his face, and punched it, hard. The man flew backwards and sprawled on the pavement, knocked out cold. The other three took one look and scurried away.

The young man stood at the ready until they rounded a corner and disappeared. Once they were gone, he turned to

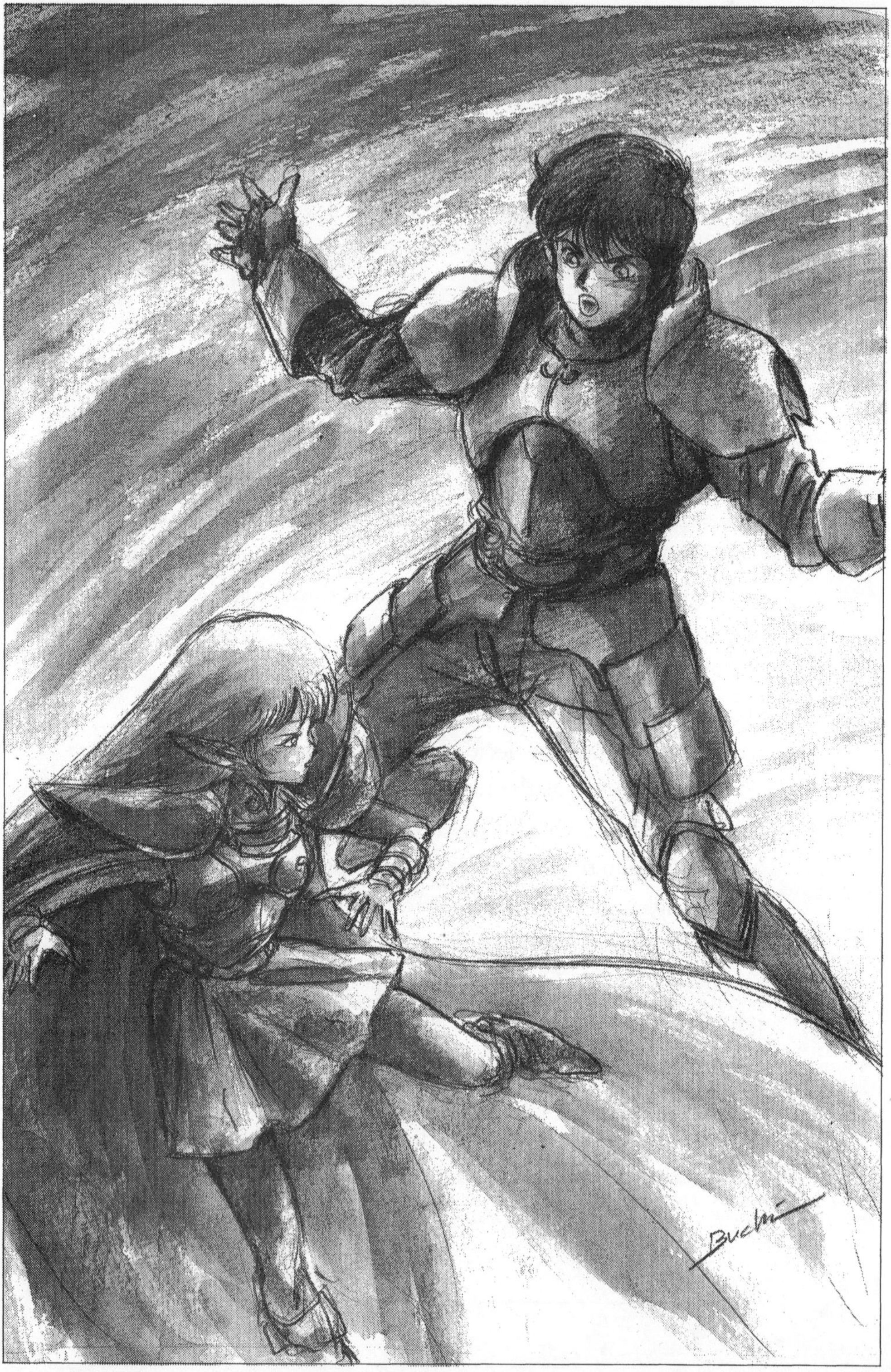

Deedlit—she was gasping for breath and coughing, the wind knocked out of her. Her long blonde hair covered her face.

Deedlit sensed someone reaching for her and leapt out of the way on pure instinct. From several steps away, she leaned heavily against the alley wall and observed her two "rescuers."

The one who'd reached out was another young man, this one in a white, loosely fitted robe and what looked like a Pharis amulet. Once she got a look at him, his priestly garb and gentle expression made her fairly certain he'd been trying to help.

The priest shrugged and exchanged a look with the armored youth, who grinned back as he dusted himself off. The warrior seemed good-natured enough, but he'd managed to dodge her full-speed kick—he had to be a highly trained warrior.

"Seems like I have to thank you," Deedlit said gently, brushing the hair out of her eyes.

"N-no need for thanks," Parn replied, trying to swallow the crack in his voice when he finally got a look at her face.

She was so small and slight that he'd thought she was a child at first. Her almond-shaped blue eyes were framed by thin, arched eyebrows. Her nose was small but shapely, and her red lips were slightly parted while she caught her breath, bright white teeth peeking out. And her ears…

"She's an elf," Etoh whispered. Her long, pointed ears twitched.

"Y-yeah…" Parn nodded. She was a forest fairy—no *wonder* she was small. Elves were shorter than humans, and female elves were often mistaken for children.

She was the first elf Parn had ever seen, and her beauty was beyond even what he had imagined. He couldn't look away.

"No need for thanks…" he repeated breathlessly. "I was just doing the right thing."

"The right thing?" Ghim snorted as he strode up. "This was none of your business."

"Dwarf!" Deedlit cried. She shot a look at the new arrival but immediately regretted it—he was a hideous mountain dweller, after all. Deedlit's face twisted in disgust.

"That's right, elvish lass," the dwarf replied, unconcerned by her reaction. He turned to the two young men. "She would've been fine without your help—that's just how elves are. Shrewd and quick. Born thieves."

"How rude!" Deedlit scowled and rounded her back like a cat ready to pounce.

"And too proud for her own good, apparently…" the dwarf continued. "I bet she started that fight."

"That does it!" Deedlit sprung towards him, but the warrior's hand shot out and snagged her left arm.

"That's enough, Ghim!" the warrior cried, seeming genuinely angry as he stepped toward the dwarf.

"Hrmph…I suppose. Sorry, I didn't mean to upset you that bad." The dwarf turned away. "You handle this—I'm going back to the inn. I don't like dealing with elves." He ambled off toward the main avenue.

The young man watched him go, deflated, and then let go of Deedlit's arm with a start.

"You finally noticed," she said, rubbing the red, hand-shaped mark he'd left on her arm and wondering how a warrior could have so little control over his strength. She opened her mouth to lecture him, but a laugh burst out instead.

Parn broke into a crooked, sheepish grin.

"My name is Deedlit," she said. "Allow me to treat you to dinner tonight as thanks."

Parn turned bright red as the elf gave him a mischievous look.

"Huh? Uh..."

"I can't have you thinking that elves have no manners." Not waiting for his stammered reply, Deedlit took Parn's arm and started walking.

3

THAT EVENING, THE PUBS WERE CROWDED WITH CELebrators. The street stalls had packed up and the throngs in the streets had thinned, but everyone who still had energy left had poured into every tavern and inn on the street. Parn wandered through them, searching for an empty table until he finally managed to stake a claim in a small tavern.

He wondered how all of this had happened. He'd left the Crystal Forest with Etoh and Ghim. Now he was out drinking with a young elvish woman—or, well, he thought of her as young, but knowing elves' longevity he had no idea of her true age.

Encouraged by Deedlit, he gulped down pint after pint of ale and started to tell her about himself.

"You're on a journey?" she exclaimed with exaggerated interest, nodding with wide eyes. Parn was already drunk and didn't seem to notice her awkward act. "You, the Pharis priest, and the dwarf?"

"There's a wizard, too. He's an odd guy, but he's also been a lot of help. I hate to say it, but Slayn's magic is much more powerful than my sword."

Slayn must be the wizard's name, Deedlit noted to herself. She put her flattering expression back on.

"You aren't giving yourself enough credit," she proclaimed. It wasn't *only* flattery—he'd been faster than her, after all. She snickered to herself as Parn scratched his head bashfully at the compliment.

Deedlit had gotten bored of her tiresome forest life and had recently left home—which made everything in the human realm new and fascinating. Foolish and uncivilized, to be sure, but she couldn't expect humans to live up to elvish standards. That understanding was what made the occasional rude or difficult encounter bearable.

At any rate, Deedlit was confident that she could handle anything humans threw at her. She knew she never would have gotten into that bind with her four attackers if the young warrior hadn't interrupted and distracted her. The fact that such a young human—not even a seasoned master—had outmaneuvered her wounded her pride.

So seeing him flounder through a simple conversation with the opposite sex did make her feel better.

Parn's story had meandered backwards as he rambled on about some goblin battle with increasingly slurred words. "I thought we were finished. But y'know what? I felt good about it. My dad said the same thing. Huh...what wuzzit...ah, I forgot... oh yeah—'s why I'm here! Dad and I've got the same purpose... I'm gonna go to Valis to make sure. King Fahn's there—he's a great hero. And lots of knights. Dad was one of them, y'know? That's why I wanna be a warrior, too. I'm just a mercenary for now—but I worked for the king of Flaim, an' he started out a mercenary like me...so I can do it just like him, yeah? I could be a King...nah, prob'ly not that, bein' a hero'd be enough..."

As Deedlit listened to him ramble, one thing in particular jumped out at her. "What are you trying to find in Valis?" she asked quietly.

"Huh? Dunno..." he replied. "I haven't been able to find it yet."

"Sounds like a riddle to me."

"Slayn's s'posed to solve riddles, not me," Parn said. "He's got this weird name, Starseeker. They say it's 'cause he's looking for his star. I like the name my parents gave me—Parn. But I don't mind when people give me nicknames." Parn rubbed his eyes and gazed blankly at the beautiful creature next to him. "Wanna come with us? It'll be fun! I got friends, too. Ghim's a grump, but he's okay deep down. Slayn's a weirdo, but he's real powerful, even more'n my sword...oh wait, I said that already. An' Etoh's so nice, an' smart—he's gonna be High Priest of Pharis someday, an' he'll bless me when I get to be a knight."

As the night wore on, Deedlit figured she should bring Parn back to his lodgings while he could still walk on his own. He had mentioned he was staying at the Crystal Forest—maybe she could find a room there herself.

When they made it to the Crystal Forest, Slayn, Etoh, and Ghim were seated around a table at the pub on the first floor. Drunk patrons were singing the national anthem and toasting the King.

Slayn watched Parn stagger in, clearly drunk and accompanied by a female elf. He rose from his chair in surprise—Etoh had warned him, but seeing her for himself was something else. Ghim snorted his displeasure, and Etoh just smiled wryly.

Slayn shook himself and looked over the impishly grinning elf. She seemed young, but her eyes had an uncanny glint. He reached quietly for his staff.

The motion didn't escape Deedlit's notice. She assumed this was the famous Slayn who Parn had mentioned—she slid her left hand to her hip and touched the drawstring water bag that hung at her belt. Inside, she kept the water elemental Undine—not particularly powerful, but she'd be able to stop the wizard from casting a spell. A long, tense moment drew out between them.

Slayn disarmed the moment. He'd been on edge since learning about the demise of the Academy—but once he had a moment to think, he realized there was no reason for this elf to harm them. Their group had no money, power, or status. And though he thought for a moment that she might be from the Thieves' Guild, he knew an elf would never join up with thieves.

"Nice to make your acquaintance," Slayn said in his usual slow, gentle tones. "We were just talking about you, to tell the truth. Thanks for bringing Parn back." Slayn propped his staff back against the table where he'd had it before.

"I'm fine!" Parn signaled unsteadily to Slayn.

"How is this fine? You should get to bed. Etoh, could you…?" Etoh nodded and got up, pushing under Parn's arm to support him.

"Drunk on ale? Pathetic," Ghim muttered. "Or maybe it was exposure to the elf," he continued, loud enough for Deedlit to hear.

"Comparing a human's constitution to a dwarf's isn't fair. Humans might be lightweights, but at least they aren't poisonous—like dwarves." Deedlit smiled and gracefully saluted Ghim.

At that, Ghim actually grinned. "You've got a fiery streak! I like you. Let me apologize for what I said earlier—it's not our fault that our kinds don't get along." The dwarf laughed and raised his mug to Deedlit. "A toast to an old adversary. We vowed to accept each other after the Demon Wars, after all."

"True…" Deedlit half-heartedly agreed, watching as Etoh lugged Parn upstairs.

"Come—sit with us," Slayn pulled up a chair and gestured to Deedlit. She hesitated, but after a moment shrugged and sat down. "We should talk and clear up some misunderstandings," the wizard said, looking into her emerald eyes.

"Y-yes," she replied, averting her eyes from his gaze. "My name is Deedlit," she began, and started to tell her story as if under a wizard's spell.

4

THE MORNING AFTER A FESTIVAL ALWAYS FELT EMPTY, and the streets of Allan that morning were much quieter than usual. Woodchuck wandered the city, avoiding the main avenue—after all, staying to dark, quiet places was habit for a thief.

He wore a dark brown shirt and pants, black matte leather armor, and black leather boots with fur-lined soles for maximum stealth. His only worldly possessions were the clothes on his back, the dagger and three knives at his hip, and a few coins in his pocket.

"So much for the mercy of the Guild," he grumbled, watching the streets of Allan for the first time in years. He hadn't been away, though—he'd spent the last twenty-odd years within the city walls.

Those years, however, had been spent entirely in the dungeons of Stone Web. His only view for all that time had been the cell across from him, the tired old man within, and the grumpy prison guard who delivered his meals twice a day.

Woodchuck took a deep breath of fresh morning air and wondered how he'd managed to not suffocate in that stifling dungeon. He'd been pardoned after the birth of the prince, allowed to walk right out of prison—but he'd lost twenty-two years of his life, and his youth.

It was just breaking and entering, he thought, fury rising up. He'd broken into a mansion twenty-two years previous, but had messed up and gotten caught. He'd been put on trial by the young Kadomos VII, who took one glance at him and handed down a thirty year sentence without even giving Woodchuck a chance to explain.

With just a few words, Kadomos had doomed him to live the best years of his life behind bars.

Despite the recent pardon, he still held a grudge. During the festival, he'd been tempted to spit on the celebrating people— he quieted the urge by stealing their wallets instead. He didn't make any mistakes but quickly learned that his pickpocket skills weren't what they used to be. He'd been able to exercise his body during his years in the dark, but there'd been no way to practice his thieving skills. His advancing age was slowing him down, too.

The only other option he'd been able to come up with was going to the Thieves' Guild to ask for a seat on their board. But the Guild's leadership had changed in the last twenty-two years— and the new, unfamiliar leader had brushed him off, saying he'd need to pay 10,000 gold for the privilege. If he hadn't wasted those years locked up, Woodchuck could've been a top executive in the Guild by now, rather than having to beg for a place on the board.

Woodchuck was angry, but he knew he couldn't afford to burn his last bridge. He'd swept aside the slight with a smirk.

The Guild leader had taken pity on Woodchuck, giving him a lead on a good money-making job.

Problem was, the job was much too difficult for one thief to pull off alone.

"I need companions," he muttered to himself, "and a skilled warrior, too. But first, I need some grub," he said, glancing up at the sign of the Crystal Forest.

Parn groaned and drank more water, hoping he could keep down the bite of bread he'd managed to eat. Etoh meditated beside him, absorbed in morning prayers that could easily stretch into the afternoon if they weren't interrupted. Ghim, meanwhile, was still working on breakfast—he was on his second slice of cornbread and his third glass of ale. Deedlit was sipping sweet wine and nibbling on fruit while trying to avoid looking at Ghim. She ended up staring blankly in Parn's direction. Slayn sipped a cup of milk and reflected on his conversation with Deedlit the night before.

The elvish girl was endlessly exasperated at the elves for doing nothing to stop their race's slow decline, which had spurred her to leave home. Slayn was impressed at Deedlit's mindset—that kind of impulsiveness was rare for an elf, but Slayn respected it.

After her momentary outburst at all elves everywhere, she'd lowered her eyes bashfully, arranged a room for herself, and hurriedly retired upstairs.

The door to the bar opened. Slayn looked up at the sound and bristled. The man who had entered was clearly a bandit, and of course must belong to the Guild. Slayn watched him carefully until he settled into a seat at the counter.

"Something light, please," he said to the barkeep.

The tension subsided. Slayn went back to reading his ancient tome. Parn rubbed at his head to relieve his nasty hangover headache.

"Pathetic," Deedlit laughed.

"Oh yeah, Slayn," Ghim said, piling up his empty plates. "I meant to ask—how was the Wizard Academy? Was it worth skipping the festival for?"

"It was terrible," Slayn replied sadly. Closing his book, he leaned on the table and told them what he'd found.

He had quickly discovered that all the Academy's normal activity had stopped. In despair, he searched the empty buildings to investigate. After a short search, he managed to find Juggle, the old Sage, looking after the collapsed Academy all by himself.

Juggle told him that the troubles had begun several years previous. One of the school's most accomplished students at the time was a wizard named Wagnard—his reputation was so great that even Slayn had heard of him, and he'd earned the title of wizard extremely quickly. But after a while, he desired an ultimate mastery of his magic, leading him to dabble in dark magic powered by evil gods. This went against the cardinal rule of the Academy—that magic should only be used for good, and dark magic was strictly forbidden.

The schoolmaster at the time had been Larcus, one of the great wizards of modern times. As soon as he discovered what

Wagnard had done, Larcus confronted him. The schoolmaster cast a powerful forbidden spell on Wagnard that would cause him unbearable pain whenever he tried to use magic. Then, he expelled him and sent him away.

But Wagnard endured. He learned how to focus through the pain and cast his spells, fueled by his desire for vengeance against Larcus and the Academy.

He used magic to acquire enormous wealth in Kanon, traveled to Marmo bearing gifts, and made himself court wizard for Beld, the Dark Emperor who had conquered the island.

Three years ago, Larcus died—and after his death, Wagnard's revenge finally came to fruition. His dark machinations steadily undermined the Academy like a disease. Young students and wizards were murdered on the streets of Allan, and none of the Academy's attempts to fight back worked. One of the masters was killed. The library and treasury were raided; priceless books and ancient artifacts were stolen. Everything that remained was reduced to ashes in a fire.

And with that, the venerable Wizard Academy was totally destroyed. The surviving masters and wizards scattered all over Lodoss. Only Juggle, the eldest of them all, stayed behind.

"How terrible," Etoh said, clenching his fists in anger.

"It truly is," Slayn said, laying his hands on his knees. "In a way, it was fortunate that I'd already left Allan and was never a target for Wagnard."

"Didn't the kingdom do anything?" Etoh asked.

"What could it do against ancient, powerful forces? Even if

they'd posted hundreds of guards, it wouldn't have changed their fate. That's how dangerous Wagnard is."

"You're not in danger anymore?" Deedlit asked in a small voice.

"Probably not." Slayn answered simply. "The Academy is destroyed, Wagnard's revenge is complete—though he may have new evil plots in the works. He *is* working for the Dark Emperor, after all."

"I can't forgive this Wagnard," Parn suddenly shouted. The others turned to him in surprise as he jumped violently to his feet, shoving a fist into the air. "But if the wizards all knew he did it, why didn't they stand against him? They have *magic*! Are they really that cowardly?!"

"They're not like you," Slayn said, placating him. "Magic isn't like a sword. It can be used to kill, true, but wizards don't study magic to win battles."

"But what about Wort? He was a Sage *and* one of the Six who defeated the Demon King!" Slayn didn't reply—Parn had the same look on his face that he always did when he mentioned the legendary heroes.

"I just don't understand why they didn't band together," Parn said, quieter. "I would've—"

"'I would've beat the stuffing out of that Wagnard,' is that it?" a voice cut in from behind them.

Parn flinched and looked around, hand on his sword hilt. "Who's there?!"

A man stood behind them. "Oops, sorry for startling you," he said, hopping back and waving his arms—signaling that he was harmless. The thief who'd been sitting at the counter had managed to slip around them and sneak up behind Parn without any of them noticing.

Woodchuck had been eavesdropping on Parn—a useful habit for a thief. He constantly listened to other people's conversations, hoping for leads on rich-sounding targets or to overhear people planning out lucrative-sounding schemes to weasel into. Even a totally neutral conversation could be plundered for useful information.

Of course, this time he didn't even have to *try* to listen in— Parn's enthusiasm and volume made it easy.

"Listening to you talk, I thought, *this young man could very well be the hero who'll defeat Wagnard!* And I know the *perfect* place for you to start—*and* work off some of that anger." Woodchuck peered into Parn's face with his best salesman's smile—the surprise had melted off Parn's face and was replaced with obvious interest.

"Listening to a thief is dangerous," Slayn warned, surprisingly sharp.

"I should think *you'd* want to hear about this too, Mister Academy Wizard." Woodchuck turned to the wizard with a thin smile, aware that *this* was his moment. "There's a rumor that the treasure stolen from your Academy is hidden at a particular place. If that's true, maybe it's possible to rebuild your school. You'd be lauded as a hero."

Despite his misgivings, Slayn had to admit he was tempted.

He knew he'd never be able to totally rebuild, but recovering the books and treasures would be an important start. And it'd bring a smile to Old Juggle's face.

If only it were true…

"Ears to discern truth," he said, whispering a spell. He felt magic course through his body, then concentrate in his ears. The spell was cast—if the thief lied, Slayn's ears would hear through it immediately.

"I'd like to hear more of what you have to say," Slayn said to Woodchuck. He gestured the thief to an empty chair.

Finally! Woodchuck smiled to himself as he sat. *My luck hasn't failed me yet.*

"I'll tell you, but I expect payment in return," he began, then beamed at them. "You've got an elf and a dwarf? That's a fearsome fighting combination."

"Give us your story already," Parn said haughtily. "I only draw my sword for justice."

"Of course, young warrior. I guarantee that this won't harm your good name," laughed Woodchuck.

"That wasn't a lie…" Slayn muttered to himself. "Except the flattery about his 'good name.'"

The more Woodchuck talked to Parn, the more he thought the younger man would be perfect for his purposes—and so decided to tell them everything. "You're adventurers, right? I've always admired your sort."

As he spoke he had to remind himself—*Play nice, these people are your meal ticket, and you're out of options.*

5

THE THIEF WENT BY WOODCHUCK—NOT HIS REAL name, of course, but a nickname used between fellow thieves. Parn and company moved upstairs to their room to talk privately. They brought food and drinks, which Ghim started in on right away. The room was fairly large, but six people was a tight squeeze.

"There's an old mansion in the forest about three days east of here," Woodchuck began, sipping his wine. "The lord of the manor kicked the bucket twenty-five years ago, so it's been abandoned. But some suspicious people started squatting there a few years ago…right around the time the Academy's treasures were stolen."

"They're not bandits—or at least, if they are they're some fly-by-night crew and not right with the Guild. So one of my colleagues went to check it out and found something interesting—a dark elf and an ogre standing guard outside. After he watched for a while, a man in a fancy suit of armor came out—with the emblem of Marmo on his chest."

A shudder ran through the room. Marmo was infamous—and known as the home to dark elves, ogres, and trolls, so that checked out.

"The Dark Island?" Etoh groaned. "Why are they in Alania? Are they plotting something?"

"I don't know," Slayn said with a shrug. "But if Emperor Beld is as bad as the rumors say, it could be anything."

"I heard that he's trying to conquer Kanon. Is he after Alania, too?" Parn gulped.

"We can only speculate at this point."

At Slayn's words, Parn crossed his arms in thought. It was a reasonable assumption that these soldiers could be the advance guard of an invasion force. Maybe Wagnard destroyed the Academy not just because of a personal grudge, but because it would be a threat to Marmo's attack.

"I think we should check this out," Parn concluded, crossing his arms.

"Why do we have to stick our noses in this business?" Ghim asked glumly. "Leave it to the Alanian soldiers."

"No soldiers," Woodchuck said, shaking his head. "This is valuable information! Think of the rewards we'll get for bringing back the treasures and thwarting this conspiracy. How much do you think I had to pay the Guild for this sweet piece of intel?"

He didn't pay anything, Slayn thought, though he didn't bring it up to the group. "A dark elf and an ogre—sounds dangerous. Dark elves use magic."

"They're elves, too," Ghim muttered.

Deedlit bristled. "Dark elves are wretched, *evil* creatures who sold their souls to the Devil! They're nothing like us."

Elves like Deedlit despised dark elves. Legend said that, as their name implied, dark elves had made a pact to serve the Dark Gods. They fought each other in the ancient battles between Light and Darkness.

For humans, those battles were the stuff of myth, but in

Deedlit's elf clan some elders who'd fought in them still lived. Those elders passed down their memories of the cruelties they'd seen—dark elves killing men and women mercilessly, offering up maidens as sacrifices to the Devil. Siding with the hideous, supernaturally strong ogres, who would *eat* elves like a snack.

"I'll show you how different we are," huffed Deedlit.

"I think..." Parn turned to Slayn, looking thoughtful. "I think we should handle this ourselves. I doubt the Alanian mercenaries will believe us without proof. And we don't want to cause a panic by spreading rumors about dark elves and ogres."

"R-right," Woodchuck squeaked.

"I see we have little choice," Slayn sighed. "We'll go with Parn. The chance of regaining the Academy's treasures is worth it... and we can't let dark elves and ogres roam the countryside, either."

"I'm in," Ghim said simply. "I'll lop that dark elf's head off myself. Dwarves don't like *dark* elves, either." He flexed his thick arms at Deedlit, who seemed offended for a moment before realizing he was just teasing. She returned a tentative smile.

"That's the spirit—you'll all do great!" Woodchuck yelled with a grin. "And I'll help, of course. I'm pretty handy with a dagger, after all."

Slayn could imagine—he knew that the biggest thing to fear from a thief was a stab in the back in the dark. His old friend had been a fierce warrior, but had been killed before he could even respond.

"You can have half the reward. Does that sound fair to you?" Parn tried to sound savvy and dignified.

"Sounds great," Woodchuck nodded in gratitude, and smiled thinly. Slayn couldn't help but see it as a sickening leer.

He stood to get ready, and resolved to *always* stay at the back of the group. Better to keep an eye on things, after all.

With their new additions, the group settled their bill at the Crystal Forest and made it to the outskirts of Allan by the afternoon. The east road wasn't as crowded as the one that ran north-south, since the only destination this way was the fishing village of Margus. The only other traffic was the occasional wagon that passed them by, reeking of fish.

They hiked at a comfortable pace, led by Parn and Deedlit. Ghim followed behind them, Woodchuck walked with Etoh for some reason or other, and Slayn trudged along at the back, always with an eye on the thief ahead of him.

It's getting hot out here, he thought, pulling his hood low over his eyes to block out the blazing early-summer sun.

The group continued that way for two full days and reached the edge of the forest on the third.

"Here we are," Woodchuck gestured at a trail leading into the forest. "This takes us to the mansion."

"How long to get there?" Parn asked.

"About an hour."

"What a weird place for a house," Deedlit murmured, looking wistfully at the trees.

"Well, I didn't build it," Woodchuck replied.

"We'll have to be careful from here on," Slayn said, his voice muffled under his robe. The sun was at its highest, and his face was completely in shadow.

"Yeah," Parn replied with a grimace. "Let's get going."

Deedlit happily agreed.

They walked single file through the forest, with Parn leading the way and stamping down the path so the rest could follow easily. The forest teemed with life, and the smell of leaves refreshed them all—well, except one. Slayn slid on the dew-damp ground, and his rope kept snagging on branches and was starting to fray—a real problem, since there was no longer any place to buy Philosopher's Rope in Allan.

As they got closer to the mansion, they slowed down to move as quietly as possible. Even so, the metal of Parn and Etoh's armor jangled.

Ghim had bragged earlier that the mithril armor he wore didn't clank the way ordinary armor did. Deedlit also wore armor over her clothes, but though it appeared metal at first, it was actually tanned leather. It had been dyed purple with wild grapes and was etched with a beautiful pattern.

Finally, a huge mansion came into view. They hid in the underbrush and peered out at the entrance.

The most obvious thing before them was the huge, man-eating ogre guarding the door. The other guard, the dark elf, was half its height—but the evil glint in his eye was unmistakable. The ogre held a giant club, the dark elf, a spear.

"What should we do?" Parn murmured to his companions. The

view was limited from their hiding place, but if they crept forward to learn more, they'd be discovered immediately. "Bow and sling?"

"It didn't work when we tried it on the goblins," Etoh replied, wincing at the memory. "There's no way we'll knock out foes like these."

"Then *what?*" Parn snapped, unhappy to be reminded.

"Magic won't work," Slayn said. "Dark elves are resistant."

"In exchange for selling their souls to the Devil," Deedlit reminded them, words dripping with contempt. She drew her rapier from its sheath and felt for the throwing knife in her shoulder armor—coated in paralytic poison. Ghim unstrapped the battle axe from his back.

"I think...I have a way," Slayn whispered.

"Let's hear it," Parn encouraged.

"A spell that acts on an individual won't work on a dark elf. But I can use magic to direct their attention elsewhere."

"An illusion," Deedlit smiled.

"Yes, except only sound. If either guard leaves their post, we won't have to deal with both at once, and we should be able to take one down without their raising the alarm."

"What if they both leave?"

Slayn shrugged at Parn's question. "Then we'll sneak right in."

"No doubt," Ghim quietly chuckled, his beard shaking.

Slayn focused on the thicket opposite them. He whispered a spell, made a complicated gesture with one hand—and gave the underbrush in front of him a violent shake.

"Slayn!" Parn shouted in surprise—but Parn's voice and the rustling didn't sound from their hiding place. Instead, it could be heard coming from the thicket Slayn was staring at across the way. The two guards both turned to look, then the dark elf gave the ogre a brief command in a strange language. The ogre nodded and picked up its club while the dark elf grabbed his spear and glided away toward the sound.

"Wow, that's convenient. You'll have to teach me sometime," Woodchuck said with a smirk. "That would be a *really* handy trick for breaking and entering."

"On my signal—" Slayn started to say, but Deedlit was already on the move. She looked back at Parn, threw him a wink, then ran cat-like for the entrance. Parn stood frozen for a moment, shocked by her daring.

"Gentle forest spirits, that ogre is my friend," Deedlit whispered as she ran—a spell in a different tongue from Slayn's ancient language. The ogre opened its mouth to roar, but the moment the spell was complete, it froze, slack-jawed and blank.

To the creature's mind, everything was normal—except that Deedlit was its dear friend. She seemed much more soothing than the dark elf, who constantly barked orders.

The ogre was twice Deedlit's size, bulging with misshapen flesh, and wore only a ragged loincloth over its clay-covered skin. Its sharp fangs and disfigured nose repulsed Deedlit. "*Bark,*" she mumbled—"ugly" in Elvish. Then, she charged, speeding even faster toward the monster with her rapier aimed squarely at its heart.

The monster stared blankly at her as the blade sank deep into its chest. At that moment, the ogre finally recognized her as an enemy, but it was too late—Deedlit used all her body weight to yank her blade from the ogre's body. Dark red blood gushed from the wound as it lurched forward. Deedlit jumped away to avoid being splashed and turned to follow the dark elf.

"Deed, look out!" Parn's warning snapped her attention back, and she jumped on pure reflex. Beneath her, the dying ogre swung its thick arm, nearly hitting her. The monster thrashed and tried to regain its feet—if it had hit her it could have done serious damage. Bloody foam bubbled from its mouth whenever it opened, struggling to cry out.

Deedlit felt cold sweat run down her back, and her delicate frame shuddered like a branch in the wind. She couldn't deal the final blow.

6

THE DARK ELF KNEW HE'D BEEN TRICKED. HE COULD hear unfamiliar armor clanking in the distance, though the lack of battle sounds made him think that the ogre had already been defeated. He knew returning to his post would be risky at this point.

"Tiny, invisible spirits, lend me your form," he said. As he finished the spell, his figure faded and turned invisible. He ran, cautiously and silently, back to his post.

"The dark elf isn't coming back," Parn said, looking around restlessly. Deedlit was like a shadow behind him, having finally shaken off her fear—the ogre might have been able to attack with its heart stabbed through, but after Ghim finally lopped its head off with his battle axe, it had at last stopped moving—mostly, at any rate. It still twitched occasionally, a sign of its extreme vitality. Etoh, Woodchuck, and Slayn all assembled near Parn, who began to direct them. "Ghim and Deedlit, head inside quickly—whoever's inside might've heard us. I'll take care of the dark elf."

"Don't be foolish—you can't handle a dark elf's magic," Deedlit replied. "You head inside—leave this to me and the wizard." She stepped forward, shoved Parn toward the door, and pulled open the strings of her water bag.

"Pure and noble water spirit...your eyes can see the dark elf. Where is he? He must be hiding." Undine, the tiny blue spirit, slipped out of the bag. She spread out wide like a piece of cloth and fluttered through the air.

There, Slayn thought and aimed his staff toward where the water spirit was drifting. He uttered a deactivation spell—a spell that counteracted any magic—toward the spirit and gestured with his staff. Bright white light flashed from the end, right past Undine.

The dark elf reappeared with a grunt. He cursed his luck, having to fight an elf and a wizard, both with powerful magic—but he still had his spear. The elf was a diminutive girl, and the wizard seemed thin and weak. He still had a chance if it came to a melee.

That thought collapsed the next instant as he screamed in agony. Three searing bolts of pain bloomed in his back—he spun and saw a black-clad thief holding a dagger in a reverse grip. He must have snuck up behind him.

"Heh, I haven't lost it yet," Woodchuck grinned. His three throwing knives were still sticking out of the dark elf's back— three deep wounds, though not fatal.

Deedlit charged like lightning. The dark elf saw her coming and turned to meet her attack with his spear, but Deedlit sidestepped to the left, stretching her upper body toward him to stab her rapier into his side. The dark elf might have managed to dodge if he'd been uninjured, but the knives in his back slowed him down. He collapsed in a heap, his dying scream echoing through the forest.

Parn, Ghim, and Etoh slipped into the mansion, but they'd barely made it inside before they ran into four enemies. The men were clearly taken by surprise—they weren't wearing armor, but they were all armed with weapons and shields, and were skilled enough fighters that Parn and Ghim were struggling.

"Holy light!" Etoh cried and raised his left hand in prayer. It flashed brilliant white for a moment, blinding all four of their opponents without harming Parn or Ghim, who'd been looking away. Taking advantage of the distraction, Parn and Ghim each quickly finished one opponent, and the other two enemies stepped back, disoriented.

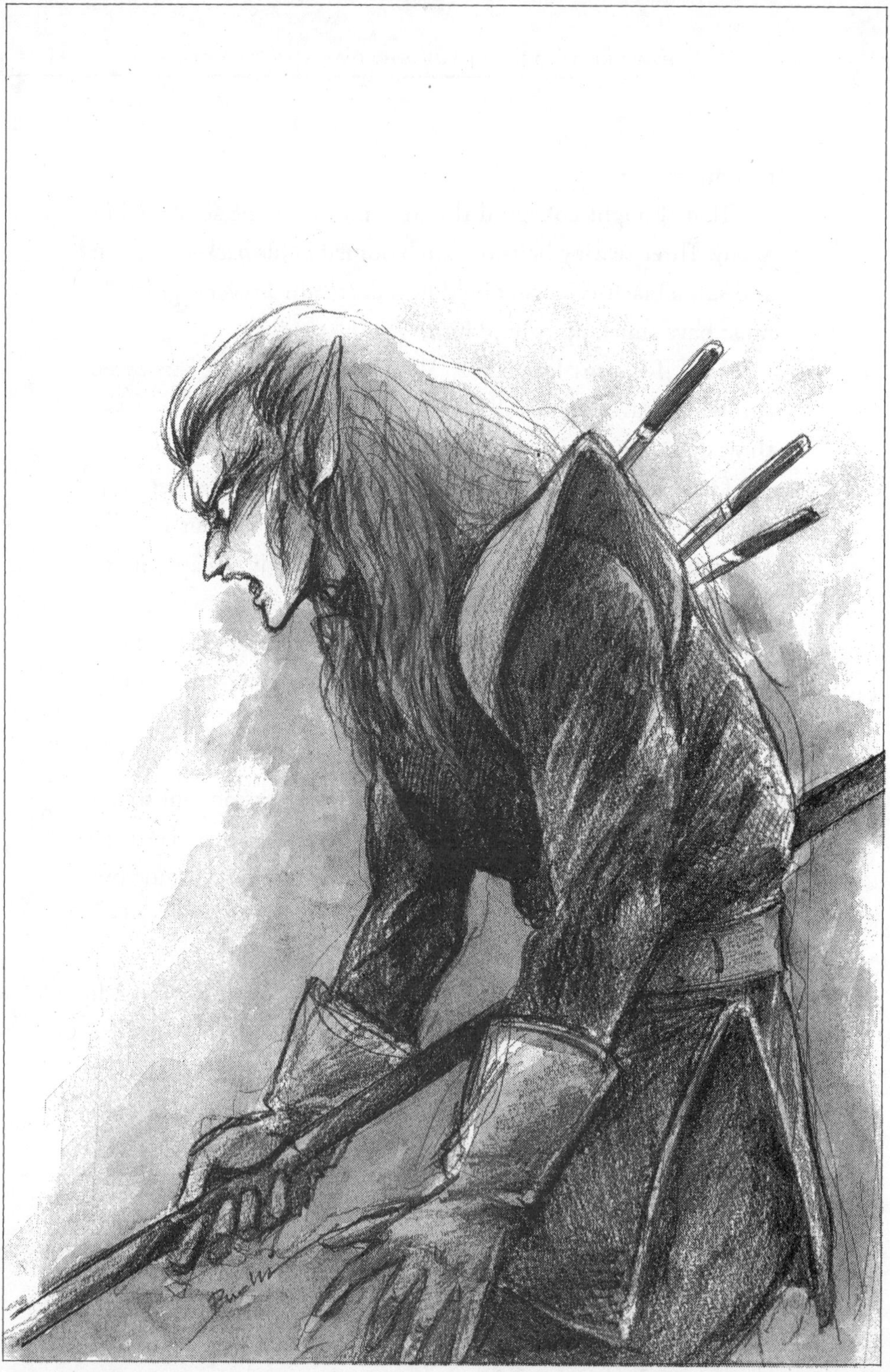

That moment, Deedlit, Woodchuck, and Slayn burst in, and the last two were finished quickly.

The mansion was empty. They checked the corpses for possessions, then cautiously began to search. The first floor was divided into four rooms, but they found nothing besides some food and a few bottles of wine.

"This is a treasure in itself!" Ghim chuckled as he filled his backpack with all the food it could hold.

"I'll check upstairs," Parn called as he headed to the second floor. The mansion seemed clean and well cared for, with new furniture. It seemed that the new residents had transformed the abandoned building into a comfortable home.

Deedlit followed Parn upstairs at a trot.

"Well?"

"I haven't seen anything yet. Be careful."

"You, too." Deedlit peered down the hallway. The afternoon sun shone through the window, showing two doors—the closer of which was open.

"Going in?"

"Of course." They stood in the doorway and looked inside.

The room still smelled of the men who'd been there earlier. It was a large room, with a rectangular table in the center surrounded by eight chairs. Some of the chairs had been knocked back messily as though they'd left in a hurry.

"What's that?" Deedlit asked, noticing the documents on the table. She ran over and picked up the four sheets of parchment.

"What's it say?" Parn moved closer and looked over her

shoulder—but he was distracted by the smooth skin on the slender nape of her neck. He shook his head to clear it.

"What's the matter?" Deedlit asked.

"N-nothing," Parn said, forcing his attention to the parchment.

The papers were about Kadomos VII, King of Alania.

First, the documents listed well-known facts: the king was an avid hunter, and the woods around the mansion were one of his favorite hunting grounds. He generally brought only a few attendants with him on the hunt.

It seemed that these enemies had bribed one of his guards—his name and a detailed description appeared lower on the page.

"What *is* this?" Parn asked, hand shaking.

"I think…it's an assassination plot," Deedlit replied.

"It must be. This is *awful.*"

Deedlit nodded her agreement. She could tell that this plan would have likely succeeded if they'd tried it.

She folded the parchment, tucking it away. Parn was too worked up over this, so she took the lead. "Let's check the next room."

Based on the layout of the mansion, the next room had to be much smaller than the first. Parn carefully put his hand on the door handle and pushed. It didn't budge. Next, he pulled more forcefully—still nothing.

"It won't open," Parn said to Deedlit, then ran back to the stairs. "Slayn! Woodchuck! Come here—the door is locked!" Parn ran back without waiting, and Deedlit tried to open it a few times, but to no avail.

"Good idea to call both the thief and the wizard," Deedlit said, peering through the keyhole under the handle. Parn grinned sheepishly.

"Don't put your face up to a keyhole," Woodchuck said dryly as he, Slayn, and Ghim approached. "A poisoned arrow could shoot out."

Deedlit jumped backwards.

"Is Etoh all right by himself?" Parn asked, worried.

"There's nobody left. He's fine," Ghim said as he carefully checked around the door.

"Doesn't look like it's booby-trapped." Woodchuck inspected the keyhole, then inserted a wire, moving it in every direction. He knocked around the handle carefully, listening to the sound.

Slayn stood behind him, cast a spell, and grumbled.

"Something wrong?" Ghim asked.

Slayn nodded and murmured, "The door is enchanted."

"Seems like," Woodchuck said, moving out of the wizard's way. "The door's not locked, and there's no trap I can find. That makes this your job."

With a slow gesture, Slayn cast an unlocking spell and knocked on the door with his staff. The door shook for a moment, then opened inward—and light suddenly flared up inside. Parn reached for his sword, but Slayn held out a hand.

"Don't worry, it's just a rudimentary magical mechanism. A light set to turn on when someone enters." He stepped forward into the room and looked around.

There was no one inside, just an old, ornate desk near the

back and bookshelves to either side.

"Books from the Academy?" Slayn moved closer, opening a cupboard that turned out to be full of glass vials and scrolls tightly wrapped in oiled paper. Slayn's hopes turned into disappointment. "No..."

It was frustrating, but not unexpected. If he'd been in Wagnard's place, he would've had the stolen magical objects brought to him at once.

"Ooh, a treasure chest!" Woodchuck exclaimed, springing over to the wooden box by the desk. "I was looking for this!"

Slayn began carefully opening the desk's drawers. In one, he found a beautifully adorned dagger and a letter. He unfolded it to see only a few short sentences.

> *Everything is going smoothly here. How is it on*
> *your end? Keep in touch via the usual method.*
> —*Karla*

"Not much to go on," Slayn mumbled to himself, then tucked the letter away. He glanced up to notice Ghim looking toward him—not *at* him, but above his head. He followed the dwarf's gaze to the back wall.

There hung a large portrait of a beautiful woman. She wore a low-cut purple dress and a circlet on her forehead. She was seated before bright red curtains, and a window showed a detailed scene outside.

The woman's skin was as pale as Deedlit's, but her hair was

the color of midnight. She seemed to look right at Slayn.

Is that Karla...? he wondered. The name sounded familiar, but he couldn't place it.

He looked back at Ghim, who was still staring at the portrait, totally rapt.

"It...it looks like *her*."

7

THREE DAYS LATER, THEY MADE IT BACK TO THE Crystal Forest. The plans they'd found were handed over to the castle guards, and they were awarded a thousand gold coins for their efforts.

Parn was in high spirits—not because of the money, but because he'd been acknowledged for what he'd done. The bribed guard was put on trial, the plot to assassinate the King was foiled, and Parn had even been praised by Duke Persia, the Prime Minister. He took another swig of ale and moved on to the next off-key verse of the song he'd been singing.

"Hey, could I come with you guys?" Woodchuck asked Parn. "You saw how useful I was, and I think we get along. My life'll be a whole lot more interesting if I stick with you."

"I don't see why not," Parn answered simply. The thief had been a big part of their success, and he'd already shown how his skills could be valuable on their journey. "Just don't break any laws."

The party continued on into the night, with everyone but Deedlit and Slayn drinking quite a bit of ale.

"Six hundred coins for the jewels still seems awfully low," Woodchuck groused yet again.

"Nah, that's market value," Ghim cut in. Woodchuck had wanted to barter, but Ghim had quickly settled the deal, and the thief hadn't wanted to argue gem prices with a dwarf. Anyway, the books and scrolls had brought an unexpectedly high price from a wizard the others knew, so Woodchuck couldn't be in too bad a mood.

Truth be told, the only one of their party who wasn't cheerful was Ghim. He sat slightly apart from the rest, sipping his wine thoughtfully.

Just when their celebration party was at its merriest, a man burst through the front door. Everyone turned to look at him as he took a few gasping breaths and staggered into the room.

"B-big trouble..." the man choked out. "Kanon has fallen. It was Beld—Emperor Beld of Marmo."

"What?!" Parn's cheerful mood crashed hard into despair. He sprang up from his chair.

"So, it's begun," Slayn muttered solemnly. "This will mean war throughout the island."

A cold shiver ran through the entire group, and they sobered immediately.

The news reached Kadomos VII at Stone Web, and the King immediately summoned his nobles to an emergency meeting.

Kanon and Alania had been allies since Kanon's founding 250 years previous, and marriages between their royal families were common—the most recent being King Kadomos VII's mother, who had come from the Kanon royal family.

That made Marmo's invasion a grave insult to the Alanian royal family, and several senior vassals took the hard line that they should declare war on Marmo immediately. There were also treaties to consider—King Fahn of Valis had led a Kingdom's Conference where they pledged to rise up and fight together in the case of any invasion.

But Kadomos VII sent no troops to Kanon. He decided to blockade the southern roads, prepare for an invasion, and wait and see. He ordered the army not to recruit mercenaries or muster the militia so as not to provoke Beld. His inaction basically acknowledged Beld as the new ruler of Kanon.

The next day, reading the official proclamation, Parn gnashed his teeth in fury. "Why?!" he bellowed, forgetting he was in public.

Slayn gently put a hand on Parn's shoulder, hoping to comfort him. "What should we do now?"

"They're all cowards," Parn choked out, and Slayn could actually see tears in his eyes. He rubbed at them with one hand, and when he looked back up his eyes blazed with determination. "Let's go to Valis," he said.

"But the roads are closed, and there's still a sandstorm in the western desert. There's no way through to Valis right now."

"We'll get there somehow. Even if we have to go through the Forest of No Return," he said, glowering fiercely.

"Are you serious?" Etoh objected. "Parn, you know how dangerous that place is. They call it that because *nobody returns!*"

"Then I'll be the first!" Parn shouted.

"They say there's an ancient Elvish curse there," Ghim added with a glance at Deedlit.

"Parn..." Slayn began, hoping to offer some calming words.

"Actually, I think it's a good idea," said Deedlit, who'd been silently watching Parn for a while. "Let's go through the forest. That way's the quickest, after all."

"You can get us through?"

"Of course," Deedlit stated proudly with a glance at Ghim. "I'm an elf. Ancient or modern, we're all still of a kind."

8

THEY LEFT ALLAN THREE DAYS AFTER THE NEWS OF Kanon's downfall.

Following Deedlit's plan, they set out on a route that would take them through the Forest of No Return. Other than Parn, none of them were happy with the plan—the sinister name was no mere legend, and no one who entered had returned in the past several hundred years. Many brave heroes took up the forest's challenge, but their fate was always the same. The Dark Forest remained unchanged as it destroyed every life that entered it.

No one knew exactly what dangers the Dark Forest held— whether it was an Elvish curse or just some deadly flora or fauna.

Nobody knew—except perhaps the victims.

By the third day, they could see the forest in the distance. But rather than entering as soon as they reached it, Deedlit kept them on the road, the forest to their right.

Two days further down the road, Deedlit stopped them with a cheerful shout.

"Here!" she proclaimed.

The others turned to her with skeptical, exhausted faces. Deedlit sighed, and wordlessly pointed toward the forest.

There, barely visible, was a narrow path, overgrown from disuse. Slayn couldn't believe that this was a road that people actually used.

"The path I was talking about starts here. But no matter what happens, promise me: you must not rest in the forest. And try not to act too surprised—strong emotions have a bad effect on the trees."

"That's all we have to do?" Parn asked, unable to hide his unease.

"Yeah. Just follow me, and we'll make it to Valis," Deedlit said, looking straight into Parn's eyes. "Let's hurry."

Despite the elf's confidence, the rest of the team's anxiety grew the more the forest loomed about them. They walked the path for an hour before they finally made it to an opening.

From close up, the forest looked normal—though there was an increasing tension and vague sense of evil all around them.

At the end of the path were two identical pine trees. Their height, thickness, and even the forks of their branches were exactly the same. The space between them looked almost like a gate.

"This is it. This is where we go through." Deedlit could barely contain the joy in her voice. "Remember—keep your promises. Don't leave my side, or the 'Elvish curse' will get you."

"*Fom alanis katoru!*" she shouted in Elvish. The view between the trees shimmered and faded, and a golden glow took its place.

"Follow me, before the gate closes." Deedlit said and jumped into the light. Parn steeled himself and did the same, followed by Etoh, Ghim, and Woodchuck. Slayn went last. He resigned himself to his fate, closed his eyes, and ran into the glow.

"Whoa!" He bumped into something and almost dropped his staff. His eyes snapped open to stare right into Woodchuck's back.

"Don't scare me like that. I almost had a heart attack," Woodchuck complained.

"Where are we…?" Slayn asked, too fascinated to notice what his companions were saying.

It was a golden, shining forest, with low evergreens dotted throughout. The thorny shrubs and fern thickets they'd seen earlier were gone, and the ground had a layer of fallen leaves that cushioned their feet.

"This is the Forest of No Return?" Parn gulped. "It's like a different world."

A different world…! Slayn mused, then cried out, "This *is* a different world! Am I right, Deedlit?" He poked the ground with his staff and looked up at the sky. The sun wasn't visible, but the entire firmament seemed to glow.

"What does *that* mean?" Parn looked back at Slayn.

The wizard glanced at Deedlit and chose his words carefully. "Not many people know this, but the world is made up of three domains. One is where we humans live. Wizards call it the material world. The second is where the spirits live—it is divided into sections, but the collective term is the spirit world. And then there is a middle world that connects the physical with the spirit world. That's the world of fairies. That's where we're standing."

"If I'd known you were familiar with the concept, I would've explained it to you. I just wasn't sure if humans would understand," Deedlit said guiltily. "But yes—like you said, this is the fairy world."

"But Deedlit, didn't the elves lose their home? I thought they were bound to the physical world and couldn't return to the fairy world. How are you here?"

Before responding, Deedlit jumped up—so high that the others could barely believe it—and landed gently on the ground. "We'd better get going," she said, and motioned for them to follow. She glided through the forest, floating on air. It was then that she answered Slayn's question. "We never lost our home," she said. "The fairy world is where I really live."

"I see…" he replied, his brain feeling like it had broken down. "You're a high elf. I had no idea—I thought they were gone."

He couldn't believe what he was hearing. High elves were legends. Just as the people of the ancient kingdoms supposedly had a highly advanced culture, elves had their own superior ancient race. But to meet one, face to face…

"We'll die out eventually," Deedlit said. "But that's in the future, when the souls of the gods die out and the dragons decay into the earth."

Parn frowned, confused. He didn't fully understand what was being said, but it seemed that Deedlit was special, even for an elf.

"We dwarves also used to live in the fairy world, or so they say," Ghim said. "But we left long ago, because we discovered the gifts of the land. Not fool's gold, but *real* gold." He raised his battle axe—but the blade was missing. "Fairies don't like iron," he grumbled. "It doesn't exist here."

Hearing that, Parn checked himself over—but found his armor gone. Only his padded under-armor remained.

"But I can feel its weight," he protested. He hadn't even noticed its absence.

"It's fine," Deedlit reassured him. "Iron can't exist here, but all that *really* means is that, if you did bring some in, you simply can't see it—just like how you can't see most of the spirits in the physical world." Deedlit nodded ahead. "But we'd better hurry. I told you—we can't rest here." With that, the elf rushed onward.

Parn picked up speed to keep pace with her. "Why's she in such a hurry?" Parn asked Slayn beside him.

"Simple," the wizard said. "Time passes more slowly here than in our world. If we lose our way, hundreds of years could pass back home."

"That's awful!" Parn cried, the color draining from his face. "Deedlit, get us out of here!"

"Huh? I don't want to get even older!" Woodchuck shouted, clearly misunderstanding what Slayn had said.

"I told you to hurry," Deedlit replied. This whole situation was annoying, but she couldn't help but laugh at Parn's desperate expression.

Deedlit led them through the forest at a jog for a while longer, then stopped and chanted some words. The same identical trees appeared, and they passed through them to exit the fairy world.

It was night outside. "But it was midday when we left..." Parn said, his voice full of surprise and wonder. He gripped at his chestplate to make sure it had come back, and relief swept through him.

He sank to the ground breathing heavily, their run catching up to him. There was a sudden flash beside him, and a pallid magic light illuminated Slayn's blue robe.

"How many days has it been?" Slayn took off his hood and looked around. In the faint light, he could see that they were surrounded by hills, the Forest of No Return rearing behind them. In the darkness, it seemed even more threatening and enchanted, as if it could reach out and snag them in its tentacles.

"At that distance, probably three days. We could've gotten out sooner if you hadn't taken so long."

"I'm just glad I got a chance to see it—frightening and strange though it was," Slayn said. "Many humans may have entered the fairy realm, but few have managed to safely return." He stood and brushed the dirt off his robe.

"Where are we?" Etoh asked anxiously, looking back at the forest.

"About three days east of Valis," Deedlit said. "We can cross the southwest hills to reach the northern road between Kanon and Valis—but it'd be better to travel through the western mountains. We're less likely to get caught up in the war with Marmo that way." She looked up at the stars to orient herself properly.

"Let's get going," Woodchuck said with a nervous glance back at the forest.

"Yeah," Parn agreed. "It's night, but I'm not sleepy." He shouldered his pack. "We should keep on until we're tired. Hope you're all ready for a mountain hike!"

No one objected, so they quickly gathered their things and started off along the gently sloping road.

"Skipping all that time will be tough on us," Etoh said, looking reproachfully at the night sky, wondering how many morning and evening prayers he'd missed.

"Definitely," the thief said with a chuckle. "The moon is so high, but I'm not tired at all. I am hungry, though."

"I feel like I haven't eaten in three days," Ghim said, and everyone finally laughed.

CHAPTER III

Rescue

1

I T WAS NOON OF THE THIRD DAY WHEN THEY REACHED the road connecting Kanon to Valis. Though it was a major thoroughfare, the mountainous land it cut through meant steep hills and a rough, uneven surface. The summer sun beat down on them mercilessly, and the loud buzz of cicadas could be heard in the distance as they made their way down another ragged slope.

Slayn was nearing his breaking point in the heat and was dizzy with fatigue. "It's just going to get hotter," he said, sighing deeply from under his hood. Just thinking about walking all day was getting depressing.

"Well, it *is* summer," Woodchuck smirked with a sidelong glance at Slayn.

"Thank you for that. I didn't realize," Slayn said sarcastically.

"What's this?" Deedlit stopped suddenly. "They look like hoofprints. Unless this is just a very bumpy road..." She knelt and ran her fingers along the ground. "They're definitely hoof-prints—a huge number of horses passed through here. They were coming from Valis."

"So Valis has risen..." A smile broke on Etoh's face. "Marmo's dark army goes against everything Pharis stands for. I *knew* they'd fight back!"

"Of course!" Parn cried triumphantly. "King Fahn and his invincible Holy Knights would *never* let Beld's actions stand! It's only a matter of time before he falls!"

I hope you're right, Slayn thought. He wasn't convinced that things would be resolved so easily—Valis's knights were formidable, but Marmo's army was full of monsters who could use the powers of darkness. Their recent run-in with dark elves made it clear how deadly they could be—Slayn knew that without help from Deedlit and Woodchuck, he never would have survived.

A chill ran down his back, making him sweat uncomfortably in the summer heat.

This war will drag on for a long time, he thought, though he didn't say anything. He didn't want to ruin Parn's good mood.

They made it out of the mountains the following day. The terrain flattened out, which made walking much easier, though the sunny, cloudless weather continued to torment them. As always, Parn and Deedlit led the way, followed by Ghim, then Woodchuck and Etoh, and Slayn bringing up the rear. Slayn struggled along as fast as he could, huffing and puffing and leaning hard on his staff.

A quaint pastoral landscape stretched out from the road in all directions. They had already passed the border into Valis, and long stretches of farmland were dotted with peasant houses and the occasional landowner's mansion. No matter how far they walked, however, there were no people to be seen. The residents were either hiding indoors in anticipation of impending battle or had already evacuated.

"Valis must already be at war with Marmo," Etoh said to Woodchuck. "They must be east of here, since we haven't seen any soldiers yet."

"You mean Valis is dominating?" Woodchuck asked.

"Probably…" Etoh replied.

"Valis *must* be winning," Parn said without even turning back.

Something up ahead caught Woodchuck's eye. "Heads up!" he called, squinting into the distance. "There's something coming!"

Tension gripped the entire group, but Slayn said, "Let's keep going—they'll be suspicious if we act strangely."

"True," Parn replied, straining to see. There was a cloud of dust—riders on horseback and one carriage. Heat radiating from the road shimmered and distorted the outlines, but it looked like a merchant caravan. Or was it part of the Valis army's supply lines?

The group tried to stay calm as they pushed forward. Nobody

said a word—just kept their pace steady and watched the on-coming group.

"Lady Karla, there are people up ahead," a nervous voice interrupted Karla's meditations. She opened her eyes and raised the carriage's sunshade.

"Hm?" she asked, and one of the mercenaries surrounding the carriage moved closer.

"There's a group on foot coming this way. They appear armed, but there's a child with them."

"A child? I'm not sure what that implies. They're not Valis soldiers, then?"

"Probably not…"

"All right. As long as they don't make a move, do nothing. But remain vigilant."

Karla leaned back in her seat again, feeling the carriage sway beneath her. *We're so close*, she thought with a sigh and a glance at the girl sitting beside her. The girl stared vacantly ahead, no sign of life in her gaze. Karla nodded, satisfied, and closed her eyes to ponder her next move.

The caravan drew closer and closer, moving at a brisk trot. Once he could see them clearly, Parn bristled at the warning signs—the fancy two-horse carriage was surrounded by seven horsemen in mismatched armor. While they were clearly mercenaries, it was also apparent that this wasn't a merchant group, since the carriage was built for passengers and had very little space for luggage. The large guard implied that the passengers were nobles.

The mercenaries seemed strangely uncomfortable with the carriage they were flanking. "What do you think?" Parn asked so only Deedlit could hear.

"I don't know... They're a strange group—though, you could say the same about us..."

"True," he replied with a smile and a glance at their bizarre mix of companions, then collected himself quickly as the tension of both groups washed over him. They were all on high alert, confused by each other's appearances and ready to spring into action.

As the group on foot, Parn's party stepped aside to allow the riders to pass.

"It's getting hot out, yeah?" Woodchuck greeted the lead outrider as he passed. Parn was impressed—the exchange seemed to put the rider more at ease.

"Must be tough on foot," another rider called back with a relieved smile.

"Tell me about it," shrugged Woodchuck. He looked away, feigning disinterest. "Get going, already," he muttered under his breath.

The carriage creaked by. As it passed their group, Slayn peeked out from under his hood. It was ornate, and he could just make out two figures inside—from their clothing, they seemed to be women.

Before he could see more, one of the riders moved to block his view, glowering at Slayn. *Someone we're not allowed to see?* he wondered, now suspicious, and watched carefully as they passed.

"Don't scare us like that," Woodchuck spat after them once the other group was far enough away.

"That was weird. Don't they know there's a battlefield up ahead?" Parn said, stepping back on the road.

"I could see two figures inside the carriage. Women, I think," Slayn said, still watching them move down the road.

"Women? Aw, I should've snuck a look," Woodchuck joked. He started walking again, shrugging and seemingly unconcerned. The others fell back in line.

"It was odd that the rider moved to block my view," Slayn muttered as he walked.

Ahead of him, Woodchuck threw up his hands in exasperation. "Again?!"

"What's wrong?" Slayn asked. He'd put up his hood again to escape the relentless sun but raised his face to see what was happening.

Woodchuck simply pointed down the road. There was another cloud of dust—another group on horseback. Considering the size of the dust cloud and the thundering hooves, the group was moving *fast*.

"Looks like knights of Valis," Woodchuck said—he had sharp eyes. "White horses and white armor. The only people that conspicuous are the Holy Knights."

"Holy Knights of Valis?!" Parn shouted, straining his eyes toward the group. Though they were still far away, he could tell that the horses were white.

The gallant riders spurred their steeds elegantly onward, galloping through the countryside like a white gust of wind. Parn scrambled off the road.

He couldn't totally hide the complicated feelings he felt toward those knights—both admiration and anger. He looked from their armor down to his own, which was time-worn and dingy, closer to brown than white but still the same shape. The center of the breastplate shone silver, a symbol of his father's disgrace. He remembered what Moto, the owner of the general store back home, had said—and the shame he'd felt.

What hopes did my father pin on that white armor?

As they loomed larger in his field of view, the surge of emotion swept over him.

"What's wrong?" Deedlit whispered close to his ear. The concerned tone of her voice soothed his worries.

"Nothing. It's fine," Parn turned to her with a gentle expression, then took a deep breath, head held high. He snapped to attention, facing the oncoming knights again.

The five knights came to a stop when they reached Parn. Slayn and Etoh bowed respectfully, and Parn gave a knight's salute.

"Where did you come from?" one of the knights asked, stepping forward.

"We're travelers from Alania," Slayn responded, head still bowed. "We're trying to escape the war in Kanon."

"That's right," Woodchuck chimed in.

"You escaped from Kanon?" The knight seemed suspicious. "I

can't take you at your word. Excuse me..." He began whispering a prayer.

Slayn was impressed—as a Holy Knight, the man was highly skilled with a sword and could also perform the holy magic of Pharis. Slayn didn't see it as a threat—any Pharis spell would be harmless.

But Etoh, who'd been standing respectfully beside him, glared sternly at the knight. "Casting holy magic unprovoked? It's *blasphemy* to use your holy powers on people who haven't threatened you in any way. I am Etoh, a priest of Pharos based out of the temple in Allan."

"I wasn't aware that one of your party was a Pharis priest. You're right—I was overly hasty to rely on Pharis...but you've resolved our doubts. I apologize for the rudeness. We'll be on our way..." the knight spurred his horse onward.

"Are you in a hurry because of the carriage that just passed by?" Slayn asked the knight.

"What?" The knight pulled abruptly on his reins, making the horse rear up and whinny in protest.

"We just saw a suspicious-seeming procession go by. Who were they?"

"That is a matter of national security—keep what you saw to yourselves."

Slayn protested, but the knight ignored him and took off. The group whizzed by like pale lightning, leaving only a billowing dust cloud in their wake.

Parn watched them go. Once they disappeared from view, he

turned to Slayn. "What was that?"

"It's disconcerting," the wizard said. "The caravan was so strange, and the knights were in such a hurry..."

"Maybe we should follow them," Parn said.

"It's not my decision to make—but if you want my *opinion*, I'd say we shouldn't get involved." Slayn kept his reply as emotionless as possible, but he doubted his words would have much effect. Parn would always follow his heart.

"Those knights said it was a matter of national security. If it were about the caravan..." Parn folded his arms, deep in thought.

"Uh oh. Parn's *thinking*—and he looks serious," Ghim grumbled. "We might as well just accept it—we're gonna be retracing our steps in this heat." Without another word, he pulled his pack over his shoulder and started walking back the way they came.

"Well, that's annoying," Woodchuck said as he followed the dwarf. He turned back to Parn. "What are you waiting for? Even if the rest of us refused, you'd go anyway—right? So don't waste your time thinking about it."

"Sounds about right," Deedlit said, trotting up to Parn and reaching a hand out to him. "Let's just go. It's not like you to mull over something this long."

"What? Lies!" Parn protested, though he grabbed Deedlit's hand as she passed. "I am a very thoughtful and serious man, I *always* think things through!"

"Sure you are," Woodchuck laughed.

"We'd better hurry, or we'll lose sight of them," Slayn said, collecting himself. It was going to be a difficult march.

"I wish we had horses, too," Deedlit commented from her spot at the head of their group. Her long hair flared out behind her, sparkling like a rainbow in the summer sun.

A little ways down the road, Deedlit stopped abruptly and cupped her hands around her pointy ears. "What was that?" she said, voice keen.

"What's wrong?" Parn asked. He scanned their surroundings, but didn't see anything amiss.

"Quiet," Deedlit hushed him. "I can hear something from over there, but your armor's too loud."

Parn froze in place, not even daring to breathe. Elves were renowned for their hearing—it was said that they could pick out the faint rustle of a tiny animal stepping on fallen leaves.

"Sounds of combat—screaming, clanging metal. There's no mistaking it."

"The Holy Knights are fighting! We have to go!" Parn broke into a run, Deedlit close behind. "They must be fighting the caravan—the Holy Knights may be outnumbered, but I doubt mercenaries can beat them…"

"We don't know that—let's just hurry."

"Right!"

"Don't fall behind," Deedlit said with a smirk as she danced out in front of him. She was quick and agile, and—with her light armor—far faster than him.

Parn's heavy gear weighed him down, and soon Etoh, Slayn, and Woodchuck caught up. Ghim fell behind even further, jogging along on his short legs.

"Warn us first," Etoh called out breathlessly.

"The Holy Knights are fighting!"

"We should see what's *really* happening before jumping in," gasped Slayn.

Deedlit had to pause for the others to catch up, jogging in place. The sounds of battle were much clearer now that they'd run all that way, and she could just barely make out the shifting shadows of a melee up ahead.

"There," she muttered to herself and fixed her eyes on the shadows.

At that same moment, red light flared up, and a heartbeat later a resounding *boom* sounded, loud as an avalanche. Deedlit cried out in pain and dropped to the ground, covering her ears.

"What was that noise? And that red light?!" Parn called out as he sprinted to Deedlit's side. He placed a hand on the elf's shoulder but kept his eyes trained on the battle, careful not to miss a thing.

Slayn scowled as he caught up. "That light—I'm almost certain it was a fire spell."

"Magic? But *whose*—the warriors guarding the carriage or the Valis Holy Knights?" Deedlit laid her hand unconsciously on Parn's as she spoke, seeking out Slayn with her eyes.

"I have no idea. But that spell is *dangerous*. It's forbidden by the Wizard Academy, and it can only be taught to a Master or the equivalent. I didn't recognize any of the carriage guards or Holy Knights from the Academy—though I suppose one of them could have transformed their appearance. That said, wizards generally dislike using swords. I don't know about Wagnard of Marmo, though."

"Was Wagnard in the carriage, do you think?!" Parn cried.

"But weren't there two women in the carriage?" Woodchuck said, frowning. "Is Wagnard a woman?"

"Hold on—the battle's over." Deedlit stood, still holding onto Parn's hand. "I can't hear the sound of combat anymore."

"*What?!* Who won?"

"I obviously can't tell that from sound alone. Hold on, I'll ask the wind."

"Wind? You mean Sylph?" Slayn said. "My farsight spell will give us more answers."

"Wait, why didn't you use that in the first place?" Woodchuck asked exasperatedly. "Why save it?!"

"Seriously," agreed Ghim, finally catching up.

"Magic shouldn't be used indiscriminately," Slayn said, then he controlled his breathing and slowly began to chant in the ancient language.

2

SLAYN'S SPELL RANG ON QUIETLY.
The spell of farsight enhanced human vision many times over, but it took a while for the brain to get used to it. Slayn looked up at the sky, closed his eyes to adjust his vision, then looked toward the road.

When he finally saw the scene laid out in front of him, he let out a groan.

"This is *awful…*"

The ground was stained black; charred bodies were strewn over the smoking earth. Slayn could almost smell the acrid stench of burnt flesh.

Slayn aimed his sight at the carriage. A woman in a purple dress stood there, waving her hands busily and ordering the men about. She wore a circlet on her forehead—clearly the craft of the ancient kingdom—and multiple clunky rings that were likely not mere jewelry. The staff she held was not a Sage's staff, but was crafted from quality oak and carved with magical runes that he couldn't quite make out.

She must be the one who cast that spell, Slayn thought.

"How is it?" he could hear Parn ask.

Slayn kept watching the woman, knowing it would be too difficult to readjust his line of sight, as he replied. "The Valis knights have been defeated. The only people moving right now are four of the warriors with the carriage and one woman. She must be the one who cast it." Slayn paused, then said, "Destroying those Valis Holy Knights—she has some formidable power, indeed."

"How could this happen…?" Parn whispered.

"I don't know, but it did," Slayn replied, matter-of-fact. He carefully scanned the area around the carriage again, then returned his focus to the woman still giving orders.

She seemed younger than Slayn, and quite pretty. The outward appearance of a wizard—especially a female one—couldn't be trusted, of course, but demeanor could not be disguised, and the way she moved seemed youthful. It was possible that she was as young as she appeared.

Slayn was surprised that he'd never heard of such a powerful wizard…though looking at her, he couldn't help but think that her face seemed familiar. He'd seen it recently…

"I remember now!" he shouted suddenly. "She was the one in the portrait—the one back at the abandoned mansion near Allan! The purple clothes, the circlet… She was even dressed the same. I think her name was Karla… Ghim, do you remember? You seemed quite taken with her."

"I don't even know what you're talking about…and I can't see this woman now, so it's not like I can say," Ghim grumbled, then said, "Let's just hurry over—she's our enemy, right? We should capture her before she escapes." He pulled his battle axe off his back.

"Yeah!" Parn cried. "I bet she was sent by Marmo to infiltrate Valis for some reason! She must've done something *really* evil for the Holy Knights to be chasing her!" With that, Parn set off at a run.

"Wait!" Slayn commanded, uncommonly sharp. Parn skidded to a halt, like he'd been caught in a spell.

"What good will it do us to charge in now?" the wizard said. "She's far more than you can handle. Did you forget? She just *annihilated* five Holy Knights."

"But…" Parn started to protest, but Slayn's severe glare stopped him.

"If you want to throw your life away, I won't stop you," Slayn continued. "But dying a pointless death is *not* courage. You need to live on to achieve your goals. Endure for now and wait for an opportunity."

"But what if the opportunity is lost?" It was Ghim, not Parn, who spoke—his voice was quiet but simmered with intensity.

"I'm just saying that this is not the time. Why are *you* so worked up about this, anyway? I would understand if it were Parn..."

"I have my reasons," Ghim mumbled, and started running along toward the battlefield again. Parn glanced apologetically at Slayn, then started after Ghim. Deedlit and Etoh followed right after.

"Made him mad, huh, Mister Wizard?" Woodchuck whispered, sidling up to him. "I, for one, agree with you—so let's stay back here, yeah?" The thief's voice in Slayn's ear was almost like a devil on his shoulder.

"I can't do that," Slayn answered—mostly to remind himself—and ran after the others. "I won't make the same mistake twice..." Slayn bit his lip hard and gripped his staff. He yanked his hood down so he could see better, and a blast of hot air assaulted his face. Still, he kept moving despite the heat and light, running desperately to keep up.

What a load of suckers, Woodchuck thought to himself, and trotted along slowly, far behind the others.

For better or worse, Slayn's worries didn't come to pass. When they made it to the scene of the tragic battle, the carriage was long gone. Ghim argued in favor of continuing their pursuit, but Parn insisted that they couldn't abandon the terrible scene—and that they'd never catch up to a carriage on foot. Ghim finally caved when Slayn reminded him that they'd have to camp at night.

They all intend to attack the carriage, Slayn thought. Knowing he had to steel himself for the inevitable—that he would have to use magic for destruction—he ran through the fire spells he was familiar with.

Parn was stricken speechless by the horror of the scene. Deedlit shrank behind Parn's back, only her face peeking out, her small hand trembling on his shoulder. She whispered words of mourning in Elvish, and her eyes welled with tears.

The intense fire had turned the road black. There were eight fallen figures, five in Valis armor. Several horses had also fallen victim to the flames.

Etoh crouched down and examined each corpse, his usually gentle face contorted in rage and pity. The charred skins of the corpses sloughed off at a touch, revealing red flesh underneath.

May their killers be judged in Pharis's name, his mind screamed.

When he reached the last body, he was shocked to find that it was still warm.

"He's still alive!" Etoh shouted. He could faintly see the man's chest moving up and down.

Everyone ran up and crowded around Etoh and the man.

"As long as he's still breathing, I might be able to do something," Etoh said, and glanced up at Parn, signaling with his eyes.

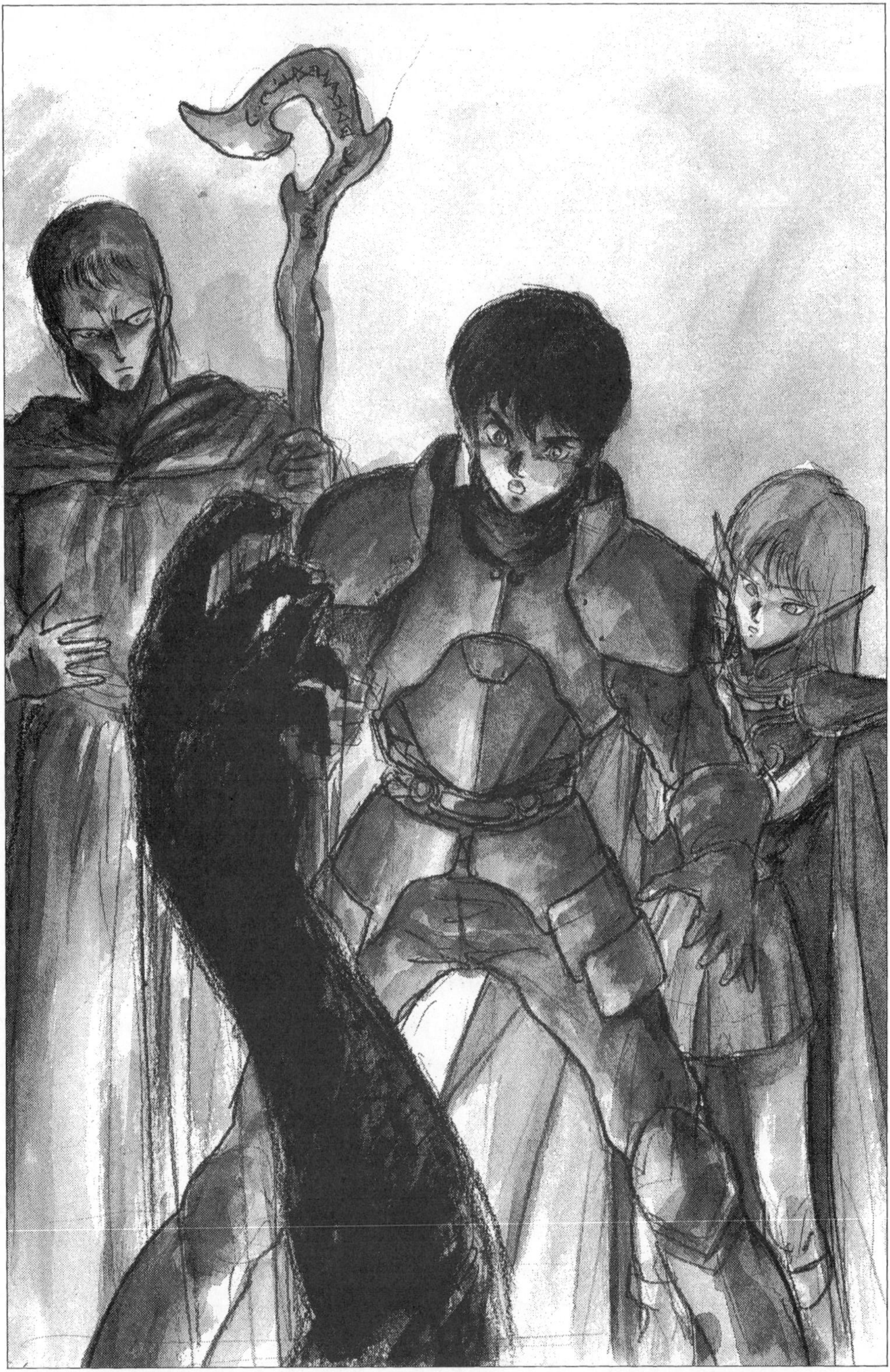

"Everybody, step back," Parn said. "Let Etoh work."

Deedlit looked dissatisfied, but Slayn reassured her. "Etoh uses Pharis's magic."

Parn frowned. "We should bury these other poor souls. We can't just leave them here."

Ghim nodded silently and unstrapped his axe. The side opposite from the blade had a sharp, hooked tip. He held the axe with that side down, chose a suitable spot, and swung it hard into the ground. The steel claw tore into the earth, breaking the packed soil apart. Meanwhile, Parn found a wooden board and started digging out the dirt. The small hole grew steadily.

Slayn sat down with his back to the road so he wouldn't have to see the horrible sight and stared instead out at the beautiful fields spread out before him. Questions swirled in his mind. The sorceress, of course, was foremost in his thoughts, but Ghim's behavior was also bothering him. The dwarf had clearly been transfixed by the portrait in the abandoned house. How could he claim that he'd forgotten it now? For someone who showed little interest in anything but food, he was suddenly charging ahead like a man on a mission. Why would Ghim care so much about Marmo's minions? There was also the fact that it was odd for a dwarf to go on a journey in the *first* place—they usually preferred to spend life underground, perfecting their crafts. When Ghim had first visited Slayn, however, he'd been doing research— looking through books of riddles and maps of Lodoss.

Does Ghim have some purpose he's not told us? Did he find a clue?

Etoh's chanting filled the air without pause while Ghim, Parn, and Deedlit dug graves. They carried the corpses with as much reverence as they could manage and thrust the knights' swords into the ground as grave markers. A little distance away, they buried the bodies of the caravan guards. As their somber work continued, the sun started to set, and the blue sky faded into dusk.

"This wizard cast a spell knowing it would kill her own soldiers?" Parn asked bitterly.

"I don't think so," Deedlit responded. "I checked over the bodies, and the caravan warriors died from stab wounds. The spell was cast *after* their deaths. The parts of their bodies in contact with the ground weren't burned."

"Still—even if they were already dead, I can't believe she'd use magic on her own people."

"Magic shouldn't be used for destruction at *all*," Slayn said. "But what do we do now?"

"We keep going, of course," Parn declared with complete certainty. Next to him, Ghim nodded.

"You want to fight this sorceress?" Slayn asked, just to make sure. "She's powerful enough to slaughter multiple foes in one attack. I hate to say it, but don't you think you're in over your head?"

"Maybe, I guess," Parn said with a shrug. "But we can't let her get away with this."

"Say we *do* defeat her," Woodchuck said, unimpressed. "What do *we* get out of it? I'm not working for free."

"Your reward will come from within your own heart," Etoh answered, coming up behind him.

Woodchuck turned to face the priest. Etoh was clearly exhausted from the effort he'd put into his magic, but his work had paid off—behind him, shaky with pain but standing on his own two legs, was the surviving Valis knight.

Parn beamed.

"The King of Valis will reward you," the knight said quietly.

"Can you tell us what happened?" Parn asked.

The man nodded. "I am a Valis Imperial Guard—my duty was to protect Princess Fianna."

"Princess Fianna, princess of Valis?!" Parn interrupted in surprise.

"Let him finish," Deedlit chided him.

"Yes, exactly. Princess Fianna is King Fahn's only daughter. This war had a profound effect on her. She wanted to encourage our men on the front lines. Everyone in the castle, the King included, was against the idea—but the princess insisted. She ran away…"

The knight paused for a moment, so Deedlit prompted him. "So, you went to search for her?"

"That's right. We found out that a merchant had helped her sneak away. We discovered where they'd gone and caught up with them to take her back…and *this* is the result."

"We slew a few guards who attacked us as we approached. When we got close to the carriage, that woman came out—she chanted some strange words, and as soon as she finished there was a huge explosion. I was blown off my horse, and I'm ashamed to say that I passed out from the pain…"

Woodchuck leaned in to peer at the man's face.

"Will there really be a reward?" he asked.

"If you can rescue the princess, I promise you will receive whatever your heart desires."

Ten thousand gold coins. The words flashed through Woodchuck's mind—the payment he needed to become an executive of the Thieves' Guild. *I'll just have to hope it all works out,* he thought to himself, and went to retrieve his pack. *I guess I'm a sucker, too.*

The group took a few moments to talk. Parn and Etoh had already decided to help, of course—reward or no. Ghim and Deedlit had no objections, and mention of the reward had obviously brought Woodchuck around. Slayn was still worried, but he'd made his decision—he'd do what had to be done to take that sorceress down.

Parn went to the knight and represented the entire group to formally offer their help.

"Thank you," the knight said with a deep bow. When he raised his head, he glared in the direction the carriage had gone with rage in his eyes, like his glare could somehow reach the woman through the darkness.

Parn's anger also burned, though not as fiercely as the knight's. Deedlit stared at him in wonder. How was he able to take someone else's anger as his own? How could he risk his life for another person's cause?

The night was dark, only lit by weak starlight—Deedlit was sure the humans would have a tough time. She cast an elemental

spell, intoning, "Shining things that live in light, gather here and show yourselves…" A small ball of light floated above her in response, growing steadily brighter.

It was Will-o'-wisp, the light elemental.

Slayn recited his own spell, and a magical light glowed from the tip of his staff. Thus guided by their magical illuminations, they left the burning stench of the battleground behind—though their trepidation remained as they started east down the road to Kanon, accompanied by the Valis knight they'd rescued.

3

It was late at night when they came upon the carriage parked in front of an old mansion—a solid two-story building surrounded by a fence. The knight told them that all the Valis citizens in this area had evacuated to the city of Adan to escape the war, and the carriage's occupant probably knew that this building would therefore be empty when choosing a place to stop. The horses were sleeping in the straw under the eaves.

"We're lucky—they don't expect us," Slayn whispered. He muttered a phrase to extinguish his magical light. Deedlit released her light elemental, which flickered a few times and disappeared into the night.

"What should we do now, Sir Knight?" Parn asked, quietly drawing his sword as he threw with a sideways glance at the Holy Knight.

"No need for tricks. If we rush in and surprise them while they're asleep, we have a good chance of victory."

The knight squared up, staring at the entrance, and tried to get his breathing under control.

It was eerily quiet, with no sound but the faint clink of their armor. A shaft of light shone through a crack in the door—it seemed there was a lookout just inside.

The knight advanced cautiously, followed closely by Parn, Ghim, and Deedlit. The other three trailed further behind.

"Be careful," Slayn whispered. His palms were damp with sweat...and who could blame him? They were about to challenge a wizard far more powerful than he.

Once they were close to the door, the knight brandished his sword and broke into a run. The sound woke the horses, and they startled with a shrill whinny.

The knight didn't hesitate—he used his momentum to kick down the door and leapt inside. Parn and Deedlit followed, and Ghim jumped through a moment behind.

The two lookouts clearly weren't expecting an attack—they stared blankly at their attackers for a moment, then scrambled for their swords.

"Deed and I will take these two—you and Ghim go upstairs!" Parn shouted as he readied his shield. He measured up the lookout on the left and provoked him with a flourish of his sword. Deedlit circled to the right and thrust her rapier toward the other man. By the time they crossed swords, the Valis knight and Ghim were already running up the stairs.

The second floor was a gallery corridor jutting out along the wall above the large first floor room. There were five doors lined up on the right.

One of those doors opened, and a woman in nightclothes swayed out.

Karla snapped awake to the sound of the horses whinnying. She hadn't expected an attack, but she wasn't unprepared.

Valis soldiers?

She tossed her blanket aside and grasped the ivory gown she had laid out to wear over her sleep clothes. She heard thundering footsteps approaching before she even managed to tie the sash.

Karla opened the door and stepped out into the hallway, glad she'd left the lights on. One of the Valis knights from earlier that day had somehow survived and was charging up the stairs toward her. A dwarf with a battle axe followed close at his heels. She knew she had to stay calm. The knight was likely the more formidable of the two, considering he'd survived what she was sure was a fatal attack. She had to be wary.

I'll use my most powerful magic to smite him. Karla raised both hands and waved them in a complex pattern, chanting in the ancient language.

"Mana is the source of all. All is born from mana, all is connected through mana, all returns to mana!" Her spell complete, she flung her hands toward the knight.

Blinding light shot from her hands and struck him right in the chest. His body shone with iridescent brilliance, then burst into a sparkling mist. When it dissipated, his body—as well as his armor and sword—had all faded into nothingness.

Ghim's eyes widened in shock, but he didn't flinch. He didn't give her enough time to cast another spell—he swung at her head with the flat of his axe.

But she anticipated his attack—she deftly jumped backwards, pulled herself together, and started another spell. While she was chanting, Ghim prepared to leap at her, glaring as he aimed carefully, knowing he could attack before she completed her spell.

However, when he looked at her face, he froze, mouth agape.

She looks just like her...

The sorceress completed her spell, and a white mist rose around Ghim, surrounding him. He instantly slumped forward, unconscious.

"Ghim!" Slayn yelled from where he stood on the first floor. He knew it was futile but rushed to cast Sleep Cloud nevertheless.

Karla's attention was drawn to the wizard downstairs, who seemed to be trying to cast a spell on her—a lower class version of the narcosis spell she'd just used. The two mercenaries she'd stationed downstairs as lookouts had already been defeated—a young warrior and an elf maiden were heading upstairs. Down below, she could see some kind of priest giving them assistance, as well as a thief who seemed to be looking for a place to hide.

She decided she didn't need to kill these intruders—instead, she cast the same spell she'd already used on the dwarf. White mist arose again, spreading down the stairs and across the first floor.

Etoh knew a spell had been cast upon him, so he asked for Pharis's divine protection under his breath and willed himself to stay conscious. The magic swirled, and he heard Parn and Deedlit collapse at the top of the stairs, while Slayn fell in a heap. Woodchuck didn't fall, as he'd already huddled in a hiding place, but Etoh had to assume he was asleep, too.

Etoh felt his body grow heavy. He staggered to his knees and crumpled from there. He summoned every ounce of will-power he possessed to keep his consciousness from descending into darkness.

His vision was blurry, and he couldn't feel his fingers. It was like his senses had fragmented. There was no pain, but he prayed to Pharis that this loss of sensation wouldn't overwhelm him.

He won the battle—he managed to stay awake, though he pretended the spell had worked. If he and his companions weren't going to be killed, better to stay still and feign sleep.

Karla looked down at the fallen intruders as she slowly de-scended the stairs. Two mercenaries emerged from the furthest door with their weapons drawn; their breaths caught at the sight before them.

"Wh-what happened, Lady Karla?" one of them asked.

"I'm sure you can guess," she replied. "If you truly call your-selves mercenaries, you should always be prepared for battle. You would've ended up like these two if I'd been slow to awaken."

Karla then gestured to the attackers. "We can't leave them here— the effects of my spell won't last forever. Lock them upstairs, in any room but the girl's. And be sure to take all of their weapons and put them in a separate chamber."

That would take care of the intruders. They wouldn't be able to escape a room locked with magic.

But what was she to do next? She was down to two mercenary guards, and she doubted she could take the princess through Valis's front lines with so few. She'd brought mercenaries from Marmo because she'd been sure it would take sacrifices to get this far, but now she was concerned. It seemed best to return to Kanon and bring her own subordinates.

At the same time, she wondered if these intruders could be swayed to her side. They'd impressed her with their finesse, and an elf and a wizard would make formidable companions. If they were simple adventurers, she was sure she'd be able to persuade them with a few well-chosen words—promise a big enough reward, and they'd gladly become her allies. If they were sensible and ambitious, perhaps they'd understand and even join her cause. Those were her most useful allies—she had many of them spread throughout Lodoss, carrying out missions on her behalf.

She'd failed to assassinate the King of Alania, but this time her goal was almost within reach. Once Princess Fianna was held captive by the Marmo army, perhaps the tide would turn their way. King Fahn of Valis was not the type to throw his kingdom away for his daughter—he would not hesitate to sacrifice her life in the name of justice. But having their princess taken hostage, perhaps executed, would destroy the morale of Valis's soldiers and knights. The war was at a stalemate right now, both forces equal in military might. A severe drop in morale could be all it took to tip the scales toward Marmo.

Karla made her decision—her top priority had to be summoning her subordinates for help. She went upstairs to check on the mercenaries, who had just dragged the last intruder into the room.

"That's it," one of them said. "So, er… What now?"

"Continuing as we have been would be too dangerous—the fort by the border is one of the Valis army's major strongholds, and it's possible that they've been warned about us via messenger. We need more manpower to push through. I will return to Kanon and bring back reinforcements."

"I get that we need more people, but what should we do until you get back?" The mercenaries looked uneasy—they'd known this would be a dangerous job, but they hadn't expected so many of their number to die. They'd known about the sorceress's fearsome powers and trusted her to use them. Now, they couldn't shake the suspicion that they were being abandoned.

"Don't worry, I'll return soon. For now, stay here and keep watch over the girl and the intruders. I'll summon a magical guard for their room, so you won't need to interact with them at all. Just be careful that nothing happens to the girl." She gazed at them steadily as she gave her instructions. "If you're attacked by Valis soldiers, you may escape or surrender. I won't blame you, and I promise to rescue you from prison. However, if you leave this place for *any* other reason…" She continued to stare at them both, face serious. "No matter where you go," she said, "I will find you, and your lives will be forfeit."

Both men gulped and quickly told her that they understood.

"Good," Karla said with a smile. "I need a moment to prepare, but then I will depart at once. I hope to return as quickly as I can." She turned then to the door. "Just in case," she said, "I will tell you how to open the lock on the intruders' door. Say the word 'Lasta,' and the door will open—without it, even trying to destroy the door itself will not work. Magic will make it as strong as iron and seal it as tight as solid rock."

Next, Karla began casting spells. As she finished the first, the doors closed slowly. As she completed the second, she took a dragon fang from her hair and tossed it onto the floor of the hallway. It shattered, and a white mass grew from it—the mass became an armed skeleton, frozen in position with a sword held limply in its hand.

The mercenaries recoiled in horror. "Wh-what *is* that?!" one of them stammered.

She gave the Spartoi a command in the ancient language, then said, "Don't worry—though this skeleton warrior's entire purpose is to fight, it won't attack you—only your enemies. It is both more skilled and more staunch than you, for it knows no fear and will thus neither falter nor run away."

The two mercenaries were so shocked by the Spartoi's appearance that they didn't notice the insult. They shared a glance and wordlessly vowed to stay away from that room at all costs.

"I'll be leaving now," Karla said. "Stay vigilant…" With that, she retreated to her room. When she reemerged, she was wearing her usual purple dress and carried a staff in her right hand. She descended to the bloodstained first floor and cast a spell with fierce arm gestures.

When the spell finished, she vanished.

The two mercenaries sighed deeply and started carrying their comrades' bodies outside for burial.

4

ETOH WAITED UNTIL THE TALKING HAD FADED, THEN stood up cautiously and looked around. His body was still numb from the spell, and he was exhausted both physically and mentally—from their forced march the day before, and from having used such advanced holy magic.

But he didn't have time to be concerned for himself. They had to escape as quickly as possible. He'd heard the entire conversation between the sorceress Karla and her two minions, and knew they only had a small window of time in which they could escape.

They had to hurry, but there was nothing he could do by himself. He could tell his companions were alive from the quiet sounds of their breathing and the rising and falling of their chests. He could try waking them, but since they'd been knocked unconscious by magic, he decided it would be safer to wait until they woke naturally.

Etoh sat hugging his knees and lost himself in thought.

Karla had been sent by the Marmo Empire and had been part of covert operations in Kanon and Valis. But Slayn had never heard of her. There was that powerful wizard in Marmo, though—the one called Wagnard. Could he have disguised himself as a woman?

Whoever she was, it was bizarre that they'd gotten sucked into two of her plots. It seemed too strange to be coincidence... Could this be a test from the gods?

That answer actually made Etoh feel better. It meant Pharis was watching over him.

It took a full two hours for the others to wake up. Ghim was first, then Deedlit, Parn, Slayn, and Woodchuck. Once they were all conscious, he filled them in on everything he'd overheard.

After he finished, Etoh turned to Parn. "What should we do now?"

"Do you even have to ask?" Parn said. "Rescue Princess Fianna and get out of here before that witch gets back!" He shook his head, still bleary from the spell.

"Right—the sooner the better," Deedlit said. "Those two men should be tired by now. At least *one* will probably be sleeping," She checked her shoulder armor and drew out the hidden dagger within—fortunately, it was still there.

"This is gonna be a bit dicey if that's our only weapon," Woodchuck commented, looking at the dagger. "The skeleton outside is pretty tough, right?"

"A Spartoi? They're more skilled than the average warrior," Slayn said—the prowess of the Spartoi was why they'd been used as sentinels at the Wizard Academy. Slayn crept quietly to the door and peered out through the crack—the armored skeleton stood there, its hollow eyes watching the door. Slayn turned back to the group. "It's definitely a Spartoi."

Parn stood up, fists clenched. "We'll still have to beat it," he said.

"*This* could be used as a weapon." With a huge crack, Ghim pulled a leg off the room's table. "They're not great, but we can use these as clubs. Better than nothing, at least."

Parn took two of the clubs, and Etoh took one. Deedlit kept her dagger, despite claiming, "Though it won't work on a skeleton." She slid next to the door and prepared to leap out.

"Leave this to me and Ghim," Parn said, brandishing his dual table legs.

Ghim and Parn stood side-by-side in front of the door, with Etoh a few steps behind them. When they were ready, Etoh said the word Karla had told the guards: "Lasta."

The door slowly creaked open, and the Spartoi appeared beyond. It seemed to know that the time had come to fulfill its purpose. The dangling scimitar was slowly raised, and it readied the circular shield at its chest.

Ghim and Parn leapt out to face the Spartoi. For the first blow, Parn aimed for its defenseless head, but a quick block by its shield deflected his attack. The skeleton struck back, wielding the thin scimitar like a skilled swordsman. Parn parried somehow with his left table leg and thrust the right toward the Spartoi's ribs, only for his strike to be blocked again.

Indeed, the Spartoi blocked every blow he attempted. And while Parn also managed to block the *skeleton's* blows, with every block, the table leg in his left hand was gradually being chipped away.

I won't last much longer like this, Parn thought, cold sweat dripping from his brow.

Behind him, his own table leg gripped in both hands, Ghim stood stock-still and waited for an opening. That was his preferred fighting style—cinching a victory in a single blow. He calmly followed the skeleton's movements, sizing it up. He doubted that this monster would be felled with his makeshift club…but there *was* a way. Parn just had to hold out.

"Ghim, what are you doing?! Parn's in danger!" Deedlit cried out from behind.

"Quiet!" Ghim yelled back. "Dwarves have our *own* way of fighting." Etoh and Deedlit were poised behind Parn, ready to jump in if necessary—but hoping they wouldn't need to.

"I can't last like this!" Parn cried out in despair as one table leg took a direct hit and finally snapped in two. The scimitar swung right through it and into Parn's torso, clanging hard against his armor. Deedlit screamed and looked away.

But the moment Ghim had been waiting for had arrived. The skeleton wasn't prepared for its sword to swing so far forward—it overbalanced and staggered a step toward Parn.

The moment the skeleton began pulling its sword back,

Ghim leapt into action. He swung low, then quickly struck upward toward the Spartoi's sword arm. He hit his mark on the humerus, which shattered with a dry crack—though Ghim's table leg shattered, as well. The Spartoi's scimitar clattered to the floor.

Ghim tossed his useless weapon aside. With a fearsome battle cry, he charged the Spartoi, leading with his right shoulder—the skeleton tried to block with its shield. There was a sickening crack and though Ghim grimaced at the sharp pain spiking through his shoulder, he didn't slow. Instead, he shoved the Spartoi up, hoisting it into the air.

The skeleton flailed its limbs, but it couldn't grab on to anything. With another angry roar, Ghim heaved the Spartoi over the gallery handrail and sent it crashing to the stone floor below.

The Spartoi tried to struggle to its feet, but after a few moments its crushed limbs fell limp to the floor, and the skeleton stopped moving.

"We did it," Parn said with a smile.

Ghim chuckled in return, then peered over the balcony. "Looks like our sleeping friends are up."

Parn joined him in looking downstairs. The two mercenaries had come out into the hallway of the first floor, one armed with a sword, the other carrying a spear. They looked at the crushed skeleton with trepidation, but after a moment they seemed to notice that their enemies were unarmed and dashed up the stairs.

"Leave this to me!" Deedlit cried as she slid past Parn. She brandished her dagger and quickly cast a spell. The room was engulfed in darkness for a moment, and then the spirit of light floated out. The little glowing sphere darted playfully toward the stairs.

"I'll go get our weapons!" Etoh yelled and dashed off—they were likely in the room next to their prison.

The Will-o'-wisp danced wildly across the width of the staircase, between Deedlit and the mercenaries. The elf readied her dagger.

"What's that?" asked the sword-wielding mercenary, taking an experimental swipe at the sphere of light. The moment his blade touched the light, he cried out in pain and rolled down the stairs, clutching his right hand—Will-o'-wisp had delivered a powerful shock to it before vanishing.

The man with the spear paused, distracted by his companion's screams. That turned out to be a fatal mistake—Deedlit let her dagger fly, and it buried itself right in the man's throat.

The first mercenary overcame the pain in his hand to challenge Deedlit with his sword, but Deedlit took up the dead man's spear and finished him off.

By the time Etoh returned with their weapons, it was over.

"Here's your rapier, Deedlit," Etoh said, handing the weapon over. He couldn't keep the impressed look off his face.

Deedlit sheathed her rapier at her hip, smoothed her disheveled hair with both hands, and turned to Parn. "Now what?"

"We rescue the princess, of course," Parn declared, heading back into the hallway.

It didn't take long to find the room where Princess Fianna was being kept. It was locked, and they could detect neither noise nor light from within.

Parn and Woodchuck exchanged a look. The thief sidled silently over to the door, took a wire from his pocket, and inserted it into the keyhole.

"Doesn't seem to be trapped," he murmured. He jiggled the wire a few times, then the lock opened with a click.

Parn opened the door. The faint light from the hallway illuminated the entryway, but it was pitch dark thereafter.

Parn started to step forward, but Deedlit stopped him.

"This is a *princess's* bedchamber," she whispered. "You *men* need to stay out."

Deedlit stepped forward into the room. With her excellent elvish night vision, she could make out a small, trembling figure hiding beyond the bed. Deedlit couldn't blame the princess for being frightened. She sighed and opened her arms wide.

"It's all right, Your Highness. My name is Deedlit, and my friends and I are here to rescue you. Please come out, there's no need to be scared." She paused, waiting for a response, but the girl said nothing. Deedlit could only hear the sound of her quick, strained breathing.

"*Lauma adonia moile de Pharis,*" Etoh called out from the doorway. Deedlit glanced back at him.

"*Moiros rahm,*" a young woman's hoarse voice replied. "Is there a Pharis cleric here?"

"I'm still only a priest, actually," Etoh replied, reverently bowing his head toward the darkness.

"We're here to rescue you, so please come this way," Deedlit repeated. A small shadow in white sleeping clothes rose from behind the bed and walked over hesitantly.

The moment she caught sight of Etoh's priest robes with the holy symbol of Pharis, she slipped past Deedlit to leap into Etoh's arms, letting out a high-pitched wail.

Etoh staggered backwards, and Parn had to support him so he didn't topple over under the girl's weight. Parn blushed deeply when he took a closer look at the girl—her nightgown was extremely sheer.

Deedlit scowled at Parn and unbuckled her cloak to drape over the girl's shoulders. Etoh was also blushing but didn't pull away from comforting the girl.

"Your Highness," Etoh said, "you need to prepare to leave this place. We don't know when the sorceress will be back, so we must go as soon as we can." Hearing that, Slayn stepped away to retrieve their things, Ghim and Woodchuck following close behind.

"Wonderful. Another midnight march," Woodchuck grumbled. He wasn't sure if it was the long day of walking or the lingering effects of the spell, but he felt much more sluggish than usual.

"You're welcome to stay here and sleep, if you want the witch to eat you," Ghim said, glaring at Woodchuck. "*Everyone's* tired. Stop complaining."

"All right, all right," Woodchuck sighed.

"I hope we can use that carriage," Deedlit mumbled to herself as she headed to the staircase. Parn followed after her to help.

"So do I," the princess stammered. She made to follow Deedlit and Parn and lend a hand, but Etoh stopped her.

"Don't worry, Your Highness—we can handle this ourselves. You should get ready to leave." With that, Etoh followed the others downstairs.

Princess Fianna headed back to her room. Once there, she at last noticed how immodestly she was dressed. Her face flushed with mortification—if Elmore, the Grand Chamberlain, found out she'd embraced a young priest while dressed like this, she would get *quite* a scolding.

Embarrassment aside, she was truly grateful for the priest's presence. She was relieved to be rescued, of course, but she still felt anxious surrounded by such strange people. Hearing someone recite Pharis prayers was a welcome taste of home. The others were so odd to her—she'd never met anyone at *all* like them back at Roid Castle. She shivered. She wanted to go *home*.

Before, she had wanted to travel to the front lines to encourage the troops—but instead, she'd been tricked and captured. Magic had kept her subdued and captive during the day, and at night, the guards made escape impossible. She had basically resigned herself to her fate—that of being taken to Marmo and used as a hostage—but omniscient and omnipotent Pharis had not abandoned her. He'd sent her angels of salvation, though they weren't exactly what she would've expected.

Fianna traced the sign of Pharis over her heart and offered a prayer of gratitude, then quickly flung off her nightgown and reached for the dress left folded on the table. *They're my only hope,* she told herself, but still couldn't shake the doubt that gripped her heart.

By the time Etoh made it outside, Deedlit was trying to calm a restless horse in a language he'd never heard. Another horse was already hitched to the carriage, waiting quietly. Parn was leading another horse, saddled and ready to ride, in a circle.

Deedlit brought the now-calmed horse over to Etoh and glanced at the priest. "Etoh, why don't you get into the carriage and take a nap? You look like you're about to fall over."

"But—" he tried to object, but the elf shook her head.

"You'll make yourself most useful by climbing into this carriage, wrapping yourself in a blanket, and going to sleep." Deedlit spoke gently but firmly. From the moment she'd woken from the spelled sleep, she'd noticed that Etoh looked completely exhausted—sick and deathly pale.

Etoh nodded and, without another word, climbed into the gilded carriage. He felt around the dark interior to find the seat and lie down.

A moment later, he slipped into a deep slumber, as if Karla's magic had only been delayed.

Dressed and ready to go, Princess Fianna came outside and climbed into the carriage, Deedlit right behind her. Parn forced an objecting Ghim onto a horse behind him. Once astride, the dwarf howled his protests at the terrifying height. Woodchuck took the carriage reins; Slayn sat beside him on the driver's seat. They were all exhausted, but the thought of Karla made them forget their fatigue. They would be killed if they met her again, and with her powerful magic, she might already know they'd escaped.

With that terrifying thought, they headed out.

Slayn's staff cast a wan glow on the path ahead. Dawn was still hours away, and their goal—the city of Adan—was even further off.

The journey through darkness seemed to last forever, but eventually the eastern sky brightened and the morning sun rose over the horizon. The tension abated with the darkness. Parn started to drift off despite being on horseback, and Ghim had to keep him awake for fear of sliding off along with him. Woodchuck handed the reins off to Slayn and fell quickly asleep. Slayn left the horses mostly to their own devices, trusting them to follow the path with only a light touch on the reins. They were travelling through fields, beneath the trees planted along the path, their leaves spread wide to receive the sunlight's blessing. Roosters crowed in the distance.

"We're still half a day from Adan?" Parn asked Slayn, giving the rising sun a gloomy look.

Slayn nodded. "We might get there before noon. It'll be another hot day."

"We should stop for a rest."

"We should," the wizard said. "We're all exhausted, as are the horses. It would be nice to rest in the shade during the heat of the day and then keep going this evening."

Despite their words, they pushed on. They didn't know how far the witch was behind them, after all. Around noon, however, the horses started to foam at the mouth, and they had to stop.

Etoh and Woodchuck were awake by then. Deedlit and Princess Fianna woke soon after and emerged from the carriage.

The group chose a large tree along the road and settled down under its branches. Ghim dismounted, relieved to feel the earth beneath his feet once more. Parn stretched out next to him and immediately started snoring. Deedlit looked on warmly. Slayn started to doze off where he sat.

"We're not out of the woods yet," Etoh said, slow and languid. "We won't have truly escaped Karla's clutches until we reach the Valis army. We'll be safe once we make it to Adan, so we'll just have to stay on our guard and keep moving forward." Etoh glanced at Parn's snoring form, then at Slayn, who was still sitting up but dead asleep. "Before we rest, we should decide who's going to ride next and who's going to drive. I could probably manage the latter."

"I'll ride next, then," Deedlit offered. "The princess can stay in the carriage, but Slayn and Parn should join her. Wood can drive with you, Etoh. Do you think Ghim would fit next to you both?"

"Not with my girth," the dwarf replied.

"Then you can sit behind me. There's a grip on the saddle. Just don't touch me, or I'll throw you off the horse."

"I'll keep that in mind," Ghim answered, looking serious. He'd had to cling to Parn's waist for dear life while sitting behind him—a horse's gait was *bouncier* than he'd expected.

"We'll rest a little while longer," Etoh said. "But then we have to get going. We shouldn't be too far from the city." He looked at the sunlight coming down through the trees. The supreme god Pharis ruled the sun, and its light was his blessing...but its heat was almost unbearable already. It would be a rough afternoon.

5

THE GROUP DEPARTED NOT LONG AFTER THE SUN HAD reached its zenith, in the hottest part of the day. The horse carrying Deedlit and Ghim led the way, followed by the carriage driven by Etoh.

There was nowhere for the witch to hide in the bright afternoon, but they still couldn't shake the feeling that they were being watched. Parn and Slayn probably felt the same despite being asleep—crammed uncomfortably on the carriage seat, they both moaned in their sleep with every bump in the road.

"Shouldn't be long now," Etoh murmured with a glance at the sky. There were several huge, pillar-shaped clouds to the west—it would likely rain that evening, but they would probably reach Adan before then.

Etoh glanced behind them on the road. There was no one there.

As he turned forward again, however, he noticed a black speck high in the air. He blinked to clear his eyes—it was still there.

He had a bad feeling.

Woodchuck was lost in thought, staring blankly at the unchanging rural landscape. He was mostly daydreaming about the reward from the Valis royal family. The Holy Knight who'd promised them a reward had died, but returning a princess to her family *had* to be worth a lot. He could use that money to become an executive of the Alania Thieves' Guild—or maybe he'd open an inn somewhere. Or he could even spend the rest of his life doing absolutely *nothing.*

That made him smile for a moment, but then he shook off that train of thought. Surely he was capable of doing something *more.* If he convinced himself to be satisfied with an ordinary life, he'd never make up for the twenty-odd years he'd lost in prison.

I gotta do something big...

His thoughts were interrupted by a poke to his side.

"Woodchuck—what do you think that is?" Etoh asked.

Woodchuck looked where the priest was pointing. He narrowed his eyes. "That black dot?" he asked. "Hm. It's pretty far, so it's hard to tell—but it's gotta be a bird." He snorted, annoyed that Etoh had intruded on his happy fantasy for something so trivial.

"Just a bird?" Etoh said. His heart pounded in his chest, and he couldn't shake the bad feeling. "Let's wake Slayn and Parn, just in case. There's no way that's just a bird—it's so far away, it must be *huge,* whatever it is. And it keeps getting bigger—I think it's heading straight for us!"

Woodchuck looked again. As Etoh had said, the bird *did* seem strangely large. "It better not be a dragon," he said in a shaky voice as he opened the small window. "Slayn! Parn! Wake up— we've got a job for you!" He pulled out his dagger, though he knew it'd be useless against whatever beast flew at them.

"Whoa!" Etoh cried, stopping the carriage in the middle of the road. Deedlit turned back with a questioning look.

"Hm? What's wrong?" Slayn asked sleepily, thin face peering out the window. He was still groggy, but upon seeing the alarm in Woodchuck and Parn's expressions, he climbed out of the carriage, putting up his hood to escape the oppressive sun.

"Look!" Etoh pointed, and Slayn strained his eyes.

"I can't tell from here…" He shook his head, then mumbled a spell under his breath. He focused on the black mass again, then his mouth opened in astonishment. "That's a roc! It's a legendary bird, extremely rare—only ever seen in the desert east of Flaim. They say they're messengers of the gods… But why would there be one flying around here?!"

"A roc?! There's no way!" Etoh cried. "It *has* to be the witch transformed. Look at the size of it!" Etoh was almost screaming, his calm demeanor overwhelmed by the panic the thought of Karla's fearsome powers roused.

"That does make sense," Slayn admitted. He gripped his staff and prepared to cast a spell.

Just as Parn and Fianna emerged from the carriage, the roc flew over their heads, flapped its massive wings, and landed before them in the middle of the road. The wings blew a huge cloud of dust into their faces; they crouched with tears in their eyes, rubbing to get the grit out.

Once they could all open their eyes again, the giant bird was gone—and in its place was a woman in a purple dress, a staff in her hand. She walked forward slowly, a faint smile on her lips like she'd found a new toy.

The witch Karla stopped quite close to them, the circlet with its eye-gems gleaming on her forehead. "I suppose not enough time has passed to say that I missed you," she said in a gentle voice.

Parn drew his sword and stepped forward to protect the others, ready to spring into action. Slayn held his staff out sideways and recited a spell in his mind, tapping his foot to enhance his focus.

"Why are you here?" Etoh asked in a hoarse voice. In the light of day, he could see the witch's pale, strikingly beautiful face. Her coal-black hair that seemed to absorb the light. A powerful magic emanated from her whole being—and while he couldn't suppress his fear, he *could* overcome it. He refused to surrender to her power.

Slayn thought she looked strangely sad. But a moment later, the woman's eyes shone blue and cruelly intelligent. Her red lips began a bewitching dance.

Parn heard a strangely musical murmur. He braced himself, sword and shield prepared, determined to take on her magic with his entire body. Anger welled up inside him at the thought of all that power used for injustice.

But somehow, the witch's strange words seeped into the anger he was feeling. Parn blinked. The witch was smiling at him, not the frosty expression from earlier—her gaze was full of tolerance and patience, like that of a goddess of mercy. Parn realized she would never harm him. His weapon drooped in his hand.

"Stay alert!" Slayn warned. "She's casting a spell on you!"

The voice seemed like it came from far away, but it snapped Parn back to his senses, and he willed himself to stay grounded.

"None of your tricks, witch!" Parn shouted in rage. He swung wildly, as if trying to destroy the spider's web entangling him. Etoh half expected Parn to charge her then and there, but the young warrior simply resumed his original stance, burning eyes locked on the sorceress.

"You stole this girl from the mansion, *and* you have the strength of will to shake off my magic...you have proven yourselves worthy adventurers." Karla looked at them with honest admiration for a moment, then her ice-cold gaze swept over them. "It would be a *pity* to kill you now. Will you join me? You may not understand it right now, but everything I am doing is for the benefit of Lodoss in the end. I can give you all that you desire— wealth, fame, knowledge, or perhaps a beautiful companion?"

"No way!" Parn shouted, furious.

"If you don't desire anything, that's fine. Hand over the girl and leave this place at once. If you refuse, I will show no mercy. You will die here, your corpses charred to cinders!"

Karla waved her hands and chanted spells one after another in a flowing melody. With each incantation, a flaming red sphere appeared above her and started spinning like a living thing.

"Unbelievable," Slayn whispered, his voice steeped in despair. "Each of those is a fire spell. Just *one* would be enough to kill us all."

"Isn't there something we can do?" Parn asked.

"No. It would take all my mental capacities to produce just *one* of those orbs."

"Okay." Parn made up his mind. He'd rather die fighting like his father than live in disgrace. He forced his breath to calm, scanned the landscape between him and the witch, then raised his sword to his shoulder and pointed the tip straight at her bosom.

Deedlit noticed what he was doing, gulped, and opened her mouth to speak.

"Wait!" a voice called out—it was shaky, but resolute. "If I go with you, will you spare them?"

Princess Fianna stepped forward. Etoh watched as her eyes turned to the witch, unwavering, with royal pride and dignity—though he also saw how her slender limbs trembled.

He edged discreetly over to the princess.

"Your Highness, we'll buy you time," he whispered quickly. "She won't use magic that will harm you—if we all run, we might distract her long enough for you to escape. Take the horse, gallop through the fields and into the forest, then head for Adan. Have faith in Pharis's protection." Etoh raised his arms. "Now go!" he cried, and the holy light of Pharis flickered above his head. For a moment, a bright flash outshone even the sun, and the witch was forced to avert her eyes.

Fianna stared at Etoh as if she had no idea what to do. "Go!" the priest cried, and Fianna ran for the horse.

Slayn cast darkness and put the cloak of night behind the princess, blocking her from the witch's view. He then stepped sideways to prepare his next spell.

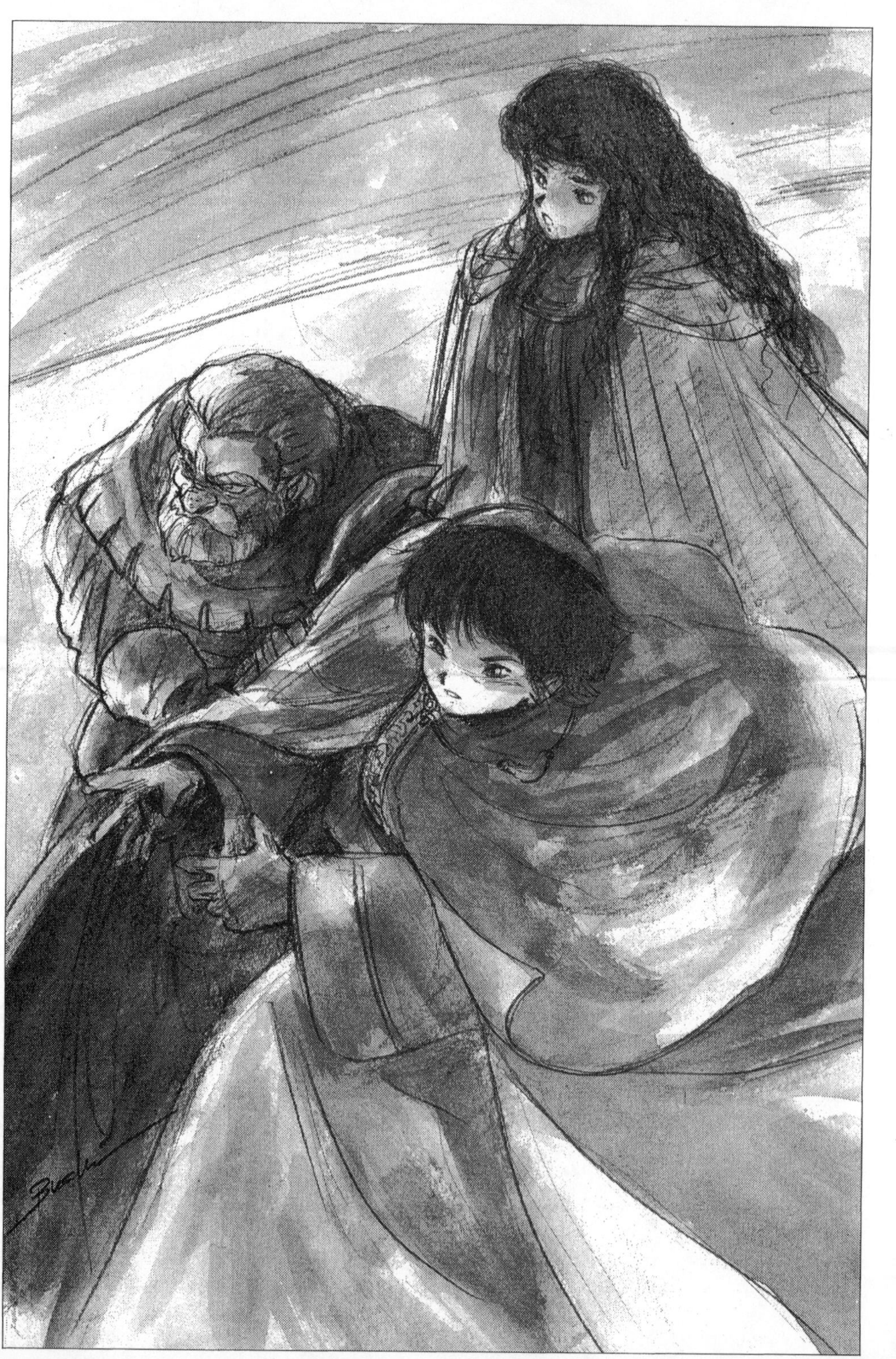

Deedlit stepped up next. "Wind maiden unfettered, stop the air's vibrations and muffle all sound," she said, casting the spell of silence where the witch stood. Then she drew her rapier. Parn and Ghim were already running.

Karla gestured with her hands and tried to send the balls of fire smashing down on top of them—but when she opened her mouth, no sound came out. She recognized the elvish magic of Sylph, the wind elemental.

Impertinent fools! Karla shook the ring on her left finger and erected invisible magic protections around her. She stepped back out of the area affected by the elemental's spell.

Parn ran in to stop her escape. He thrust his sword at her, but the blade was stopped by an invisible wall. The impact stung his hand, almost making him drop his sword.

"If you want to die that badly, I'll indulge you!" Finally able to speak, Karla focused and spread the magic wall around her in order to cast her next spell uninterrupted.

Parn and Ghim were propelled backwards. Parn fought to resist the unstoppable force, furious at his own powerlessness. He knew they couldn't win.

But then, in his moment of despair, a cloud of dust rose beyond the road.

Slayn's eyes were still keen due to the farsight spell, so it was easy for him to see what approached. He removed his hood and called out joyfully to Etoh and Woodchuck, who were hiding under the carriage. "It's the Valis Order of Knights—at least twenty of them! And those robes in front…that's a wizard from the Academy! It must be Lord Elm, the Valis court wizard!"

With a quick prayer of thanks to Pharis, Etoh relayed the information to Parn at the top of his lungs.

"Amazing!" Parn's face brightened, the despair and hopelessness disappearing.

Karla overheard—no, the obnoxious priest had made *sure* she heard. Rage coursed through her but dissipated quickly.

I suppose fate is on their side. She switched to another spell as she glanced behind. As the priest had said, a group of armed horsemen were galloping toward her at full speed, calling out for Princess Fianna.

Karla smiled. "Cherish your good fortune—just don't let it go to your heads. And never appear before me again. Miracles don't repeat themselves, after all." She dissolved her magic wall and activated another spell—one that sounded quite different from her usual incantations, spoken in the ancient language.

Truth be told, it sounded very similar to Etoh's prayers.

"That's Marfa's holy magic," Slayn said to Etoh in wonder.

As they watched, Karla vanished, her smile unwavering the entire time.

"That witch must be a priestess of Marfa," Slayn explained. "The spell she cast is known as the return spell and can only be used by Marfa priestesses."

Etoh wondered why a wizard would be more familiar with holy magic than a priest like him. He'd heard that most wizards worshiped Rahda, god of knowledge—but he'd never seen Slayn pray.

"A Marfa priestess?" Ghim asked with a grave look as he pressed closer to the wizard.

Slayn nodded, surprised by the dwarf's intensity. "And a high-ranking one, too. At least from what I've heard."

"I *knew* it!" Ghim shouted.

"What do you mean?" asked Slayn. "You know something, don't you? Something you've been hiding."

"I'm not hiding *anything*," Ghim scowled. His stomach heaved with emotion—joy and anger twisting together. "I didn't think it could be true...but how is she casting magic? And why would she side with Marmo?"

6

SLAYN SIGHED IN RELIEF AND WALKED OVER TO PARN. He knew Elm from his time at the Academy, though they had only overlapped for a few years. They were more than a decade apart in age, but Slayn had been accepted at the Academy when he was still a child.

Elm was a prodigy, similar in strength to Wagnard, and a passionate devotee of Pharis. It seemed natural that he was quickly welcomed as Valis's court wizard.

Slayn bowed deep to the middle-aged wizard leading the knights. "It's been a while, Lord Elm," he said. "Do you remember me? Slayn Starseeker?"

The knights were wary, but Lord Elm took one look at the

robe, staff, and Slayn's thin face—and smiled. "I do remember you—you have a distinctive face and voice. You've grown up."

"Thank you."

"I must ask—what are you doing here? Did you leave on a journey after the Academy closed?"

"Something like that," Slayn said, sidestepping the question. "Are you searching for Princess Fianna?"

"We've been chasing after a group of merchants that took her. But how did *you* know? Have you seen her?"

Slayn nodded. "It's a long story, but she is with us. The wizard we were fighting had kidnapped her, but we rescued her."

As if on cue, the princess emerged from behind Slayn's wall of darkness—she'd chosen not to escape by herself after all. The knights cheered in relief and delight, and several quickly dismounted and rushed over to her.

"Looks like we're the ones who should bow to *you*," Elm said. "Slayn, I can't thank you enough. I had no idea you'd grown to be such a fine wizard. By the way—have you found your star yet?"

"Not yet." Slayn answered. "But don't just thank me. We were only able to rescue the princess thanks to *this* young man." He gestured at Parn. "Without his skills and willpower, we never would have gotten her here safely."

"I see," said Elm, nimbly swinging down from his horse. "Then I must thank you as well. What's your name?"

"I'm Parn," he said with a knight's salute—but he was distracted by the Holy Knights' white suits of armor. His thoughts from the day before swam through his head as he continued,

"I am the son of Tessius, a Valis Holy Knight." Parn himself was surprised as he blurted it out, though once it was said, he watched them intently for their reaction. Valis knights should know why his father died.

"Tessius the Holy Knight?" Elm said more sharply than Parn had expected. It made him uneasy. "Is that true? Are you truly Tessius's son?"

"Yes. This armor is proof—it may be dirty, but it's still the official armor of the Valis Order of Knights."

"It *does* look like it," Elm said, looking him over.

"There's no mistake, Lord Elm," said one of the Holy Knights. "His armor is the same as ours."

"It must be true," said another. "No one would bother claiming to be Tessius's son."

"What do you mean?" Parn cut in. "Please tell me—how did my father die? My mother wouldn't tell me anything, just said to have faith in him. But rumors say he died a *coward's* death..."

Elm approached Parn and warmly placed a hand on his shoulder. "Your father did indeed disobey orders, but he was *never* a coward. Lord Tessius's duty was to patrol the northern border with another young knight and report the discovery of any enemies he saw. But when he learned that a small village was in danger of being raided, Tessius sent the other knight to make the report and stayed behind to fight the savages alone.

"Your father went to the village by himself, warned them of the danger, and bought the residents time to escape by fighting the savages alone. There were too many of them—he had no chance. Still, he didn't hesitate. And because of what he did, damage to the village was minor."

"Is that true?" Parn's voice was hoarse.

"It is. His bravery should have been praised. But the laws of chivalry are absolute, no exceptions—so the King had to strip him of his knighthood for disobeying his orders. Anyone who knows the truth, though, can't help but admire his courage."

"Among the Holy Knights, Lord Tessius's actions were honorable," a young knight said. "There are twisted rumors about his death because we can't openly tell the truth...but do you really think rumors such as those could keep one knight's name alive for so long?" The young knight seemed almost jealous of Tessius's son.

"I'm happy for you," Deedlit said, gently taking Parn's arm.

"And Lord Tessius brought us yet *more* honor today," the young knight went on. "For among those who rescued our kidnapped princess is none other than his son! This *must* be Pharis's divine guidance!"

"So Dad's death wasn't dishonorable after all..." For the first time, Parn felt a surge of pride that the armor he wore came from his father, who had made the right choice—the very same one *Parn* would have made. It was further proof that his father's blood ran in his veins.

Parn looked up into the brilliant sky and said a prayer. "I thank you for the blood of my father, which runs in my veins."

In return, he could feel his father's spirit looking down upon him.

CHAPTER IV

The Great Magus

1

AFTER EIGHT PEACEFUL DAYS OF TRAVEL, THE GROUP arrived in Roid, the imperial capital of Valis.

The city's streets bustled with great throngs of people, and both sides were lined with lively shops. The country may have been at war, but that was a faraway concern for the city's residents.

As it was built on a delta, the buildings were short, and even the spires of the royal castle jutting up from the cityscape were smaller than those in Alania or Kanon. Instead, the castle of Valis was a sprawling complex surrounded by a moat and stone wall, taking up the greater part of the city center.

Radiating out from the castle, streets twisted and turned

seemingly at random, and the simple, regular facades of the architecture made it difficult for newcomers to find their way to the castle gates. Waterways cut through the city, more obstacles to easy travel. Valis may have been built on flatlands, but the city's layout made it a fortress.

"This is Roid? It's smaller than I expected," Deedlit remarked rudely, not caring that Elm was in earshot. Parn gave her a glance and a sneaky nod.

"It *is* small compared to the great city of Allan. But I can promise you that these are the most loyal citizens you'll find anywhere." Elm stopped and greeted the crowd of people in front of them, who bowed their heads and made way.

After a long ride, the group finally reached the castle gates and crossed the drawbridge into the courtyard. They dismounted there—it was custom to walk the rest of the way to the castle.

The carriage carrying Princess Fianna stopped as well, and the princess slowly descended, daintily holding the hem of her dress. The castle guards who caught sight of her called her name and waved, delighted at her safe return. Fianna waved back with a bashful smile.

Elm led the princess and a small group of knights into the castle; one of the knights led Parn's group to a luxuriously decorated parlor to wait. It was furnished with plush sofas and a large table imported from the continent. A glass-doored cupboard was stocked with expensive-looking liquors, and a variety of goblets were arranged conveniently within reach. One entire wall was taken up by a massive painting depicting a battle with a demon, and the high window on the south wall was fitted with stained glass depicting the supreme god Pharis, which cast bright shapes throughout the room.

That single room was about the size of Slayn's entire house.

"I guess we shouldn't help ourselves to the booze," Parn said to Deedlit with a question in his voice and shining eyes. Deedlit flatly refused to answer and settled on the sofa as Parn gazed longingly at the bottles.

The expensive liquors didn't interest Ghim; he just fiddled with a dwarf-made craftwork and paced the room.

"It's rather nerve-racking," Slayn remarked, though he still spoke in his usual gentle manner. The furnishings didn't interest him, and he was considering taking a book out of his bag.

"A fancy room like this isn't meant for a guy like me," Woodchuck complained as he perched uncomfortably on the sofa. "I feel like I'm locked up in a gilded prison... I don't feel much like drinking, either. I hope they don't take long."

Just then, there was a knock on the door and two soldiers entered. Woodchuck nearly jumped out of his skin at the sound— the group couldn't contain a laugh at his frazzled reaction.

"His Majesty the King is ready for you. Please follow me." The soldiers bowed and motioned for them to follow.

The courteous reception from such fine royal soldiers made Parn suddenly self-conscious. The hand on his sword shook, and he couldn't help but notice every bit of grime on his armor. He tried to wipe down the dirtiest parts with a cloth, but it was too late to do much.

As they made their way toward the throne room, Parn was impressed at the sheer size of the castle, and he glanced around restlessly, trying to take everything in. At one point, they passed a group wearing different armor from the Valis knights. The two groups saluted each other in silence and exchanged watchful glances.

"Did you see those knights?" Slayn whispered to Etoh.

"I did. What about them?"

"They must be from Flaim, the desert kingdom. They had the hawk crest on their right shoulders."

"The Flaim Order of Knights! Are *they* going to war with Marmo, too?"

"It would be good news if they were," Slayn replied. The Knights of Flaim were renowned for their bravery throughout Lodoss.

Flaim had begun as a desert tribe known as the Tribe of Storm. It had been mired in a years-long war with another desert group, the Tribe of Fire—otherwise known simply as "the savages." A few years earlier, though, the Tribe of Storm finally achieved a decisive victory, crowned a king, and established the nation of Flaim. King Kashue, also known as the Mercenary King, was rumored to have sword skills unparalleled in all of Lodoss.

Flaim would certainly be a reassuring ally in the war against Marmo.

The group finally reached the end of the winding hallways and reached the throne room. They waited outside the door for a few moments and then were ushered into a large hall.

The throne room was huge and open, imposing and stately. A crimson carpet ran across the stone floor and up the steps to the throne—the back wall held a giant portrait of the king, with the silver cross, the Valis coat of arms, and the holy symbol of Pharis next to it. Valis knights, courtiers, and women in beautiful dresses lined the edges of the path. Parn felt almost dizzy at the sight.

I am the son of a Holy Knight, he told himself and did his best to stride down the carpet with confidence.

King Fahn sat before them on his throne. He wore a loosely tailored gown and had a beard that could rival that of a dwarf. He was at least sixty—the wrinkles etched into his face were a monument to his countless accomplishments. When he looked down at the six adventurers, his gaze was like the ocean, intense, kind, and overwhelming. Feeling those eyes on him, Parn felt almost suffocated. He dropped to one knee, and his companions followed suit.

Several others stood near the legendary king. First was Elm, the court wizard, who had changed into a magnificent white robe. Beside him was an old man in a gown embroidered with the symbol of Pharis—Genart, the high priest of the Pharis temple. Etoh was dazzled to be in such a holy presence.

Another man in a crown sat in a temporary throne beside King Fahn. Slayn noted the hawk emblem embroidered on his attire.

That must be the Mercenary King Kashue…

The Mercenary King had a black beard and sharp eyes like a bird of prey. His seat beside the King of Valis indicated that they were in an equal alliance, so Flaim must be planning to join them in the war against Marmo.

The king's voice resounded throughout the hall, gentle but dignified. "You must be the adventurers who rescued my daughter. As King—and as a father—I thank you from the bottom of my heart. My daughter should be here to thank you in person—forgive me for her absence, but she is offering prayers of penitence at Pharis Temple to atone for her sins. She is a handful, but her mistakes in no way diminish what you've done. Please accept this token of my gratitude."

At his words, one of the courtiers stepped toward Parn with a heavy sack. He kneeled and presented it with a few respectful words.

Parn decided it would be rude to refuse, so he accepted it with a bow. "Thank you for this." The bag was heavy in his hands—there had to be a ton of gold coins inside.

This'll make Wood happy, he thought, handing it back to the thief.

"Be at ease. I may be a king, but I am also a father welcoming those who saved his daughter's life. I should be the one to kneel to *you*." He turned to the crowd. "I want everyone here to know that I shall punish my daughter, not as her father, but as king. For sneaking out of the castle without permission and causing this trouble, she will spend the next two months confined to her room, forbidden from going out in public…"

There were a few gasps from the crowd, but most of the gathered people nodded in acceptance. Two months' probation was a heavy punishment, and being trapped in her room would certainly feel like being in prison for a young woman.

"As for the woman who kidnapped her, she appears to be a wizard serving Marmo. I have received a report from Elm and compared it with what my daughter told me. I would like your perspective, as well—you are the only ones to survive a confrontation with her, after all."

Parn shot Slayn a look. Slayn nodded and stood, scanned the room, then bowed deeply.

"My name is Slayn. Like Lord Elm, I studied under the great Professor Larcus at the Wizard Academy in Alania. The witch Karla's magic was like nothing I'd ever seen. She used magic in the ancient language *and* Earth Goddess Marfa's holy magic, and she cast extremely high-level spells with ease. The power of her spells might even surpass that of the late Professor Larcus. I apologize for this comparison, but not even Lord Elm has the power to strike down five Holy Knights with one fire spell."

"I certainly do not," said Elm. "Fire magic is powerful, but I cannot imagine our knights being defeated in one strike."

"But that's exactly what she did," Slayn emphasized. Murmurs cut through the crowd. It was hard to believe that Marmo had a wizard like that as an ally, but if it were true…

"Silence." Fahn raised his right hand and the noise stopped. "You're saying that this witch is more skilled at magic than my trusted Elm?"

"I'm afraid so," answered Slayn, and kneeled once again to indicate he had no more to add.

"More powerful than Elm, considered Larcus's best pupil? She is a fearsome witch indeed. Do you know who she is, Elm? Her name was Karla, correct?"

"I found Slayn's story hard to believe as well, so I searched my memories to see if anything came to mind—and I recalled a legend."

"Of course you did. What was it?"

"Long ago, when an ancient kingdom ruled this land, magic was much more powerful than it is now. Wizards of that time were far more fluent in the ancient language we use for our spells today—we would likely sound like babbling infants to the wizards of long ago. When the kingdom fell, all its wizards shared its fate...except, they say, a single sorceress who managed to escape harm. Her name was Karla. Since then, a sorceress named Karla has appeared periodically throughout Lodoss's history."

Fahn shook his head. He raised his left hand from the throne's armrest and pointed at Elm. "Are you saying that this legendary sorceress is the same witch who kidnapped my daughter? It would be a simple thing for a witch to change her appearance...but if your theory is true, she would be more than five hundred years old."

"I don't have proof—only a hunch," Elm replied. "But now that Professor Larcus is gone, the person most likely to know the truth is the Great Magus Wort."

Fahn laughed. "*That* eccentric old man?"

"He may be eccentric, but he is extremely knowledgeable. And I don't know any other way to ascertain the truth of her identity."

"I suppose you're right. But who will go all the way up into the Moss mountains to ask him? The war with Marmo will only get worse—we cannot afford to lose a single soldier."

Elm looked at the king, his expression serious. "If Karla is truly a survivor of the ancient kingdom, we will be up against magic far beyond what any of us can handle. I heard that Kanon's Shining Hill fell when a giant meteor dropped from the sky, destroying its walls—even Wagnard, Marmo's court wizard, doesn't have that sort of power. We need to know what we are up against."

"You truly feel strongly about this..." Fahn shot Elm a wry smile, then nodded. "We can't send just anyone on this mission. The old man never leaves his mountain tower, and he hates visitors. To get there, whoever we send will have to pass through the dwarven ruins to the south—the Tunnel of Evil. It's infested with ogres and dragons." He turned to a man with a decorated helmet. "Leonis, I need you to select someone suitable from among the order—"

"I can do it," Parn chimed in. He hadn't been sure whether he should volunteer, but once he spoke up, he found himself sure it was the right choice. "If you choose one of your Holy Knights, they will leave a hole in your defense that can't easily be filled. I could stay here as a mercenary, but that would be much less use to Valis."

Fahn looked down at the youth kneeling before him and felt young again. "Is that Tessius's son?" he whispered to Elm.

"It is," Elm murmured in reply.

Parn *did* resemble the Holy Knight Tessius in both face and voice—and probably in action as well, as he had just chosen to fulfill a thankless but vital role over honorable service in battle. Fahn had all but assumed that the young man would ask to join the Valis knighthood. Elm had mentioned that Parn was more than willing, and had recommended him as an upstanding young man suitable for the position—though there was much he would need to learn.

His bravery in rescuing Fianna made him worthy of the title, and he *was* Tessius's son. But if he were given a knighthood for only those reasons, the young knights who had never heard of Tessius would be upset. They had spent years training as squires, after all, and were only awarded the honor of knighthood once they were recognized for their skills and character. But if Parn fulfilled this ordeal, those young knights would have to accept him. Not everyone knew Tessius, after all, but *everyone* knew of the southern dwarven ruins. That tunnel was one of the most treacherous parts of Lodoss, rivaling even the Forest of No Return.

"Parn," the king began, "I am sorry about Tessius. We couldn't give him a burial with honors, and the stress drove your mother away from Valis. I would like you, at least, to fight with me as an honorable knight. However, you need to pass a test to join our Order. I will send you with a letter for Wort. Show me that you can accomplish this task and I will ask you to serve under me as my vassal."

"Upon my life," Parn said, heart practically bursting with joy.

"The journey to Wort's mansion will be difficult—as I said, you will have to pass through ruins swarming with deadly creatures, and the witch may come after you again. You would still go?"

"Of course," Parn replied. He felt like a hero—a modest hero, maybe, but that seemed more fitting, anyway.

"Wonderful! I haven't felt such hope in so long…" The Hero King laughed, stood, and clapped his hands. "This is a great day. First we welcomed a justice-loving desert king and now a brave son of Tessius. There is no doubt in my mind that we will be victorious in this war. Everyone, prepare to feast! We will enjoy ourselves tonight!"

The crowd let out a cheer. The double doors swung open, and servants swooped from the throne room to begin the preparations. When the time came, music rang out and the banquet began.

Kashue, King of Flaim and the guest of honor, was not even thirty years old. He had been known since his youth for his brave deeds, and had defeated the enemy Tribe of Fire and established the Kingdom of Flaim when he was in his early twenties. He was crowned the "Mercenary King" as a nod to his beginnings as a mercenary, but his skills at both swordsmanship and statecraft were incredible. Though his country was less than a decade old, the hearts of his people were one with King Kashue.

The desert savages, worshippers of the Dark God Phalaris, had been constantly at war with both the Tribe of Storm and

147

the Kingdom of Valis. Immediately after the foundation of the new country, the new king had sent a messenger seeking an alliance with Valis, and Kashue himself had come to celebrate King Fahn's sixtieth birthday in person. Fahn said that his friendship with Kashue was one that transcended age.

The Mercenary King commanded the attention of the entire party—young knights gathered around to hear of his heroic exploits, and noblewomen tried to catch the bachelor king's attention.

The knights also clustered around Parn, treating Tessius's son like a long-lost friend, praising his bravery for risking his life to save their princess, and praying for his safety on his journey to the tower.

Crowds had formed around Deedlit and Ghim as well, since elves and dwarves were rarely seen in the Valis court. Questions rained down on Deedlit with barely a pause in between, and she couldn't conceal her confusion. She answered perfunctorily and wondered how human noblewomen could bear wearing such cumbersome dresses.

Ghim had no patience for the curious stares, but he could distract with his skills as a craftsman. He appraised the ladies' jewelry and even improved some pieces with a quick tweak to enhance their presentation. It was like a one-dwarf workshop had sprung up around him as the ladies of Valis brought him their jewelry, one after another.

Young ladies also swirled around Etoh, who was now wearing his priestly robes. In Valis, Pharis priests were respected even more highly than knights. He was greeted personally by High Priest Genart and offered a position at the Great Pharis Temple in Roid.

Genart explained that he was in the process of reforming the order of Pharis with King Fahn's support, but it was not progressing as planned. The order of Pharis stood for discipline and law; as a side effect of that, the organization tended to prioritize seniority and time served over ability—stodgy habits that the high priest was attempting to shake. He asked Etoh to assist, and the young priest gladly accepted. After all, if Parn became a Valis knight and Etoh joined the Pharis order, the friends could keep working together.

Slayn, clad in a brand new Sage's robe, was deeply involved in a serious discussion with Elm about the witch's identity, the war with Marmo, and the governing of Valis. Besides teaching magic, the Wizard Academy taught a variety of academic disciplines, all considered necessary to the proper ruling of a country. As the only Academy-educated wizard in Valis, Elm rarely had a chance to discuss such things with a peer.

Elm had hoped to organize a council of wizards at court, but Valis had been wary of magic for an extremely long time. Few young people aspired to be wizards, certainly not enough to form a proper school. Elm was a passionate devotee of Pharis and loyal to Valis, making him an even rarer case. Though he hadn't originally intended to, Slayn found himself offering advice.

The banquet grew more cheerful and rowdy as the night progressed. But while most of the companions basked in words of gratitude and endless offers of wine, there was one who stood alone.

Woodchuck could feel the stares of contempt and disgust. He could almost hear the whispered discussion of his occupation and wondered, *How were my actions any different from Parn's?* as dark embers of resentment flickered in his mind.

2

THE BANQUET CONTINUED LATE INTO THE NIGHT, eventually breaking into courtly dancing. Parn and his companions couldn't keep up with the intricacies of court manners, so they eventually found sanctuary together in a corner of the hall, drinking and talking among themselves as if in their own private refuge.

"So now Parn's dragging us all deep into the Moss mountains, huh?" Deedlit needled him, but deep inside she was secretly pleased that her journey with these people would continue. If Parn became a knight of Valis, there would be nothing to keep the two of them together.

"Look, I'm sorry. I don't mean to force you into this—I want you all to come with me, but I know you have your own goals. We've just gotten this huge reward, I understand that you might not want to risk your lives again—and I'm prepared to go alone." Parn's reply was quiet but determined, and his eyes never left Deedlit's face.

Deedlit was taken aback. She had expected Parn to be stunned or at least surprised at her reaction, and then she could graciously volunteer to come along, demanding his gratitude. But Parn's intense determination put a stop to that; she wrapped her lithe arm around him and gave him a light kiss on the cheek.

"You've grown into a fine warrior," she told him. "You win, for now. I'll follow you."

"I'm coming too," Ghim slurred excitedly. "Now, don't thank me—this is my problem, too."

"I'll gladly join you this time," Slayn said. "I can't pass up a chance to meet Wort."

"Do I even need to say anything, buddy?" Etoh said with a sunny smile.

They all turned to Woodchuck.

"I know, I know, in for a penny, in for a pound. I'll go with you—I know you'll end up needing me, anyway," he said cheerfully, hiding his darker thoughts.

Even if we make it back somehow, you lot will be the ones they thank.

Woodchuck turned toward the center of the hall so no one would notice his dejection. The others followed his gaze.

At the center of the great hall, King Kashue was dancing gracefully with one of the noblewomen. He had only been king for a short time, but he had perfectly mastered the etiquette and decorum of the court. The nosiest of the noblewomen were gossiping about where he might have gotten lessons. Some speculated that he might be Kanon's third prince, who had run away more than seven years ago, or a royal who had drifted in from the continent. Kashue himself never discussed his origins. When asked about his past, he replied that his present was everything.

King Fahn stayed at the banquet for only a short time, retiring early. Without the king's attention presiding, the ceremony and formality of the party loosened as the night grew later.

Woodchuck, Ghim, and Slayn crept away and withdrew to their guest rooms, but Parn lagged behind, not wanting the night to end. The crowd around him had thinned until the only one left at his side was an unexpectedly cheerful Deedlit. She hadn't eaten or drunk much and wasn't speaking to anyone—she'd refused all requests for a dance from the knights, saying that elves had no such custom. Yet she seemed unexpectedly happy just to sit beside him.

Etoh had tried to return to his room several times, but each time he was stalled by one of the young ladies, asking for Pharis teachings or stories of his adventures.

"He's so popular," Parn pouted, watching his friend.

"Of course. He's attractive enough—and considering the devout Pharis following here, it's no wonder a young priest is drawing attention," Deedlit chuckled, leaning against the wall beside Parn.

"May I join you?"

The sudden greeting interrupted their peaceful bubble, which annoyed Deedlit. She turned to the newcomer harshly.

"What do you want?" she huffed.

"What a stubborn elf," he laughed loudly.

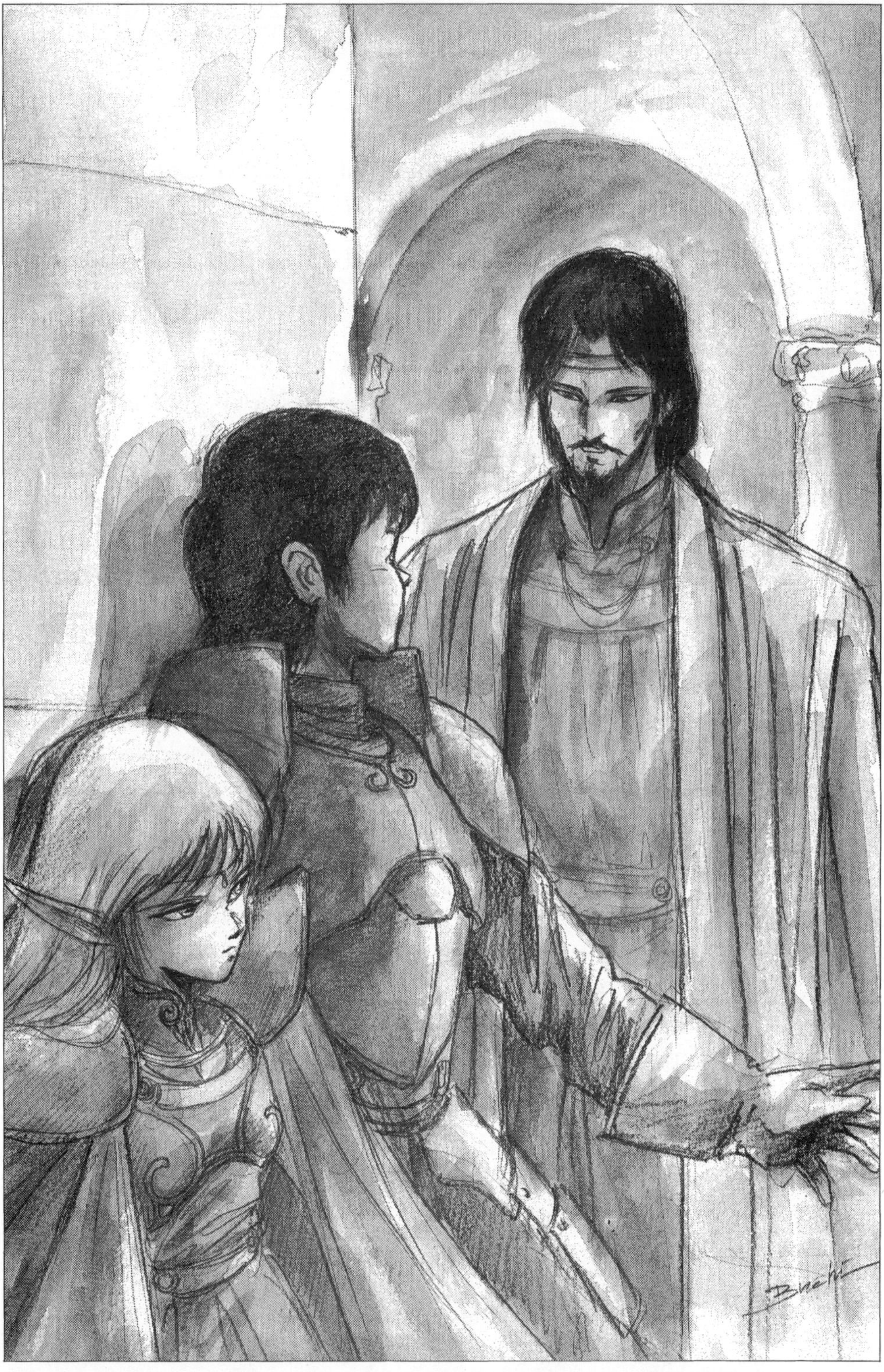

Parn was struck silent—the man talking to them was the King of Flaim himself. "F-forgive me," Parn quickly apologized with a bow.

"At ease," the king replied. "No need for decorum—I was once a swordsman for hire, just like you."

"I-is there something I can do for you, sir?" Parn couldn't help but be nervous, but Kashue's frank manner was helping to relax him.

Deedlit, on the other hand, wasn't bothering to hide her displeasure—she pursed her lips, vowing not to speak to him at all.

"Nothing in particular," the king replied. "I was just in the mood to talk to a young warrior about his adventures."

"O-of course..." Parn said. He began to tell the story of their rescue of the princess. While he talked, he watched the King of Flaim, hoping to observe how he was different from Parn himself, thinking that he might become a better man if he could just bridge the gap between them.

Kashue seemed to enjoy Parn's story, even giving advice during the battle scenes based on his own experiences. He had a wealth of knowledge about battle tactics for one-on-one combat and had survived countless chaotic melees. He even offered to give Parn a sparring lesson the next day.

As Parn's story wrapped up, the clear voice of a troubadour rang out. The man picked out harmonies on a lute as he sang a song of heroic deeds—an epic poem about the war against the demon gods.

Brought to this world through our most dire mistake,
the fearsome Demon King whose tale I tell,
left death and dire destruction in its wake.
With kingdoms destroyed, the world to darkness fell.

But light then gathered there to fight its war,
the humans rose, armed with shield and sword,
the elves with bows arose from forests far,
and dwarves joined in with axes freshly forged.

Forces of light, a shining sun of hope,
banished the awful darkness from this land.
A shout of triumph rang from shore to shore,
from forest, mountain, ocean, sky, and sand.

Abysmal labyrinth hid the kingly demon,
its final stronghold, the city of the damned.
From hidden portal by its horrid throne,
the fiend's hand reached and cursed the land.

A hundred chosen heroes ventured there,
challenged the fell labyrinth—and died.
Corpses grew cold, but their inner light flared,
a radiance that left evil no place to hide.

Seven heroes fought the Demon King,
six survived and thus the world was saved,
the knight, the royal hero with sword a-shining,
Fahn of Valis, chivalrous and brave.

The warrior, Beld, who smote the demon lord,
and lost his soul when he struck the killing blow,
the priestess, Neese, Marfa's child, dearly adored,
and the wizard, Wort, who knew all there was to know.

The dwarf there was, too—Flebe, the last one of his line,
a lost country of stone, and he the king—
and last, the nameless warrior-mage long gone.
Together, all put to right the evil of which I sing.

The song ended, and the room fell silent. Then someone clapped and raucous applause broke out—the Valis knights cheered their Hero King and called for the overthrow of the Dark Emperor Beld.

Parn knew that the events of the song had really happened—the epic battle against demons had occurred only a few decades before—and now, *another* war was about to break out on Lodoss between two of the heroes of that last war.

What an ironic fate, Parn couldn't help but think. Why had Beld abandoned his heroic nature and become Emperor of the dark island? Why had he destroyed Kanon? Parn just couldn't wrap his head around it.

The dancing resumed with no end in sight. Kashue ignored the ladies vying for a dancing partner, seemingly content to keep talking to Parn, who couldn't imagine a better opportunity. He had the personal attention of a legendary king who had started out as a mercenary just like him. Parn remained rapt, absorbing every single thing the king said.

Deedlit listened to their conversation with her back to them. She watched the dancing, which was reminiscent of the time she had met Parn, during the festival in Allan. However, it also roused nostalgic thoughts of her home in the forest.

She had expected to be bored and unimpressed with humans, but it seemed that there were leaves of truth and insight scattered through their short lives. It would take some time to sift through what she'd discovered. Deedlit glanced back at Parn, who was still talking to Kashue with a serious look on his face, and found herself thinking that she wouldn't mind taking the time to watch over this young man's life.

3

A HIDEOUS, HUNCHED GOBLIN SOLDIER MARCHED BACK and forth before the castle gate.

Emperor Beld of Marmo looked on, wondering which was more normal—the goblin's wretched nature or his own twisted heart. The demonic sword at his left hip rattled as if mocking his thoughts. Beld gripped the handle forcefully, like he was strangling a hated enemy.

"What's wrong?" a voice came from behind. "Odd to find you so thoughtful in the middle of the day."

It was Wagnard, the court wizard and Beld's most trusted advisor.

"I was considering the hideousness of that goblin gatekeeper. Shining Hill was once called the finest castle in Lodoss—now look what it's become under its new master." Beld's jet-black cloak billowed around his blood red armor. The demonic sword let out another unearthly cackle.

"I heard that Karla's plans in Valis have failed."

"Yes. But no matter. I will defeat Fahn without having to re-sort to cheap tricks."

Beld took a moment to look at his advisor. Wagnard wore black robes. It was rumored that he'd dyed his Academy robes with the blood of a dark elf.

Like the dark elves, Wagnard used the black magic of Phalaris. Physically, he was also much stronger than the traditional wizard and was an expert swordsman. To most sword-hating wizards, that alone was enough to brand him a heretic. Despite his great power, however, Wagnard only used magic under the most extreme circumstances. In truth, he was unable to use it most of the time. His master, Larcus, had cast a forbidden spell on him—whenever he cast a spell now, no matter how simple, his body was wracked with unbearable pain. Most people would immediately lose consciousness when experiencing pain that intense, but Wagnard had endured. He even learned how to conduct complex, hours-long rituals without his concentration slipping.

It was that sinister strength of will that gave Beld complete confidence in the wizard—and that had earned him the title "The Black Mage."

"The witch failed in Alania, as well. It seems she has less talent for scheming than she does for magic."

"You think so? She has always been shrewd, and she has plots within her plots. She still says that all but Valis will self-destruct."

"That'll save us a lot of trouble, if it's true."

"Did you bring a report, Wagnard? I thought I saw a messenger arrive on horseback."

Wagnard laughed dryly. "You see everything, Your Majesty. I did receive a report from the spy I left in Valis. King Kashue of Flaim recently arrived there with a hundred knights. It seems that King Fahn will soon bring the battle to us."

"So the day has come." Beld smiled thinly and looked up at the sky. "Hide the sun during the battle. Goblins don't like sunlight."

"Understood. Where is the witch now?"

"She should be in Moss. She said she had a scheme to finish up there, after which she wanted to see an old friend."

"She sounds busy," Wagnard said. "Why is she even working with us? What is she after?"

"Why indeed?" Beld remarked mysteriously. "It's more interesting when you don't know." With that, the Emperor turned with a flip of his cloak and went inside, footsteps ringing on the stone floor. Wagnard followed his lord as silent as a shadow.

Deep in the mountains of Moss, Parn and his companions struggled up the steep mountain path. Two weeks had passed since the group left Roid. They had made it through the ruins of the dwarven stone kingdom, battling evil creatures on the way, and were now getting close to Wort's tower. Due to the dangerously steep path, however, they had to pause every few steps to avoid losing their footing. They were all sweating hard from the effort.

"What a terrible place to live," Deedlit sighed, leaning heavily on the dead branch she'd picked up to use as a walking stick.

"Agreed. Isn't this Wort an old man? How can he live out here?" Woodchuck asked.

They scrambled along the ridge of a craggy mountain where only sparse grass grew. Earlier, Slayn had been buffeted by a strong gust of wind and slid down a slope—Woodchuck had had to pull him back up with a rope. Etoh healed his wounds afterwards, but the experience had left the wizard both wary and grumpy. Since the incident, he'd been so focused on his footing that he barely said a word.

"Is that it?" Woodchuck asked from his place in the lead. He straightened up and used a hand to shadow his eyes, staring into the distance.

Deedlit could just make out what might have been the tip of a tower—though it also might have been a mountain peak. Slayn began murmuring. They all recognized his farsight spell and so waited for his verdict.

"No mistake—it's a stone tower," Slayn said cheerfully. He quickly cast a floating spell just to confirm, floating up until his feet were about level with Woodchuck's head. "We can get there in a quarter day," Slayn continued, but no one seemed particularly relieved—at that point, even a few more hours of hiking seemed way too long.

"Let's rest a little while longer, then push through," Parn said, and he plunked himself down on a nearby rock. He pulled out a hand towel and mopped his damp brow—there was no way to escape the summer heat, especially for a man in heavy armor.

Little did Parn and his companions know, but they were being watched at that very moment. Not far from their resting spot, at the top of the tower they'd just spotted, two wizards gazed at an image inside a crystal ball.

"*These* are the ones who managed to outwit you?" an old man said with a derisive snort. He wore a grey robe and his hair— once raven-black in his youth but long since faded to white— grew long down his back. He was clean-shaven, so there was nothing to hide the deep wrinkles of his aged face, but he still had a curious twinkle in his eyes.

"Say what you want, Wort. Even *I* am powerless against fate," the second wizard replied. She wore a purple dress and her white teeth peeked from between voluptuous red lips. The jewels on the thin circlet on her forehead sparkled like a pair of eyes. She appeared more thoughtful than angry as she watched the people in the image.

She was the witch, Karla.

The dimly lit, circular tower room held only a table and four chairs near the room's center. There were two doors. One simply led downstairs, while the other was a glass door that led out to a balcony with a view of all of Moss—all the way to the faraway Lake Above the Clouds.

The crystal ball in the center of the table could allow the wizards to see even further than that. Manipulated correctly, it could show any place in Lodoss.

"What's your plan? Will you go out and crush them?" Wort asked, mouth pursed like he'd bitten into something bitter.

Karla let out a bewitching laugh. She'd used her magic mirror of truth to find out Parn's group's next destination. After finishing her business in Moss, she'd made her way to the tower a full two days before their arrival to wait for them and now, at last, they were finally here.

"You make that sound easy," she said, "but they're surprisingly shrewd—especially that wizard. He may be young, but he's quite capable. I might have been careless, but they've *still* outwitted me twice now."

"With five hundred years' experience at your beck and call, that makes them quite an impressive band of adventurers. I hope you won't kill them before I've made their acquaintance."

"Does that mean I can kill them after?"

"Somewhere out of my sight," Wort replied, his piercing gaze locked on Karla's face.

"Is there anywhere on Lodoss you *can't* see?" Karla asked with a laugh. "As long as you have this crystal ball, that won't be possible." With a hint of laughter still on her lips, she turned her cold eyes to meet the old man's. "All right, Wort. I won't kill them out of a personal grudge. That just isn't my style. At any rate, my work in Moss is done—so as long as they leave me alone, I won't make the first move. But..." Karla paused, letting her gaze fall back to the crystal ball. "Will they forgive me? And if not—if these travelers want a fight—I *will* be allowed to defend myself, won't I?"

"I wouldn't be able to stop you."

"Don't worry—I'm not seeking a fight. I like them; I'd much rather they joined me. Still, I'm sure they'll try to defeat me again. That young warrior hates me from the bottom of his heart."

"What are you thinking?" Wort asked with a stern expression.

"Hmm, what indeed?" she said. "What do you see when you look at them? He's just like you or Fahn back in the day—guided by destiny, overcoming deadly obstacles, rushing headlong toward his goal. One day, I'm sure they'll face me as deadly foes."

"Huh..."

"I'm sure they'll ask you where I am. You can tell them. You know where I live, don't you?"

"Of course," Wort answered glumly. "I'll keep my promise. I won't assist Fahn—and in exchange, you'll sever ties with Beld. If we got involved in this battle, it would just mean far more casualties on both sides. But our agreement doesn't include *them*."

"Are you going to attack me for the sake of complete strangers? That goes against everything you believe in, Great Magus Wort. You're the *only* one who knows just how futile it is to fight me."

"I do..." He had thought that he was unbeatable in a magic battle. But he could not vanquish the witch, because doing so would mean his own destruction—and not even *Wort* knew how to neutralize her without killing her.

"It's a shame," Karla said, rising from her chair and giving the adventurers in the crystal ball one last look. She then stroked the crystal ball's surface lovingly, and the image faded into darkness, leaving the ball a black glass sphere once again. "Now then, I should get ready. I'll prepare some drinks and a light meal—they're my guests too, so there should be nothing odd about me cooking for them. Let me know if there's anything you'd like to eat, Wort—my culinary skills are quite impressive."

"Not yours. Those skills belong to the woman you're controlling," Wort spat.

"Exactly—but this body belongs to *me* now. Leylia, the Marfa priestess, is gone. Body and mind, I am Karla."

Wort avoided her gaze and activated the crystal ball once more. This time, it showed an image of Beld's face—unchanged since they had gone together into the Deepest Labyrinth to defeat the Demon King. The demonic sword he bore had kept him young. He was only a few years younger than Wort, so he should have been an old man, but he was frozen in time by a curse—the same curse that bound him to become the overlord who would unify Lodoss.

In the final battle against the Demon King, a Pharis priestess sacrificed her life to save Beld. She had entrusted him with her final wish: eternal peace on Lodoss. The only way to achieve that was for a great king to unify the island.

Beld was trying to fulfill that wish.

The priestess was called Flaus, and she, Wort, and Beld had travelled through all of Lodoss together. Beld's heart had died with her; his soul still wandered the eternal abyss in the depths of the labyrinth. All that remained of him was a shell, acting only to realize her last words through conquest.

Fahn also tried to realize Flaus's dreams—though in a different way. Beld and Fahn both wanted the same peace for Lodoss, though the paths they took to get there couldn't be more different. And the dream remained elusive.

"Such tragic folly." Wort felt anger bubble up inside him, toward the grey witch who had let herself into his tower with not the slightest shame. This woman, sole survivor of the ancient kingdom, had cleverly manipulated his friends' genuine emotions just to maintain a balance in the world—the triumph of not black nor white, but the grey in between. Wort could almost see the outcome of the battle to come. He had no way to change it and Karla knew that, so she'd come to stop him from trying to intervene.

And Wort had agreed to her terms. The witch stood in the shadows of history, using brave heroes as pawns in her game. Her existence was why a unified Lodoss had never been achieved since ancient times.

Wort continued to gaze at the Emperor of Marmo, pity in his eyes.

4

"WE'RE FINALLY HERE."

Parn panted with exhaustion, bent over with his hands on his knees. Even after they'd spotted the tower, getting there had taken longer than they'd expected—there were so many switchbacks and detours on the mountain trail that they began to suspect the old Magus had done it on purpose.

Throughout the grueling day, Parn had gotten more and more annoyed with the mage and their whole situation. And annoyances aside, a peerless mage choosing a life of seclusion despite his great abilities made no sense to Parn.

"It's just like King Fahn said," Parn had complained over and over throughout the day. "He's a stubborn old man who hates everyone."

Deedlit had voiced her agreement every time Parn said it, but eventually it got so tedious that she finally snapped, "If you dislike him so much, why don't you just go back to Roid?" They'd traveled in stony silence ever since.

That kind of argument had become more common between them. Parn was becoming more assertive, which meant more bickering. And for every noble thing that came out of his mouth, he'd say something equally immature later. She didn't *dislike* that part of him necessarily, but it confused her. For every two steps Parn took toward his true potential, he seemed to take one step back.

Still, though, Parn had seemed different since leaving Roid.

Inspired by King Fahn and King Kashue, he was finally growing into a leader.

Slayn had noticed the change in Parn, too. He felt like he had to advise him less often. Slayn had told the others that, after their current journey ended, he was going to help Ghim find whatever it was he was looking for. The wizard was sure that Parn had started to walk down the right path and could practically see their futures—Parn would become a knight of Valis and Etoh would join the Pharis Temple in Roid. Slayn and Ghim would continue their journey and Woodchuck...well, who knew what Woodchuck would do next?

Deedlit was also unsure of what to do next. If Parn was knighted, there would be no reason to stay with him. But she didn't want to journey alone, and she had no intention of going back home. She just couldn't decide. She kept telling herself that it wasn't worth worrying over—maybe, once this trip ended, things would fall into place.

From the outside, the Magus Tower was unadorned and plain. For all intents and purposes, it looked like a regular castle watchtower. It was perched on an empty, rocky mountain peak, and they couldn't help but wonder how someone could live there.

As they carefully made their way to the double doors leading into the tower, their breath caught in their throats. The door handles were shaped like dragons.

Parn raised a hand tentatively to knock, but before he could do so, the door slowly creaked open on its own.

"Whoa!" Parn shouted, pulling back. "Heh...what a joker.

Does he want to give people heart attacks?" The interior of the tower was dimly lit and difficult to see, but when Parn leaned closer to look inside, the lights came on by themselves. "What the heck *is* this?!"

"It's just simple magic. He's a Magus, after all—even his basic spells are extraordinary."

"He's showing off!" Parn objected.

"Let's just go inside already. Yelling out here won't solve anything," Deedlit said, stepping through the doorway.

"Hello!" she called out. "I am Deedlit the elf, here on a mission from King Fahn of Valis!" Her voice echoed in the empty tower. The only things inside were a staircase heading down to the basement and another staircase that ran up in a spiral along the wall, ending at a single door.

Deedlit waited, but there was no response to her call. "Now what?" Deedlit turned to ask an anxious Parn.

"He better not be gone," Parn answered, shuddering at the thought. The thought that they might've come all this way only for the Magus to be out just wasn't funny.

"It seems someone's upstairs—I can hear talking." Slayn lowered his hood and stepped inside. "I can also feel magic here— many spells that only a great wizard could cast." Slayn cautiously approached the spiral staircase and stood on the first step to test it. Under his foot, the stairs suddenly flashed with pale blue light and started ascending with a low groan. "Well, this is convenient—if only they could cast this spell on the stairs of the castle of Valis. I had quite a bit of trouble with them." Slayn let out a laugh and turned to Parn as he was carried upstairs.

They had spent three days at the castle after the ball, deeply meaningful days for Slayn and Parn. Slayn had had a chance to peruse the rare and valuable books in Elm's collection—and, as he'd promised at the ball, Kashue had given Parn sword lessons. Etoh was appointed an official cleric by High Priest Genart and assigned to serve the Valis court upon his return. They both wanted to assist in national affairs. Ghim had taken ten gold coins from their reward and crafted something in the castle smithy. Only Deedlit and Woodchuck had spent their time idle.

The moving staircase carried Slayn steadily upwards. "Don't go by yourself!" Parn shouted, jumping onboard in a panic.

I guess it probably won't eat me, Woodchuck told himself as he gingerly stepped on. The other three soon joined him.

The landing in front of the door was small—not really large enough for six people to stand on. They clustered there awkwardly for a moment before Parn spoke up.

"Excuse me," he called out. "I'm Parn, a travelling warrior, and I'm coming in." He pushed the door open—this one didn't open on its own. Beyond was a spiral passageway, a gentle slope with a rough-paved stone floor for surer footing. Parn continued onward, and the others followed behind—but this time they only took one trip around the tower before they reached a pair of doors, side by side.

Listening carefully, they could hear voices coming from the door on the right. Parn wondered who on earth would visit such a place—well, other than him and his friends.

"Excuse me…no one responded when we arrived, so we let ourselves in. Oh! I'm Parn, a traveling warrior," he announced to the air again.

"Get in here already!" a gruff, elderly-sounding voice responded. That had to be the Great Magus Wort.

Parn breathed a sigh of relief to find out that the Magus was home. He slowly stepped inside, already in a low, respectful bow—but when he raised his head, he couldn't believe his eyes.

"K-Karla…" he groaned, trailing off into shocked silence.

Deedlit's hand flew to her mouth—her other reached unconsciously for her rapier. "Why are you here?" she asked, her face gone pale.

"You will *not* fight here!" the old man yelled sharply. At his words, Deedlit felt her muscles freeze by the power of an outside source.

Finally, Karla spoke. "Don't worry, I don't intend to start anything here. I just wanted another chance to speak to all of you. So, come in."

The table in the center of the room held a glass for each of them, with several bottles of wine, roast venison served on a platter, and fresh fruit and vegetables piled high. The mages had clearly been waiting for them.

"All right, we'll listen," Parn agreed. He was still in shock, but he took Karla's words as a challenge. He crossed the room and sat down, prepared to draw his sword at a moment's notice. His hateful glare never once left her face.

Ghim took the other empty chair unprompted, and the

other four fanned out behind them, still standing. Woodchuck cowered as far from Karla as he could manage, trying to look inconspicuous.

An awkward silence filled the room.

Karla offered drinks, then poured herself a glass and gracefully drank to show that it wasn't poisoned.

"The glasses and wine are from my personal collection, so don't worry," the old man chimed in.

"Let's talk first," Parn said, leaning forward. "What are you doing here? How did you know we were coming?"

Karla smiled at the furious young warrior and settled in the seat next to him. Ghim kept staring, inspecting her from head to toe—Karla gave him one glance before turning back to the warrior.

"I don't have to answer that…but I will anyway. One of the reasons I'm here is that Wort and I are old friends. We once fought together, side by side. Another reason is that I wanted to see you all again. And as for how I managed to find you—that was the simplest of all." Karla leaned her elbows on the table and clasped her hands, fingers intertwined. Most of them were adorned with rings of different shapes and sizes; they knew from the previous battle that they weren't just ordinary jewelry. The witch could wield powerful magic with the shake of a finger.

"You said you want to talk to us?"

"I have a proposal. Like I said before, I value all of you highly. Won't you join me? I'd be happy to put our…unfortunate previous encounters behind us."

Parn's eyes widened in fury. He opened his mouth to yell in a fit of anger, but restrained himself out of respect for Wort.

"There, I listened," he said. "Did you actually think we would agree? We'd *never* work for Marmo." His voice cracked with rage, but he managed to keep himself from yelling, at least. He couldn't believe she had such a low opinion of him, to think he had it in his nature to sell his soul to evildoers.

"It seems there's been a misunderstanding," Karla responded with a sigh. She swirled the red liquid in her glass, which reflected the lights of the room. "I am not Beld's minion. I cooperated with him for a time, but my goal is noble. You know of the ancient kingdom, correct? It was a magical civilization that thrived in Lodoss, and in fact, across the entire world of Forcelia. Do you know the real reason it was lost?"

"Legend says a powerful magic spell went out of control," Slayn chimed in, "though that was long years before all of our time, so we have no way to know the truth," He looked over to Deedlit to see if she had anything to add, but she shook her head.

"I wasn't born yet, and the elves don't pay much attention to human events," Deedlit explained.

"The wizard is basically correct. In the last years of the kingdom, the wizards built an enormous device that would generate inexhaustible magical power to use for infinite spells. By implanting a small crystal ball into their foreheads, connected to this device beyond space and time, they shared this infinite magic power. The experiment succeeded and the civilization prospered—spawning an age of great magical invention. Entire cities were lifted into the skies or floated in the oceans. They had complete control of the spirit world, even using dragons as servants. But the wizards lost the ability to use magic without relying on the device. When they attempted the ultimate spell, the device couldn't sustain it and was destroyed—leaving no wizards left who could use magic."

"Around that time, the savages began to attack in earnest. The powerless wizards couldn't defend themselves and were wiped out. It took less than five years for all that they'd built to be reduced to nothing..."

Parn listened with his arms folded across his chest. His gaze was locked on the witch's pale face and blue eyes so intensely it was like he'd forgotten to blink.

A long moment passed. When Parn realized that Karla was likely waiting for an answer, he mumbled, "So what?" He didn't understand the point of her story.

"You don't understand why it fell into ruin?" she asked, closing her eyes and searching through her memories. Images of the greatest wizards slaughtered one after another came rushing back to her like it was yesterday. Her memories never faded because her existence was memory itself. "The world should never rely on a single power. No matter *what* it is, it will ultimately lose control and lead to catastrophe. The ancient kingdom perished trying to establish a supreme magical civilization, but magic isn't the only dangerous power. Fahn's ideals, Beld's ambition—they are equally dangerous.

"There must always be balance. Once that breaks down,

catastrophic destruction is unavoidable. But it's impossible to maintain a perfect balance—the scale will tip one way or the other, even more so when trying to balance the entire world. But what if the scale is endlessly rocked back and forth, so neither side can ever attain full victory?" Karla paused, thoughtfully swirling the wine in her glass, following the liquid with her eyes.

"Look at it at any given moment," she went on, "and it will seem that one side is winning. But looking at the greater pattern, it might as well be balanced in the middle. I have meddled throughout history to tip the scales because it's what's best for Lodoss. Fahn's faith in the light of law, Beld's destructive power... if either gained supremacy, Lodoss would stabilize under a single power. But that stability wouldn't last forever. In the future, when it finally crumbles, the destruction would be so great that the war between the gods pales in comparison, and civilization would collapse again. It could even cause the end of the world."

"You must realize that what I'm saying is true," she said, "so I'll ask you again—join me, and save the world from destruction—"

"Is that it?" Parn asked in a low voice. Karla nodded, waiting silently for his reply. "Then here's my answer—*no*. We're not going to join you. Maybe there's some truth to what you're saying, who knows? But no matter the reason, toying with people's hearts and lives is never right! How many have died in the battles that you caused?!" Parn stood up and slammed his fist on the table. An empty glass fell over and rolled into a wine bottle with a *clink*.

"Even if many more lives are lost when the day of destruction arrives?" Karla asked, her expression unchanged. She met Parn's furious gaze unflinchingly.

"Even if that's true, a single human being shouldn't be allowed to manipulate destiny! That should be left to the gods!"

Karla simply nodded once, then stood. Everyone braced themselves, but Karla simply walked past them, straight toward the door.

"Then I'll leave it at that. If you disagree with what I've done, fine. Try to stop me if you want. I'll take you on any time."

"Then we'll settle this right here and now!" Parn shouted, hand on his sword.

"I told you, no blades here!" the Great Magus said sharply.

Karla waved her right hand at Parn, preparing to meet his attack—but before she could activate her magic rings, Ghim grabbed Parn from behind.

"Parn, wait! Just wait!"

"What're you doing, Ghim?! You're going to let Karla escape?!"

"Ghim's just saying *not here*," Deedlit said, helping the dwarf hold him back.

"I apologize, Great Magus Wort," Slayn said to the old man with a bow.

"You should mind your manners," Karla said with a cold laugh, and continued on.

"May I ask one thing?" Slayn asked. Karla paused and looked back.

"What is it?"

"Have you really lived for five hundred years? There's no known spell for eternal youth—at least, not among Academy wizards."

"Why do you want to know? Would you seek out this spell if you found out it existed?"

"I don't know. I'm just surprised that you've lived so long, even for a wizard of the ancient kingdom. Even in ancient texts, I've never seen an immortality spell mentioned. Just the knowledge that one exists would be a great motivation for the wizards."

"What an interesting way you think."

"Is it?" he said. "Perhaps not as interesting as you. With your powers, there could be other methods to save the world from destruction."

"There aren't. I'm not omnipotent. I can only affect the balance on this island, and I can only exist like this because I've always remained hidden in the shadows of history. If I had stepped out into the open even once, someone would have killed me. My role in this modern era is over—everything has already been set into motion, so I will retreat into the shadows until I am needed once more..." Karla turned back to the door. "Wort, I will take my leave. Brave adventurers, may you receive Marfa's blessings." At last, she opened the door and left.

Ghim, keeping with his grip on Parn, continued to stare at the door until her footsteps had faded.

"Great Magus Wort," Parn said, turning his furious glare on the old man. "We have a *lot* of questions for you. That's why we're here."

5

AFTER KARLA LEFT, DEEDLIT EASED HERSELF INTO THE now-empty seat. She took a glass and poured herself some wine. Behind her, she heard Etoh let out a long, relieved sigh. With Karla gone, the mood was significantly lighter, but the encounter with her had been such a shock that no one had regained their composure yet.

Parn was conflicted. After what happened, he couldn't trust the old man—he seemed just as bad as Karla. Wort seemed unconcerned about Parn's wary attitude. He took a glass of wine and a piece of meat from the platter and began to eat.

"I don't blame you for distrusting me," Wort began, his mouth stuffed with food. "All I can say is—I'm the one and only Wort, and I'm not Karla's ally." He raised his glass to Parn in a mocking toast; in response, Parn's glare grew even angrier. The old man kept speaking, not responding to his change in mood. "There's some truth to what she says—I did once fight at her side. But so did Fahn, Beld, and Neese. We fought our way through the Deepest Labyrinth. Though back then, Karla didn't look like the beautiful woman she is now—she was a warrior in a clunky mask and armor..." Wort paused to look around the room, and grinned.

"What?! How?!" Parn exclaimed. "I know the saga of the Six Heroes...the last of them, the unnamed warrior-mage. That was Karla?! She was really one of the heroes of the Demon Wars...?!"

"The demons definitely changed the balance of the world," Slayn said calmly, but his wide eyes betrayed his astonishment.

"Wait, what do you mean?" Woodchuck asked, confused.

"Like the young man here said, Karla was the warrior-mage, one of the Six Heroes." Wort laughed and raised his glass to his lips. "You might have assumed that she's lived for the past five hundred years looking exactly as she does now, but that's a mistake. That kind of magic has never existed, not even in the ancient kingdom. She is powerful, but even the greatest ancient wizards could only extend their lives for two hundred years at most. But Karla came up with a way around that limit."

"Is it to control someone else's body?" Ghim mumbled, sinking into his chair.

"Ghim!" Slayn was surprised at Ghim's insight, but it also made a strange kind of sense, considering some of the dwarf's behavior. "Does this mean you're ready to tell us what you're looking for?"

"Yes," the dwarf said with a deliberate nod. "It's time."

"I didn't expect a dwarf would be the one to figure this out!" Wort said with a gleeful laugh. "Have you researched ancient magic?"

"Of course not. My kind have nothing to do with magic."

"And yet you're the one who first arrived at the truth. Good for you," Wort replied. "Like this highly intelligent wine barrel of a dwarf says, Karla transferred her consciousness into an object and has kept existing all these years by controlling the mind of anyone who wears it. Did you see the circlet on her forehead? *That* it Karla's true form, though whether or not she is truly alive is up for debate. Her consciousness has stayed unchanged for the past five hundred years—since she abandoned her original body. I wouldn't consider her human; she's a ghost."

"So the woman we're seeing is Karla's victim," Parn said. He was slowly beginning to believe the old man, at least a little. He reached for the food and accepted a glass of wine when Deedlit offered it.

"Exactly. When Karla's latest body is destroyed, the circlet casts a spell to take over the mind of whoever destroyed it. The magic is so powerful that nobody can escape. That's why Karla can never be defeated—even when someone succeeds, they just turn into the next Karla."

"I don't want her defeated. I promised I'd bring that girl back home," Ghim said glumly.

"You mean the woman Karla is controlling?" Slayn asked.

"Yeah. I know who she is. I couldn't believe it when I first saw her portrait, and even after we met her, I still had my doubts. But when she cast a holy spell of Marfa, I knew it was true. Her name is Leylia, and she's the daughter of Neese, Marfa's high priestess—and one of the Six Heroes. Neese is a friend of mine; I told her that I'd bring her missing child back to her if I could." Ghim sighed. "This also explains the riddle she told me—that her daughter is alive, but doesn't exist. That really does describe Leylia in her current state. After all, Karla isn't alive, but she certainly *does* exist."

"So that's your story," Slayn sighed, struck with admiration.

"Hold on…so we *can't* beat Karla? But we can't just let that witch get away with this!" Parn shouted in frustration.

"Were you listening?" Deedlit huffed in exasperation. "We *can't* fight her! Even if we win, the magic of the circlet will take over our minds!"

"Then how do we rescue the girl?!" Ghim shouted, looking at all of them for help.

"There may be a way," said Wort, glancing at each of them in turn. "It's very dangerous...but not impossible if you have the courage." Wort stood up, strode to a stone wall, and tapped it. The wall shuddered and opened, revealing a small room full of what looked like useless clutter. He disappeared into the room but kept shouting back to them. "The magic of the circlet activates when the body is destroyed, so all you have to do is tear it off her while she's still alive."

"Easier said than done," Etoh chimed in, calling out in Wort's general direction. "I'm sure you know how difficult that would be. The witch uses powerful ancient magic. Capturing her will be far more difficult than killing her."

"Obviously," Wort replied. They could hear him rummaging through something. "Ah, finally!" he exclaimed, sounding delighted. He emerged from the room, holding a small stick. "Like the priest said, you have no chance of beating her head-on. And, no offence, but you lot aren't heroes like Beld or Fahn—even your wizard here isn't as well versed in the ancient language as I am." Wort casually tossed the stick onto the table. "So I'll give you this magic wand—it's a relic of the ancient kingdom. Cast the spell correctly, and its magic will be released."

"What does it do?" Slayn asked, picking up the stick with

great interest. It wasn't made of any metal or wood he recognized, and it had ancient runes carved into its surface. "*Te-u-ra?* Is that the spell?"

"Yes. I think you'll find it quite useful—it nullifies all magic around it. Of course, that means you won't be able to use your own magic, either."

"So we can use it to keep her from casting any spells and capture her alive!" Parn said excitedly.

"I'll be useful at that point, I bet," Woodchuck declared. "I can sneak up behind her and snatch that thing off her forehead." He'd gotten bored listening to them, but he knew it was finally his time to shine. "But what will we do with this circlet?" he said. "Destroy it? Sell it? It looks like a valuable piece of jewelry."

"It would be wise to destroy it while the wand's magic is in effect. Leave it and who knows when it'll find another victim."

"But isn't there a way to resist its control? You know, take her magic powers but leave your own consciousness intact? Maybe there's a way to defeat the spell that takes you over if you know what's coming. Then you could bring back some of this lost ancient magic."

"Are you out of your *mind*, thief?" Wort glared at Woodchuck. "If you could resist the spell, then yes, you would obtain all of Karla's knowledge and memories. And that would be priceless. But it's impossible. Think about it. Many of the people who Karla has dominated over the years must have been powerful—they had to defeat her, after all. But they all fell to the circlet's spell. You shouldn't entertain such foolish thoughts."

"I guess," Woodchuck said with a shrug.

"That's all I have to say to you. Return to Fahn and tell him all of this. And make sure he knows—I will not pick a side, and Karla will no longer assist Beld, either. You all, however, can fight to your hearts' content."

"Can you tell us one more thing?" Parn asked, leaning forward.

"What is it?"

"Tell us where to find Karla."

CHAPTER V

The Final Battle

1

IN THE AFTERNOON, THE BLAZING SUNSHINE WAS ABRUPTLY replaced by a sky full of dark clouds. Lightning flashed, and large raindrops began to fall.

The soldier guarding the Roid castle gates didn't even have time to put on his rain gear—instead, he quickly took refuge in the shed to continue his duty from within.

He tensed as he saw a cluster of dark shadows approach through the sheets of rain.

"Who goes there?" he called out nervously to the six figures.

"My name is Parn," the lead shadow answered, lowering his cloak to show his face and immediately getting soaked. "We've journeyed from the Great Magus's mansion on orders from King Fahn. Please send word of our return to His Majesty."

"Sir Parn!" the guard cried joyously. More than a month had passed since they had left Roid. "I'm glad you're safe! I'll have them open the gates." The guard stepped out of his shed, ignoring the rain, and waved to the guard beyond the moat to lower the drawbridge.

Fahn was in a war council with Elm and Kashue when he received the news, and he requested that the returning adventurers be brought there to speak to them all.

Parn and his companions were led through the castle and into a room containing dry clothes and steaming hot towels to wipe themselves down with. Parn finished pulling on a light hemp shirt, then caught sight of an approaching servant. His eyes widened in surprise.

"What's this?" he asked, looking at the armor the servant presented him with. It wasn't his father's breastplate, but a white one with a shining silver crest—a cross on the left breast.

"His Majesty's orders." The servant bowed.

"I'm happy for you," Deedlit said with a soft smile. She had changed into a loosely tailored grass-green outfit with a silk sash wrapped casually around her waist. Her hair still stuck damply to her forehead.

Parn shot her a grin as he buckled the new breastplate, then hung his father's sword at his hip. The sword fit perfectly against the new armor as if they'd been made as a set.

"Let's go," he nodded to his friends.

Slayn wore a white Sage's robe, identical to what Elm wore. Etoh was dressed in a Pharis cleric's gown and had been given a ceremonial mace. Ghim changed into clean underclothes but wore his own mithril chain mail and garb over it, as well as his own battle axe on his back. Woodchuck changed but also put his own armor back on—he'd dried the leather armor and long black boots by the fireplace.

The group made their way to the room where King Fahn waited, which was in one of the castle's spires. There were no windows, and they couldn't even hear the fierce rain outside. Even so, a gentle breeze somehow kept it from feeling stuffy.

Deedlit glanced at the ceiling, looking conflicted. "Thank you for working so hard," she murmured.

Parn glanced at her quizzically.

"Is it Sylph?" Slayn asked.

Deedlit nodded and raised her right hand into the air. The breeze stopped momentarily, then resumed.

The wind elemental was trapped in this room by some kind of spell, probably working to prevent any sound from getting in or out. This was not Deedlit's kind of magic. It was ancient magic, tied to a magical device built in the days of the ancient kingdom. Elemental users like Deedlit controlled them to cast spells, or sometimes confined one in an object and thus put it to work. However, they wouldn't enslave and exploit an elemental for hundreds of years. Deedlit couldn't help but feel resentful at the treatment, though she tried not to let it show on her face.

There was a round table in the center of the room, with Fahn,

Kashue, and Elm seated around it. On the table was a bottle, several unfinished glasses of wine, and a map of the area around Roid marked with colored lines.

"Well done, all of you," King Fahn declared. The group bowed their heads at the praise. Kashue rose from his seat and stood before Parn, looking him up and down.

"That Holy Knight's armor suits you now." Kashue laughed, and he shook Parn's hand firmly. "I have nothing more to teach you. I knew you'd all make it back, but it was a tough journey, wasn't it?"

"It was," Parn agreed. "The ruins of the stone kingdom are swarming with monsters. I think one day we should work with Moss to wipe them out, once and for all."

"How valiant," Kashue said, laughing loudly this time.

"Now then." Fahn motioned Parn alone over to his side, gaze solemn. "Parn will be formally inducted into the Order of Knights soon, but for now we have business to discuss. I'd like Parn, Lord Slayn, and Lord Etoh to remain here and join our war council. The rest of you can make yourselves comfortable elsewhere and receive your rewards. You have my gratitude for aiding Parn and fulfilling this quest."

"I didn't follow him for a reward," Deedlit said, shaking her head. Her stomach turned. Fahn's words made it sound like Parn was no longer one of them.

"Likewise. I don't need a reward. Give our shares to this man," Parn said, motioning toward Woodchuck.

"Hey, thanks," the thief declared shamelessly.

"How you divide it is up to you." Fahn nodded magnani-mously, then turned his attention back to the map. The guards escorted Deedlit, Woodchuck, and Ghim out, and the door closed behind them.

"There is a meal waiting for you in the guest room," a servant informed them politely.

'I figured as much,' Woodchuck said. He shot a look back at the closed doors but obediently followed the servant.

"Well, this is dull," Deedlit yawned and folded her hands be-hind her head.

"Have you lost your manners?" Ghim scoffed.

"Traveling with you lot did it to me," Deedlit shot back.

"That sounds about right," Woodchuck smirked with a sidelong glance at Ghim. "We're lucky we get to fill our bellies, anyway."

"True," Ghim replied with a sigh. "That council will go on for a while…"

2

"To THINK THAT KARLA WAS THE WARRIOR-MAGE ALL along…" Fahn groaned, then trailed off, lost in thought. He was shocked to discover that he'd been involved in one of Karla's plots, but the more he thought about it, the more it made sense. During the war with the demon gods, Karla—a masked warrior-mage at the time—had tried to use everyone around her as pawns, including all her companions and even the demon gods themselves.

Now, she had robbed a young woman of her future and prevented the unification of Lodoss. In Karla's mind, Fahn and Beld had come out of that war prepared to unify the island, so she plotted and set them against each other and pushed them toward mutual destruction.

But even knowing that didn't mean he could prevent the coming battle. A showdown with Beld was inevitable.

"The Great Magus Wort claimed that Karla won't assist Marmo anymore, but I'm not sure if we should trust him…" Parn said hesitantly.

"If the witch is truly this obsessed with balance, then she no longer has a reason to be on Marmo's side," Kashue replied with a bitter smile.

"We heard some rumors during our travels. Are things really that bad?"

"Honestly, yes." Kashue gestured to the map as he explained the current situation.

During the month they had been gone, the tide of the battle had turned over and over. The first turning point was when Moss and Alania entered the war as allies of Valis. In particular, Jester the Dragon's Eye, ruler of Highland, had rushed to their aid even before the rest of the Kingdom of Moss. He'd joined them out of his own sense of justice, and as leader of the Dragon Knights, he'd lent them considerable military power. The thirteen Dragon Knights had taken their dragon steeds and broken through the

Marmo army deployed to the south of Kanon, then used that momentum to make their way to Marmo proper and set the port city on the north tip of the island on fire. Once the news spread, the people of Lodoss felt confident and called for their own countries to join the fray—the rest of Moss and Alania finally rose in opposition and closed in on Kanon from the north and by sea.

Many thought that Marmo's fate was sealed, and for a time the allied forces had almost made it to Shining Hill, Kanon's royal castle. But several more incidents shook their alliance.

The first was the assassination of Kadomos VII, King of Alania, by his younger brother, Duke Laster. His entire family was murdered, including the infant prince, and Alania was plunged into a fierce civil war between supporters of the Duke and his opponents.

At the same time, one of Moss's factions, "Dragon Scale" Venon, rose in sudden revolt against the royal castle of Moss's ruler, "Dragon Flame" Harkane. In Flaim, the Tribe of Fire emerged from their hiding places in the mountains to attack the capital city of Blade while its king was absent.

And from Marmo itself, the main force of dark elves led by Chief Luzeev made landfall. As the armies of Alania and Moss returned home, the army of Valis was left behind to be tormented by the dark elves' evil spells. If not for Kashue's help, the Valis army might have been annihilated.

Despite the uprising of desert savages, Kashue did not bring his troops home. He'd been expecting an attack while he was away, so he'd left his land in the hands of his right-hand man, Shadam. The people of Flaim were all brave warriors, so he was confident that they'd prevail against the threat even without his aid.

The Valis army managed to return with minimal casualties, Kashue bringing up the rear. The Marmo army followed and had already crossed the border into Valis, burning villages and plundering fields as they went. The allied armies of Valis and Flaim set up a final line of defense in the plains east of Roid, and the Marmo army, led by Emperor Beld himself, drew near. The final battle was looming close.

"That's terrible," Parn sighed as Kashue's briefing ended. Everything had gone exactly according to Karla's plan. Parn had prevented the King of Alania's assassination by chance, but he'd never imagined that the king's own brother would cause an uprising. Karla had manipulated events in Flaim and Moss, too, and plunged half of Lodoss into civil wars. Valis and King Fahn, Marmo and Emperor Beld, were left to clash one-on-one just as Karla intended. The witch had probably known all along what the outcome would be.

"Even if Karla does appear in support of Marmo, it changes nothing about what we must do. We have no choice but to believe in Wort's words. Parn...your first battle as a Holy Knight is going to be crucial to the fate of Lodoss."

"I'm ready," Parn answered with pride.

"For now, don't prepare for the worst," Kashue said, his even tone intended to ease Parn's anxiety. "Just focus on surviving the battle in front of you, and you will naturally grow as a warrior.

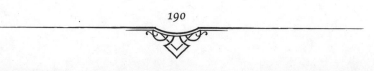

Only fools die in vain."

"Exactly. There's no need to rush into heroism." Fahn agreed.

"Oh. Of course." Parn lowered his head in embarrassment.

"King Fahn, may I take charge of him?" Kashue said. "He has never fought as a Holy Knight before. His fighting style is close to that of the people of the desert. I'd like him to take command of the newly recruited mercenaries in my army."

"That's a good idea. You will learn a lot from watching Lord Kashue fight up close. I heard that you once fought as a desert mercenary, as well. You will be better able to prove yourself there than in an all-knight regiment you aren't accustomed to. You may not like it, but you have to accept."

"I wouldn't dream of objecting," Parn answered hastily. The Valis Order of Knights was known for their unity and teamwork. Parn knew that he'd only be a burden if he joined them without training.

"Now, Lord Etoh and Lord Slayn, we have something to discuss with you two."

"What is it?" Etoh asked, sitting up straight.

"Lord Genart has appointed you a cleric of the court, but have you accepted the position?"

"Yes, respectfully," Etoh placed a hand over his heart and bowed.

"Good. Then you will handle all the religious ceremonies at court from now on. As for you, Lord Slayn—what are your plans? King Kashue mentioned that he would like to have you as his court wizard…"

Slayn, surprised, turned to Kashue and bowed deeply. "I'm honored, but there is something I must do. I'm afraid I can't serve anyone until my task is done."

"Is this about Ghim?" Etoh asked quietly.

"Yes..." Slayn nodded.

"Too bad, I like you. But if you have your own mission, I understand. Just remember that the gates of the castle of Flaim are always open to you."

"Thank you." Slayn bowed once more.

"I'm concerned for Ghim, too," Etoh said, apologetic, "but I have to do my duty as a servant of Pharis."

"Don't worry about us. We'll be careful."

"You're still going up against that witch." Parn's stomach twisted at the thought.

"Woodchuck will help us, so we'll manage," Slayn answered, unruffled.

"Then bring me, too," Parn said with determination. "I'm sure King Fahn will allow me to go kill Karla."

"Kill Karla? By yourselves?" Fahn frowned. "That's reckless. You all know what she's capable of."

"The Great Magus Wort gave us a weapon for fighting her." Slayn quickly told the kings about the magic wand.

"I see... Then perhaps you *will* be able to defeat her. We cannot allow a ghost from the ancient kingdom to keep treating Lodoss like her plaything. When the time comes, we will use all the power of Valis to defeat her, and if she appears in the upcoming battle, you will use the magic wand." But even as he said it,

Fahn didn't expect her to appear during the battle—she would know the risks of being in a melee.

"If the witch appears, I'll bring her down myself," Kashue said casually. Then he said, laughing, "Thus, I'll get a brilliant wizard for my court."

"Beld is our more immediate concern," Fahn said. "Marmo split their army into three and is heading to Roid through the eastern plains. We'll have to split our forces into three to engage them. I will take the center with Leonis, Elm will take the right flank, and King Kashue will take the left. Each of our forces will strike the enemy we encounter."

"Head on?" Kashue asked.

"The enemy won't have anything in reserve for an ambush. The rightmost of Marmo's forces is the monster army led by dark elves. The wizards will be assigned to King Kashue's army to handle them. They will likely be more dangerous than the Knights of Darkness approaching in the center, or the savage warriors from the Forest of Darkness on the left."

"I'll join Parn," Slayn offered. "I'm a wizard, too—I've earned my Sage robes, after all. I don't desire combat, but I can't retreat from this fight. So I'll use my spells in support of Parn and King Kashue."

"Will the Pharis battle-priests be fighting?" Etoh asked Fahn.

"Of course," Fahn nodded. "Lord Genart has declared this a battle between the Supreme God Pharis and Phalaris, the God of Darkness. The Holy Knights of the Great Temple of Pharis will take part."

"Then may I join in? I trained as a battle-priest when I was at the Temple of Alania."

"Yes, you can also join the left wing." Fahn nodded at Etoh, then turned to Kashue and motioned to wrap up the war council.

"Well then, Your Majesty, when will the battle begin?" Kashue asked, following protocol.

"The day after tomorrow, at noon. Send a messenger through to the front line."

At Fahn's words, Elm opened the door and left quickly to carry out his orders. Parn followed, feeling tense.

It had begun.

3

THE TIME OF THE FINAL BATTLE HAD COME.
Parn had never experienced a clash of armies so large before. He rode alongside Kashue and the knights of Flaim, watching the clouds growing in the eastern skies.

"It was such nice weather…" The sun had disappeared behind the cloud cover. It was too early for an afternoon shower, and Parn sniffed the air to see if it would rain. It didn't feel very humid—the weather was behaving strangely.

"They probably summoned clouds with magic," Slayn mumbled from behind them. He was walking carefully to avoid being kicked by horses—the battle was clearly weighing heavily on his mind, so Parn was trying to give him his space.

Etoh walked behind Slayn, Pharis battle-priests in matching armor streaming behind him like a group of pilgrims.

Deedlit rode a horse a short distance behind Parn—she'd decided at the last minute to join the battle. Woodchuck, how-ever, had stayed behind in the castle—a battlefield was no place for a rogue like him.

As for Ghim, rescuing Leylia was his most important duty.

"A large-scale battle such as this isn't like the small skirmishes you're used to, which tend to break down into one-on-one fights," Kashue said, offering guidance as he always did. "You must al-ways be vigilant and keep track of the flow of the battle. You need to know whether your allies have the upper hand or are losing ground. Even the most skilled swordsman will die on the battle-field if he isn't aware of the battle around him." Kashue frowned. "Our opponents use dark magic and elemental magic. We have no idea what they can do, so be prepared for their trickery. Use code words among allies and consider anyone who cannot answer an enemy. The deaths of a few allies will do less damage in the long run." Kashue turned to Parn. "It's not a popular strategy, but it's how I survived."

Parn understood the meaning underneath the words. *Don't waste your life. Only take that risk when it's worth it.*

When the bells in Roid tolled noon, Fahn swung his sword down to signal the attack. Horns blasted and drums beat out their low *boom, boom,* sending the signal through the entire army.

On the northern battlefield, Kashue heard the signal. With a shout, he commanded his knights and soldiers to charge through the rolling grassland and attack the enemy camp. The battle had begun.

Angry bellows rang out from soldiers on both sides, and a ringing clash of swords surrounded them. Soon, death cries could be heard as the battlefield turned into a sea of carnage.

"Deed, don't fall behind!" Parn called out to the elf. He drew his sword and spurred his horse on.

"Follow me!" Kashue ordered. "Don't give them time to cast spells!" But before they could get any further, a company of dark knights appeared over a hill and cleaved into the side of the charging Flaim army, almost exactly where Parn was riding.

"We'll get them!" Parn called as he reined in his steed. If these knights ruined their formation, they would be at a massive disadvantage.

"Leave it to me!" Deedlit called as she released Undine from the water bag at her hip. The water elemental fluttered through the air and clung to the lead knight's face like a thin film. He tumbled off his horse, grasping at his face, unable to breathe.

A moment later, a massive explosion shot through the center of the dark knights—a fire spell from Slayn. Several of the horsemen exploded and several more were knocked from their mounts. The remaining knights bravely drew closer, however.

Then, just before the lead rider crossed swords with Parn, they swerved and galloped off.

"They were a diversion," Slayn warned. "The dark elves are lurking, hidden."

Parn nodded, then rode down the line yelling, "Protect the

wizard! He'll tell us where the dark elves are!"

Etoh's battle-priests surrounded Slayn with shields facing outward.

"Thank you," the wizard muttered. From behind the shield wall, he could point out where the invisible dark elves were approaching and cast neutralizing spells to break their invisibility.

"There! Get them!" Parn shouted, pointing at the now-visible dark elves with his sword. He galloped over and used the momentum to run one through with his blade. The mercenaries of his squad followed, skillfully picking off the dark elves. Flaim's powerful mercenary army had once been led by Kashue himself, and they were on par with Flaim's Order of Knights. They were normally led by Kashue's trusted right hand man, Shadam.

"Don't stray far from the infantry!" Kashue shouted. "Support the magic-users!"

At his order, Parn turned his horse back toward Slayn and Etoh. They were already in the enemy camp, but as Parn rode up, the enemy was nowhere to be found. He could only see monsters with bows moving in small groups, roving the hills.

The monsters were weak, but their arrows flew far from their posts on high ground. Parn drew an arrow from his quiver and, with a *twang* of his bowstring, let it fly in a parabola toward the enemy. He'd only intended it as cover fire, but it was a lucky shot—one of the monsters took it in the chest and stumbled to the ground.

Several of the enemy archers returned fire. Parn raised his shield to protect his face.

"Sylph, spirit of wind…" Deedlit called out to the wind elemental, who created a gust of wind on her command. The arrows suddenly changed course and buried themselves harmlessly in the ground.

Deedlit took the lead position, expanding Sylph's influence to protect more of their soldiers.

Parn hurried over to her. "Don't push yourself too hard," he called out.

"I'll have Sylph handle the archers," Deedlit called back. "Shouldn't you be looking for other enemies?" She gestured with her rapier—Parn followed with his eyes, only to see Kashue, the mercenary king, at the front of the Knights of Flaim. He was boldly slashing his way through the enemy ranks.

"Whoa," Parn whispered, awestruck. Kashue's skill with the sword was even more impressive than the rumors had implied. Every swing of his blade felled another enemy. The knights at his back were all stalwart veterans of the long war with the desert savages and kept pace with their king.

"We can't fall behind!" Parn called out to his soldiers as he spurred his steed onwards. "Follow King Kashue—the enemy is fleeing!"

"Good to see you alive!" Kashue called to Parn, pulling his horse to a stop. A few of the desert knights were wounded, but none had died yet. Two of Parn's squad had been killed by the dark elves, but the others had all made it through unscathed.

"There were fewer dark elves than I expected," Kashue said with a wry smile. "The others must be having a rough time."

"Then we must clear this area and go assist them," one of the knights replied.

"Indeed," Kashue responded. "We have nothing to fear from a few dark elves. Cut through them and finish this quickly. Follow me!"

Parn rode alongside Kashue at the front. Enemy arrows rained down on him, but he felt no fear—being near a true hero like Kashue made him feel safe and powerful. He knew he could push past his own limits, basking in the aura of such a magnificent warrior.

Deedlit's elementals were doing their jobs, deflecting all of the enemy's arrows into strange trajectories that didn't come close to hitting their allies.

Suddenly, several balls of fire appeared ahead. As they watched, the fireballs took on the shape of lizards.

"It's Salamander, the spirit of fire! Watch out, it breathes flames!" Deedlit called out in warning.

Parn readied his shield and galloped up to one of the fire lizards. The sword in his right hand glowed pale blue.

"Is that Slayn?!" he cried in delight at his glowing blade—his wizard friend had enhanced his sword with a spell.

The glowing blade sliced cleanly through the salamander's torso as he galloped past—the fiery monster vanished without even a wisp of smoke.

"Charge!" Parn held his sword out and galloped at full speed. The salamanders' flames had knocked several knights off their horses, but the rest plunged into the enemy ranks, routing them.

"Attack while their ranks are disrupted! Have faith in Pharis's divine protection!" Etoh called. His battle-priests were clustered behind the knights, closing in on the enemy, supporting their allies with holy magic but also pushing forward hand-to-hand with their maces.

"I'm exhausted," Slayn panted next to him. "Running like this right after casting a spell? I'm not gonna last."

Etoh glanced over, then paled when he saw how badly Slayn was doing. He called over one of the fitter priests and quickly directed him to attend to Slayn. The priest laid a hand on Slayn's body and began praying to Pharis—at once, Slayn's heart beat slower and his breathing evened out.

"Pharis magic sure is handy," Slayn commented, impressed. "Thank you, I feel much better—and they still need me." With no hesitation, Slayn raised his staff and cast an ancient spell. He shook his staff to the side once, and several of the enemy fell to the ground.

"Is that the old standby sleep spell?" asked Etoh.

"Yes. I've learned that these little spells are often more useful than the larger ones. In a melee, one inattentive moment can be fatal," Slayn mumbled as he scanned the battle around him.

Etoh agreed. The formations of both armies had crumbled, melding into a massive melee. A short distance away, Parn and Deedlit could be seen wielding their swords side by side.

Etoh couldn't help but smile, thinking of how far his strong, dependable friend had come.

"This area is clear!" Kashue's voice boomed above all the other noise. "Head south to assist King Fahn's main force. Reassemble the formations. Those of you on foot—don't push too hard, you won't be able to fight if you wear yourselves out running. Cavalry in front, then the battle-priests and wizards. Heavily armed infantry will take up the rear. Only drink water on the way—you'll fight better if you're a little hungry!" With that, the fighters began their march through the trampled farmland.

The enemy army's right flank—already destroyed by Kashue's army—was likely a decoy. Most of the dark elves were in the left flank, where they'd quickly wiped out Elm's army. Elm himself had fallen to the blade of a dark elf assassin.

That triumphant enemy had charged through the decimated left flank to join the battle in the center, and they had given their side the advantage—until Kashue's army arrived. Evenly matched, the field was plunged into absolute chaos...

4

IT WAS NO HOLY BATTLE. SOLDIERS ON BOTH SIDES FELL dead, one after another—pure, unending slaughter.

Two kobolds ran at Parn, half-crazed with fear. Parn crossed swords with them and dispatched the pair quickly. Looking down at their corpses, words escaped him despite himself.

"This is terrible."

Parn and Deedlit dismounted their tired horses—they were panting hard and caked with mud and the blood of their enemies. Etoh and Slayn were still with them, but most of the battle-priests and mercenaries were scattered across the field. Even Parn understood that there would be no victor in this battle. Only Death would be left smiling at the end.

Dimly, he wondered when it would be his or Deedlit's turn to fall, staining the ground red with their blood, just like those poor, pathetic kobolds. He shuddered at the hopelessness of it all. Even so, every time he spotted another enemy, his sword swung practically on its own, in search of fresh blood.

Just then, he caught sight of King Fahn from afar. The king had dismounted, and he and a few Royal Guards were facing a throng of goblins. Beyond him, Parn could see a warrior in red armor with the crest of Marmo emblazoned upon it.

The red-clad warrior was clearly no mere mortal.

"King Kashue, there's King Fahn," Parn called out.

Kashue had abandoned his wounded horse and was fighting with his longsword in both hands. There were only a few knights of Flaim left around him—some had surely been slain, and the rest had been separated from their master in the chaos.

Kashue followed Parn's gaze. His stern expression softened for a moment at the sight of Fahn, but then his eyes widened in surprise.

"That red armor… That must be Beld," Kashue muttered and ran toward Fahn.

Parn pushed past his exhaustion in desperation to follow the Mercenary King.

"King Fahn!" he cried, slashing through goblins and kicking

them aside to reach the lord he'd sworn fealty to only yesterday.

"Parn! It's good to see you safe—and King Kashue, as well."

"I've survived, somehow," Kashue answered, knocking down one of the hideous monsters. "I'm glad you're safe, Your Majesty." Kashue slew the last goblin, then drew near to Fahn. "Emperor Beld is over there."

"I noticed." Fahn replied, biting his lip as he watched the red shadow's slow approach. There was a faint smile on Beld's mouth—and for a moment, it seemed that even the black blade in his hand wore a satisfied grin.

"That's...Emperor Beld?" Parn almost felt like he was being crushed by the Emperor's menacing aura.

Beld was getting closer—close enough that they could have run over to fight him, if they chose. Parn considered it for a moment, but Deedlit blocked him and shook her head.

"Don't get yourself killed. We don't stand a chance against him."

Slayn agreed—he urged the people around him to step back, and prepared some defensive spells.

Parn nodded, not because he didn't think he could win, but because this was clearly a battle between kings.

"We finally meet, Fahn. I haven't seen you since the end of the demon god, hm?" Beld's voice was calmer and more refined than Parn had expected.

Fahn held up a hand to stop Kashue in his tracks. He took up his sword and stepped forward.

"I suppose not," he replied, the holy sword in his hand

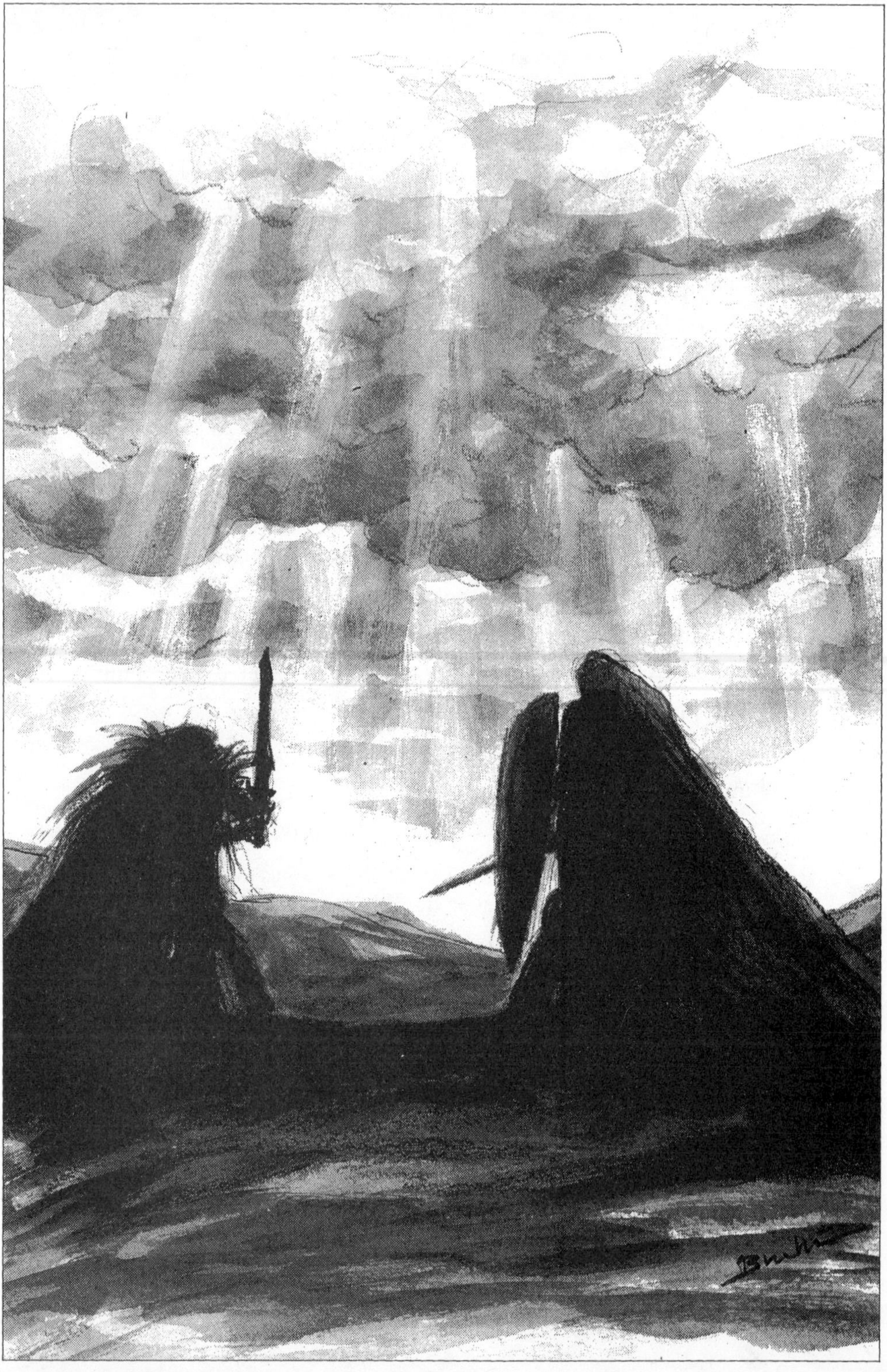

glowing with a pure white aura, the shield carved with the silver cross held high. He closed slowly on Beld.

"Ever since we fought side by side, I've wanted to see how we would fare against each other. I feel lucky to be your enemy now. We can fight to our hearts' content." Beld edged closer to Fahn, swinging the tip of his great black sword back and forth to gauge his timing.

"I never felt the same," Fahn replied. "It's a strange twist of fate, facing you like this, and I wish it weren't so. But I'll accept the challenge anyway." He pointed his blade at the sky and saluted Beld. "Nobody interfere!" Fahn shouted, then without a pause he leapt forward, swinging his sword sideways.

Beld saw the attack coming at the last moment and swung his sword from the shoulder like a bolt of lightning. The force behind his strike seemed like it would crack the earth—but Fahn simply blocked it with his shield, drove the blade back with a heave, and swung toward Beld's torso once more.

With an eerie metallic sound, the blade struck Beld's armor, making sparks fly. Beld let out a small grunt. Fahn's sword tip had cut into the armor, but there was no way to tell if it had even reached his body.

"Not bad, old man!" Once more, Beld attacked with all his strength, the giant blade like a black whirlwind slashing through the air. But Fahn ducked right under, barely seeming to move.

As the duel progressed, loud murmurs erupted from both armies. The pair crossed swords over and over, the sound of steel clashing on steel resounding through the air.

Just watching was practically overwhelming for Parn. Their skills were well matched, and neither fighter seemed to hate the other. They almost looked like close friends sparring.

"King Fahn and Emperor Beld have always been opposites in action and philosophy," Kashue whispered to Parn. "But I hear that they were once trusted comrades in arms. Fate may have made them enemies, but maybe those feelings haven't changed, even now."

"I agree," Etoh said quietly. "Emperor Beld doesn't seem truly evil to me. I believe his heart is pure—I can't help but think that Karla is behind all of this."

"Wort said that they both want to bring lasting peace to Lodoss, even if their methods are different," Slayn murmured. "That vision of peace is a threat to Karla. If she's the reason for this battle, that makes this an even greater tragedy."

Even the slain goblins strewn at their feet were piteous. If they had stayed in their caves, they would never have met such violent ends.

The whole battleground was still—Fahn and Beld were the only things moving as far as the eye could see. Few had survived to watch.

Fahn was slightly more skilled with the sword, but he was an old man, and as the duel stretched on, he began to reach the limits of his endurance and strength. Beld, though, was kept eternally young by the demon sword. As Fahn started to slow down, Beld's strikes began to get past his shield, hitting his armor with a dull clank every time.

"No…" Kashue groaned, and almost took a step.

One of Beld's guards drew his sword and pointed it at him in warning. "Are you a coward, to interfere in a duel?!"

Kashue froze—King Fahn's honor required it.

"King Fahn!" Parn cried in anguish. Kashue had glanced toward the guard, but at Parn's cry, he turned back to the duel.

The sight was heartrending.

Fahn's sword was deeply embedded in Beld's left shoulder, the wound dripping red. Beld's sword had pierced Kind Fahn's breastplate so deeply it had speared the cloak on his back.

A moment later, Fahn pitched forward in a slow collapse.

"King Fahn!" Parn cried again and turned to the man in red armor with hatred in his eyes. "How dare you?!" he screamed, and ran at Beld with his sword in hand.

But the warrior who had stalled Kashue was in Parn's way—otherwise, Parn would have been slain by Beld in one stroke. The other guards who'd been watching used Parn's attack as a signal to rejoin the fray.

"I am Kashue, King of Flaim! Beld, Emperor of Marmo, I am your next opponent!"

Beld had been staring impassively at Fahn's corpse, but at Kashue's challenge, he turned to the man with a faint smile.

"I accept," he said.

With no further warning, Kashue slashed shallowly at Beld's red armor.

"Is that all?" Beld asked, ignoring the attack. He swung his coal-black blade down at Kashue's head with ease.

Kashue dodged at the last moment and attacked again—his blade tore easily through Beld's armor. Kashue felt his sword sink into the muscle of Beld's left hip.

"That's quite the enchanted sword," Beld commented, with no indication that he felt any pain at all.

"Not as fancy as yours," Kashue replied. His longsword had been forged in the days of the ancient kingdom and was enchanted to slice through armor like paper.

"To think that a man like you was Fahn's sworn friend," Beld snorted.

"You think you know me?!" Kashue said. "I respected Fahn, I cared for him. I couldn't be a holy king like he was—just simply a king, going wherever my talent can take me. But I will *never* be a demon king like you!"

Kashue swung his longsword nimbly, putting pressure on Beld with his unending onslaught. Beld blocked each strike with his jet-black blade.

"You have some clever tricks, but all this jumping around— are you sure you're trying to defeat me? Or are you just showing off for your guests?"

Kashue's face stiffened at Beld's words. Beld used the opening to counterattack, lunging for Kashue's throat. He barely dodged, falling over backwards to avoid the blade.

Kashue rolled smoothly back to his feet and thrust. Beld had taken a step forward with another giant swing—but he stopped just short of being impaled on Kashue's blade, having noticed something out of place at the last moment.

"My audience enjoys a good comeback." Kashue smiled fearlessly, withdrew his sword, and reset his stance.

Beld lowered his blade in kind. "Was that little tumbling trick supposed to fool me?"

"You assumed you knew everything about me from my sword, but there is more to me than what you see. I am proud of my whole life. I don't hide where I came from."

"You're a more interesting man than I suspected. But after a battle with Fahn, this fight holds no excitement for me." Beld rotated the shoulder that Fahn had stabbed—it hurt, but it was nothing he couldn't endure. His left leg still supported his weight.

"Lucky for me. I'll just slay you and add that to my list of kingly achievements," Kashue said, holding out his sword horizontally in front of him.

"Good." Beld raised his sword above his head in both hands. "This would be boring otherwise."

"I will end the age of heroes. I want my people to live pleasantly boring and uneventful lives," Kashue said and struck at Beld like lightning.

He had already seen the way Beld fought. The man's strength and intuition were superhuman, and his sword moved like a wild beast. Every movement was powerful, heavy, and precise—he didn't need finesse. But Kashue could tell that his own movements were just a tiny bit faster. And his sword's enchantment meant he didn't need to swing forcefully—a light touch would slice through his enemy's armor.

Extending his elbow and flipping his wrist made a weak strike, but the point of his blade would move quite quickly. In his mind, Kashue could see himself evading the black blade and chopping Beld's head off. He could practically see how it would go.

But then, as if reading his thoughts, Beld sped up.

So, he had another trick up his sleeve. But Kashue was ready to die. And at this rate, he was sure that he and Beld would end up slaying each other. He suspected Beld knew that that was the most likely outcome, too. A thought flashed across Kashue's mind—dying here would mean he'd be called a hero, just like King Fahn and Emperor Beld.

But it was not to be. Out of nowhere, a single arrow struck Beld deep in his left shoulder. It knocked Beld's sword off course—Kashue dodge it with a hair's breadth to spare.

Their eyes locked. Beld's pupils widened as he realized what was about to happen.

Guided by that look, Kashue swung. His blade sheared through the Dark Emperor's neck and sent his head flying into the air. The headless torso collapsed on top of Fahn's corpse.

"Your Majesty!"

The warrior Parn was fighting stopped when he saw Kashue's final blow.

"Kashue, King of Flaim, you *coward!*" the warrior cried, voice dripping with contempt. "My name is Ashram! Remember this—I *will* make you pay for this someday!"

He walked over to where Beld's head had landed, picked it up, then turned and began leaving the battlefield, the other guards following close behind.

For a moment, Parn considered attacking Ashram, but threats aside, he just couldn't bring himself to strike a retreating enemy from behind. He sheathed his sword. Ashram had been a fearsome foe, and Parn had barely held out against him. Defending was all Parn had been able to manage before their fight was interrupted. Parn felt pathetic. He knew he'd have to find a way to get stronger if he wanted to protect the people he loved.

Kashue walked over looking haggard and exhausted, all of his usual spirit gone. It seemed that even the Mercenary King had his limits.

"I'm so glad you're safe," Parn said with a salute.

Kashue sighed. "I defeated him dishonorably. That's not how I wanted it to go, but that's how it played out. I suppose my destiny will be my judge." He frowned at Parn. "I know this will be an awful task, but I need you to deliver King Fahn's body to Roid."

Kashue nodded to Parn's group, then said, "You know…getting to know you all is the only good to come out of this war. I hope you'll visit my country when you get the chance. I would be happy to welcome all of you."

He fell silent for a moment to honor the two dead heroes before him. Then, without another word, he turned and began to lead his remaining knights on the long trek back to Flaim, where another war awaited them.

Twilight was descending on the battlefield. Parn stared dumbfounded at the corpses of the two heroes, vaguely aware that their deaths were truly the end of an era.

"I can't forgive Karla for this," Slayn growled—none of his companions had ever seen him so angry before.

"This is exactly what that witch had planned," Etoh commented with a scowl. "Marmo and Valis are exhausted, and there are civil wars going on all over Lodoss. Despite the influence of Pharis across the island, it will be a long time before there is any peace here." He set his mouth in a determined line. "But that is the task before me. I'm going to help Master Genart rebuild Lodoss."

"You'll do it," Deedlit said with a nod to Etoh. Then she turned to Parn and wrapped him in the tightest hug she could. After a second, Parn hugged her in return, rubbing her back gently—and struggling to breathe in her vice-like grip.

Then he let out a scream, a single word, "Karla!" That one word felt like a release for all the sick emotions swirling inside him. His voice carried across the battlefield, but there was no one left alive to hear him.

The sun was setting, bathing the ground in another layer of red.

"I heard that Elm is dead," Slayn said simply, wondering who had survived the day. "But what of Marmo's court wizard, Wagnard—does he yet live?" With Beld gone, they had no idea what would happen to Marmo...nor what Valis would do without Fahn. The entire future of Lodoss was chaos.

"Let's go home," Deedlit whispered to Parn, her voice full of tears. "Roid will be safe. Let's regroup there. I just... There's too much sadness here. Even the sight of these goblins laid out on the ground is sad. I know that if they came back to life, we'd have to fight them again, but right now...I only wish they'd get up and start moving."

"Mm," Slayn agreed, voice gentle. "We should go back, Parn. We're still alive, and the living can do more than the dead. Let's return and deal with the aftermath of this battle however we can." Slayn couldn't help but frown. He wondered if this was really what he'd wanted.

It made him think of his old friend. He'd been so certain of the divide between absolute good and absolute evil. But there was no justice left in Lodoss now. Evil didn't exist; it was covered in a grey curse forced to maintain eternal equilibrium. Parn's scream had expressed exactly what Slayn wanted to say.

"Karla." Slayn shivered as he whispered the name. "I will never forgive you. You shouldn't even exist."

They carried Fahn's remains back to Roid. The Marmo army had also attacked the capital city, destroying and pillaging parts of it. The city of Roid was mourning to begin with, but the news of the death of their Hero King, their symbol of justice, seemed to turn sadness to despair. The only kings of Lodoss were disorder and chaos.

Genart, high priest of the Pharis Temple, took on the role of defending the public for a while. He released the riches and supplies of the temple to aid the victims of the war.

This gesture did much to keep the country together. Though the windfall only stretched through Roid and its surrounding areas, it was enough to keep Valis from falling apart.

Parn and his friends had much to do. Warriors, wizards, and priests were in great demand. Deedlit, Ghim, and even Wood-chuck all pitched in to maintain public order in Valis.

Before they knew it, a whole month had passed. Valis eventually calmed, and by the time the smiles had returned to the residents' faces, the group had disappeared like they'd never been there at all.

CHAPTER VI

The Daughter of Marfa

1

NEAR THE NORTHERN EDGE OF THE WETLANDS THAT spread northwest of Roid lay Lenoana Lake, also known as Stillness Lake.

The companions were ten days out from Roid when they disembarked on a small island in the lake's center. They had one goal: to confront Karla the grey witch, wizard of the ancient kingdom who had plunged Lodoss into this gruesome war.

Slayn gripped the wand given to them by Magus Wort. Its spell was supposed to be able to neutralize Karla's magic.

The six crept through the fog, none daring to speak. This fog was common on the lake—it was rare for sunlight to reach the water's surface, especially in the winter. Supposedly, the ruins of a city from the ancient kingdom slept on the bottom of the lake.

"This is the perfect place for that witch to live," Parn muttered as he glanced around warily.

Soon, an old mansion loomed out of the fog in front of them. The two-story building was entirely grey—a fitting color for its inhabitant.

Slayn's sharp eyes noticed Ghim rummaging through his pockets. Curious, he leaned closer, catching just a glimpse of gold before it disappeared.

"Is that a new weapon?" he asked. The dwarf was skilled at creating precise gadgets, which he often used to build traps and weapons.

Ghim hesitated for a moment, but then passed over the object in his hand.

"A hairpin—did you make this?" Slayn asked. "What fine work—though, it seems a bit plain to be your handiwork." The wizard handed the pin back to Ghim. The ornament really did seem a bit simple for a dwarven craftsman. Its base had a rainbow of jewels arranged in the shape of a star, and a precise pattern had been carved into the rest of it. But beyond that, however, the only other enhancement was that the metal had merely been polished—though there was space where more jewels or more intricate embellishments could have been added.

"I made this during our stay at the castle in Roid," Ghim said. "You may call it plain, but I consider it my masterpiece. There's no point in overworking a piece like this. Why should an accessory be beautiful on its own? The important part is what it's decorating. When an ornament is adorning its owner in perfect harmony, the result is all the more brilliant. A truly masterful piece of jewelry only shows its beauty when it's worn."

"Is that so...?" Slayn said hesitantly. He didn't quite understand his friend's point.

"I'm about to accomplish what I set out to do," Ghim said. "I will free Leylia from the power of that circlet and send her home to Neese in Tarba."

"Then *that's* why you came all this way..." Slayn muttered as he gazed at the grey mansion standing before them. It was all the more eerie for how silent and empty it seemed—they'd been expecting an attack before they got this close.

Parn and Etoh both felt the tension as they scanned their surroundings, wary of an ambush. They had no idea how many minions Karla had, but they knew she'd been able to carry out several missions simultaneously all over Lodoss. She had to have many people under her command.

Slayn cast a spell, sending the eye of his consciousness flying. He was surprised to find no guards around the mansion. Slayn continued his search, slipping his consciousness inside the building. He expected to be repelled by an enchanted barrier, but he made it inside easily and checked each room uninterrupted.

"There she is!" he cried, voice shrill with nerves. "I see Karla. She's in a room on the second floor, wearing armor and holding a weapon. She...she's looking this way. I'm sure she noticed me—she's smiling..." Slayn closed his mind's eye and shuddered.

"I think she's abandoning this place. There's nobody else inside, and most of the rooms are empty."

"So she's been waiting for us..." Parn slowly drew his sword.

Even from outside, they could sense her anger. To a wizard of the ancient kingdom, the people of Lodoss were the descendants of savages. But over the past months, Parn and his friends had destroyed several of her plans, denounced her whole philosophy, and were now planning to confront her in a battle to the death. Surely, she would want to punish them *personally* for their insolence and would never imagine for a second that she might lose. Such a mindset could be a weakness they could take advantage of.

"All right, let's get started!" Parn cried, gripping his sword.

"Don't forget—we're not here to kill her," Ghim said with a glare at Parn.

"Of course not," Parn said. "I can hold my own without striking anywhere deadly." He turned to glance at Woodchuck, who stood silently at the very back of the group, and added, "Anyway, Woodchuck has the leading role today."

They had planned out their attack carefully. First, Slayn would use the wand to neutralize Karla's magic. Once that was done, Parn, Deedlit, and Ghim would fight her in close combat to keep her attention, protected by Etoh. That would give Woodchuck his chance—he was to sneak up behind Karla and remove the circlet from her head—a vital, dangerous role Woodchuck had volunteered to take on himself.

Parn opened the front door. He stepped inside and led them up the stone steps to the second floor. He was no longer wary, since he knew that if Karla meant to trap them, she would have had guards with her. He headed straight for the room where she waited, knowing that the battle for the fate of Lodoss would be waged there. If they lost, Lodoss would be cursed forever, trapped in that grey balance between good and evil.

Parn gripped the handles of the double doors and flung them wide. Beyond was a large hall built like a throne room, the walls and floor made of polished, black marble. At the very back of the room stood Karla.

"I've been waiting for you," her clear voice echoed through the large hall. She stepped forward and seemed to lock her gaze onto each of them in turn. "I will end this once and for all. Come!" She spread her arms wide, and her right hand held a dagger that emitted a magical light.

"Karla!" Parn yelled, a rush of anger propelling him forward. "You vile witch! You toy with people's fates!" Deedlit and Ghim chased behind him, trying to keep up with Parn's furious dash.

That was the moment Slayn was waiting for. "Laura!" he called in a clear voice, casting the spell of the wand he was holding. He felt a great magical power surging from it.

Karla held out a hand to cast a fire spell at the three fighters charging toward her. A red fireball flared from her graceful fingers, trailing bright flames as it streaked toward them, large and powerful enough to kill them all—but just before it reached them, it fizzled like the flame of a candle being snuffed out.

"What is this?!" For a moment, Karla was bewildered. But she'd seen the wizard wield a wand in the corner of her eye...

Was he able to create a field that neutralized magic? The face of the Great Magus flashed in her mind. Numerous powerful magical items had been created in the glory days of the ancient kingdom. Karla herself had crafted many besides her circlet. She knew that their magic was powerful, but there was always a way to counteract it. They wouldn't be able to seal her for long with such a simple trick.

Ignoring the charging warrior, Karla focused and cast another spell.

"Mana is the source of all! Magic alone can seal magic. Magic alone can breach it!" The moment she finished speaking, a dry snap rang out.

The magic wand crumbled in Slayn's hand; he shuddered in fear. He knew Karla had cast an elimination spell to neutralize the effects of other magic—but this wand should have kept working until its power ran dry, even if counteracted. Karla, however, had destroyed the wand itself. How much magical power would it take to do something like that? Slayn couldn't imagine, but he was certain of one thing: their plan had failed.

"Be careful!" he called out. "She destroyed the magic barrier!" But Parn, Deedlit, and Ghim were already close enough to cross swords.

Etoh prayed for their divine protection, ready to cast holy magic as it was needed. As he waited, he noticed the black shadow running soundlessly along the wall. *Good luck, everyone,* he called out to them in his mind.

With a cry, Parn turned to face Karla from her right. He struck out at the hand holding the dagger. Karla parried easily. Deedlit, on her left, thrust at Karla's leg with her rapier—but the wizard dodged with a light step. All the while she was casting a spell with faultless concentration— if she reached its end, they'd likely all be dead. Parn and Deedlit kept up the pressure, knowing that was all they could do. They hadn't forgotten Wort's warning not to kill her, but they couldn't afford to ease up. If they gave her any opening at all, the dagger would defeat them, no spell required.

Hurry up, Wood! Parn thought. The thief was their only hope left.

"Wake up, Leylia! What did Neese teach you?!" Ghim yelled out from his place right before Karla, his voice shaking the whole room. He was glaring at Karla, not even bothering with a battle stance.

Karla was surprised that the dwarf knew the body she was controlling but knew his efforts would be in vain. Seven years earlier, she had gone to Tarba to take the treasure of the Great Temple of Marfa for herself. She had underestimated the priestess there and, as a consequence, the body she had occupied died. The priestess was incredibly tenacious; she'd survived Karla's most powerful spell, only to strike her through the heart at the last moment.

This woman's consciousness, her memories, are all gone. Her body and mind belong only to me, Karla thought as she continued to chant her spell, never stumbling over a word. Since her magic had been sealed—even if only for a few moments—she wanted to end them with a spell.

"Remember, Leylia! Remember the teachings of Marfa! The love for all of life and all of nature!" the dwarf continued. "Remember why you married all those young couples, why you represented the goddess of matrimony for young people who love each other! You would have never wanted to bring Lodoss into chaos! You would *never* tear apart so many couples and families in such a senseless war!"

Karla's chanting did not pause, but its completion felt unusually slow. The dwarf's words seemed to drag on her more than the onslaught from the other two. When Karla had still occupied her original body, she too had been a follower of Marfa. Taking control of Leylia's body had connected her to the goddess through the priestess's soul, letting her use Marfa's magic.

She didn't know why hearing the deity's name would upset her now, but whenever the dwarf spoke, a strange, foreign feeling welled up inside her. A fierce headache assaulted her. Could it truly be that the priestess of Marfa was regaining something of herself, trying to push Karla out?

Finally, Karla completed her spell.

"Silence!" she yelled. Her left palm was enveloped in an eerie red glow, which she pressed against the dwarf's chest. The dwarf didn't try to dodge. "Remember, Leylia!" he cried and gripped Karla's wrist. The radiance moved from Karla's hand to the dwarf's body, where it faded like it was being absorbed. The dwarf, eyes wide open but unseeing, toppled slowly backwards.

He lay there, still as death.

"Ghim!" the elf girl cried, clearly shocked. Strangely, however,

Karla felt a similar shock reverberate through her.

"Ghim…?" The word left her lips against her will. Her head spun, its ache increasing with every passing moment. Any plan to start casting her next spell vanished.

At that moment, a black shadow loomed up behind her.

"Gotcha!" a victorious cry rang out. Slayn and Etoh saw it happen—the thief, with fast, nimble hands, plucked the circlet from Karla's head. Her coiffed black hair came undone and cascaded down in a disheveled mess. Karla let out a voiceless scream and crumpled to the floor like a puppet with its strings cut.

"Ghim!" Parn yelled, gathering the dwarf's limp form in his arms. He could feel the warmth leaving the other's body.

Parn repeated his name, trying to call back his spirit. Etoh ran over, already praying to Pharis. Slayn held a hand to his chest and just watched, quiet and solemn.

With tears in her eyes, Deedlit pointed her rapier at the unconscious woman on the floor. In a panic, Slayn restrained her.

"Let me go!" Deedlit cried, voice ringing hollow in the empty hall. "She killed Ghim! She *has* to die!"

"Do you really think Ghim would want that?" Slayn asked quietly. "He sacrificed his life to rescue her. I had my suspicions, but I didn't know Ghim's true goal until today. He never told me. But…years ago, he was injured in an accident in the mines. Neese, this woman's mother, was called away from home to tend to him, and she saved his life. But while Neese was gone, her daughter was kidnapped. That must have been when her body was taken over by Karla."

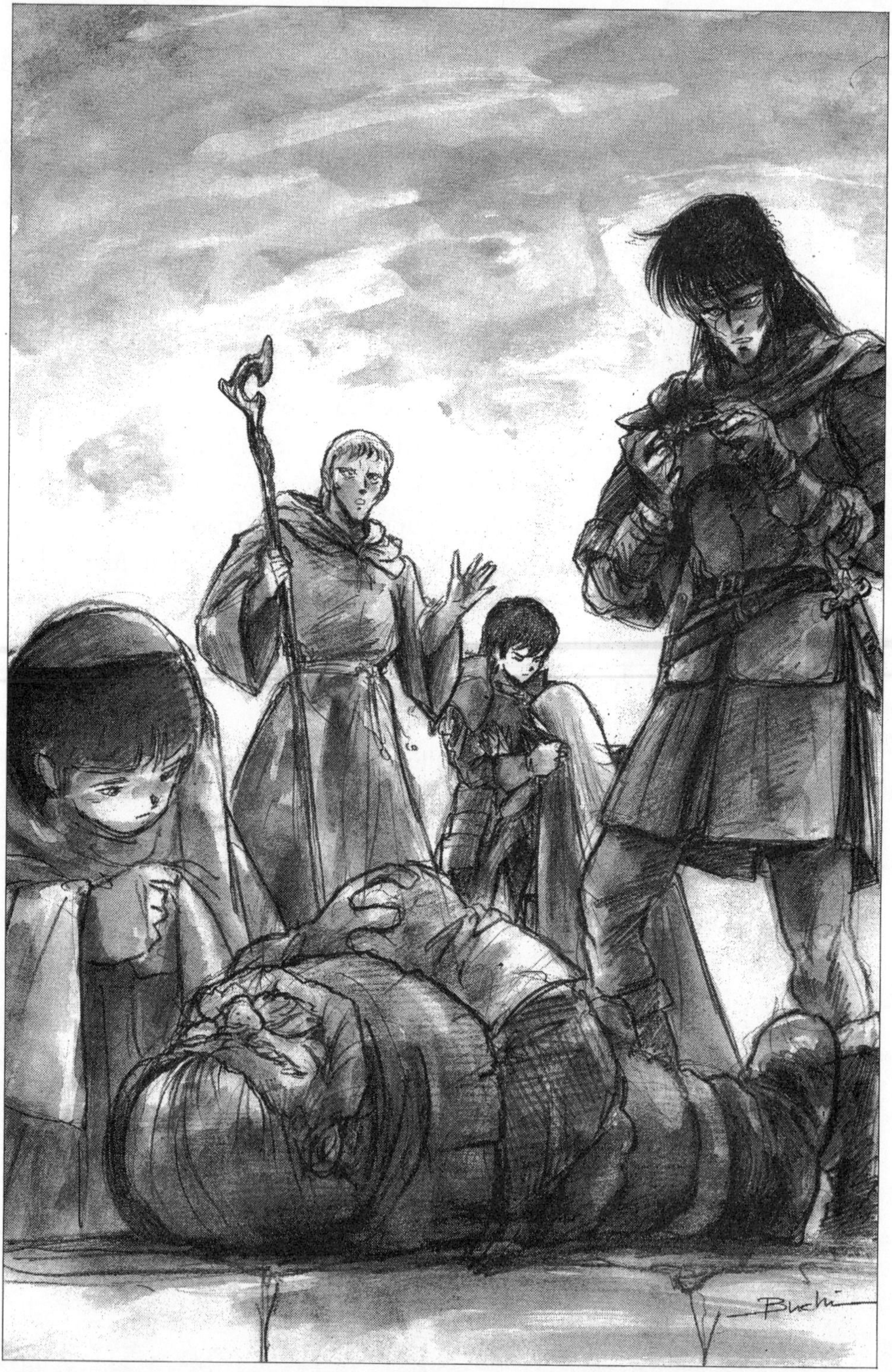

Deedlit let her rapier fall to the floor, shuddering. Parn gently wrapped an arm around her. She lay her cheek against his hand and closed her eyes against the tears.

"It's no use…" Etoh let out a sorrowful sigh. He gently folded Ghim's hands over his chest.

Slayn lowered his eyes and prayed for his friend's soul, fulfilled now that Ghim had kept his promise.

"Poor Ghim." Deedlit couldn't bear to look. She buried her face in Parn's chest, sobbing—perhaps the first time an elf cried over a dwarf in the whole history of Lodoss.

Slayn turned to Woodchuck. "Let's bring this to an end—bring *Karla* to an end. Wood, please. Smash that circlet on the floor and break it. That will finally free Lodoss from the curse, and finish this once and for all."

Through everything, Woodchuck had stood there dumbfounded. He looked down at the motionless dwarf, confused by the empty hole he felt in his heart.

But when Slayn addressed him, he snapped back to his senses and took a wobbly step backwards.

Deedlit could sense that something was wrong. She picked up her rapier.

"Wood? What are you thinking…you can't be serious!" she said sharply.

"Th-that's right," Woodchuck replied, backing away from the others with a few deft steps.

"What're you talking about? Go on, smash it!" Parn watched him, confused.

225

"You guys don't know what it's like...chained up in prison for twenty years. Yeah, I've done bad things. I'm a thief. But that was the only way I could live. I never had Parn's courage or strength, or the smarts or opportunity to study the ancient language like Slayn. I knew the gods had abandoned me before I could remember, so I couldn't follow Pharis, or Marfa, or Rahda...only the Thieves' Guild understood me and accepted me." His eyes grew wider. "But with this circlet...even *I* can be strong. I'll control Karla's power...and I'll get revenge on the world that never wanted me! The world that robbed me of my youth! *Everyone* will remember the name of the great Woodchuck Jay Lancard!"

"Wood! Don't be stupid!" Parn shouted, going pale.

"Parn, you're a good guy," Woodchuck said, his voice almost back to its usual tone. "I like how you don't have a dishonest bone in your body. But you should really learn not to be so trusting, or somebody like me will come along and stab you in the back. And Deed, the forest fairy, blessed with eternal youth and beauty...you were so insufferable at first, but I grew to like you in the end. Etoh the noble, Slayn the wise—and the dead, stubborn dwarf. Traveling with you guys was a lot of fun, you know? We made a good team. I'll always be waiting for you with open arms."

"Wood, this has got to be a joke, right?" Parn cried. "Stop kidding around!"

"Goodbye, Parn. I wish I could've been more like you."

With that, Woodchuck ran for the window. He flung it open, then turned back to face them with a lonely smile.

"Wood!" Parn's scream shook the hall and echoed in

Woodchuck's ears.

He mouthed *goodbye* one last time, then jumped out the window. Parn ran over, but by the time he got there to look out, Woodchuck had already disappeared into the forest.

"Wood, you idiot," Parn groaned, hanging his head low and leaning heavily on the windowsill. Slowly, he approached Ghim's corpse again, knelt by his head, and traced the symbol of Pharis in the air. He took Ghim's hand in his own again, now grown cold. "I swear, I'll avenge you."

Parn stood up and looked at his three remaining companions. "I'm going after him. I don't think he'll be able to control Karla. You guys, take care of the rest."

"I'll go with you," Deedlit said. "Someone has to watch your back—the next Karla will be stealthy." She jumped up and landed lightly at Parn's side.

"Thanks," Parn said with an embarrassed smile. "Um…don't laugh, Deedlit, but I always wanted to be seen as a hero, to be one of the people they tell stories or sing songs about. But it turns out I'm not that kind of person. I should be heading back to Valis to fight as a knight and bring peace back to Lodoss. But…I can't just stand by while the Grey Witch is still lurking in the shadows of history…"

Deedlit nodded silently. She'd known he wanted to be a hero from their first drunken conversation. And while she hadn't seen him as particularly heroic *then*, she thought differently now.

"Your name may not go down in history…but the people of Lodoss will be telling tales of your straightforward stubbornness for years to come," she said with a smile.

"I'm sorry, Parn," Etoh chimed in with a pained expression. "I want to help you, but...I've sworn my life to Pharis. I have to return to Roid to rebuild Valis and the Order of Pharis there."

Parn gave him a nod and a smile, and shook his childhood friend's hand.

"I can't join you either," Slayn said. "I have to carry out Ghim's wishes and accompany Leylia back to Tarba."

"Ghim gave his life for her, so make sure she gets home safe," Parn said and shook Slayn's hand, as well. "See you," he said in simple farewell to his friend. Then he took Deedlit's hand and they left, side by side.

"I couldn't save Ghim or Woodchuck," Etoh mumbled, cursing his powerlessness. He turned one last time to the dwarf's corpse and offered up a prayer for his soul to rest in peace. "This is all I can do for him. I'll leave the rest to you, Slayn."

"I guess this is goodbye," Slayn said with a wave.

"Slayn Starseeker, I hope you find what you're looking for," Etoh said with a warm smile and a wave of his own. Then he turned and left the hall.

2

SLAYN WAS THE ONLY PERSON LEFT MOVING INSIDE Karla's mansion. He sat by Ghim's corpse for a long time, waiting patiently. The dwarf's expression seemed satisfied, as if he had died proud of his life.

"Oh, I almost forgot…" Slayn reached into Ghim's pocket and took out the gold craftwork. The hair ornament was the last thing the dwarf craftsman had made, so the wizard wanted to be sure it got to the person it had been intended for. He slipped it in his robe pocket and went back to waiting for Karla—or rather, Leylia—to regain consciousness.

It didn't take long. A little while later, she stirred and moaned weakly.

"Are you all right?" Slayn asked gently, peering into her face. "How do you feel?"

The woman slowly opened her eyes. Slayn saw his face reflected in those clear blue orbs. She was beautiful—and she looked completely different from when she was under Karla's control. Karla may have controlled her body and mind, but she couldn't own her nature—and true beauty originated in the soul.

"Wh-who are you?" she asked, clearly confused. "What am I doing here?"

A moment later, her face went pale and her features twisted in torment.

Slayn knew what must be happening—she was regaining the memories of everything that had happened under Karla's control. Slayn winced in sympathy—it seemed cruel that she'd have to carry those memories. But this was her destiny; it was an ordeal she must endure.

Leylia pushed herself up on her elbows and looked around quickly. After a moment, she caught sight of Ghim's body and stared.

"Ghim...the kind dwarf craftsman..." she murmured, voice hoarse. Tears overflowed her eyes. "I do remember. Your voice... it reached me when I was asleep in the darkness, trapped deep in my own mind. I thought it was all just a nightmare...but this is real..." She staggered to her feet and stumbled over to Ghim's corpse. She took his hand gently, then collapsed beside him, clinging to the body that could never speak to her ever again.

"I wish it had all been a dream..." she said, her tears spilling silently. "If only all of this were a nightmare I could wake up from back at Tarba temple. But... But this is reality..." A sob rose in her throat, and soon she was crying and cursing herself uncontrollably.

Slayn stood by and waited for the tears to purge her sadness.

Leylia thought she might cry forever, but gradually her sobbing subsided, then stopped.

"What I've done can never be taken back," she said, voice shaky but tears at bay for now. "I killed Ghim and so many others...and brought war to Lodoss. How could I possible atone for a sin that horrible?!" She looked to the robed man who'd been sitting beside her when she woke, desperate for answers.

"Live on," he said simply but firmly. His eyes were gentle, but she didn't see pity in his gaze, just deep knowledge and understanding. Looking at him, the pain in her heart seemed to lighten, just a little.

"This isn't your sin," he continued. "You weren't the one who did all of those things. It was Karla, the witch of the ancient kingdom. You should put it all behind you, if you can...though I suspect that won't be possible." He gave her a knowing look. "So, you must confront it. Save as many lives as you can. Do whatever you can to bring peace to Lodoss. As a priestess of Marfa, there is so much you can do. But before all of that…return to Tarba and put your mother's worries to rest. Ghim's one goal through all of this was to bring you home."

Leylia sat silently, biting her lip so hard it drew blood. "All right," she murmured. He was right—her death would accomplish nothing, and the war had just begun. "I will offer the rest of my life to serve Lodoss…and I'll go home to Tarba to see my mother."

Slayn nodded and shot her a smile. "I'll come with you, Priestess of Marfa. My name is Slayn Starseeker, and I'm a wizard from the Wizard Academy. I'd like to help you."

"I remember you," she said. "I remember everything from the past seven years."

Slayn's heart ached for Leylia. It would be hard for her to move past her pain, but her smile would come back one day. He would help her any way he could. He couldn't wield a sword like Parn, but his magic would surely come in handy.

Slayn took Leylia's arm and led her out of Karla's mansion. Along the way, he cast combustion spells to light fires around the mansion, and soon the entire building was engulfed in flames.

In that fire, Ghim's soul would depart peacefully and find its way home to the world where the fae folk of the earth dwelled.

They stayed by the mansion until the last of the embers died down. After that, they started walking, Slayn letting Leylia lead.

The fog lifted, and early autumn sunlight shone down on them.

Slayn suddenly remembered the hair ornament in his pocket. He took it out, looking it over one more time.

"May I…?" he asked, and when she nodded, he placed the ornament in her hair. He took in the sight with a sigh. "Ghim was right…" As soon as it was in place in her hair, the ornament that had seemed so plain started to shine. It caught the light and turned it to rainbows, like it had finally found the one place it belonged. Ghim had known exactly what he was doing. "Beauty from harmony," he said, then explained, "Ghim made this hairpin as a gift for you."

As Slayn gazed into her red-rimmed eyes, he found he couldn't look away. The hairpin twinkled against her jet-black hair, and as he gazed upon her, a new thought gripped him.

I may have found my star.

Afterword

by Hitoshi Yasuda

*Lodoss was a remote island a fortnight's voyage south
of the Alecrast continent. [...] Some people on the
continent called Lodoss "The Cursed Island"...*

THIS BRINGS BACK SO MANY MEMORIES FOR ME. Whether you read this book in Japanese when it first came out, or became a fan later, this passage has probably always been somewhere in a corner of your heart.

When I opened the book, I thought I'd come across that passage immediately, but it turns out, it was actually at the beginning of section two of chapter one. I thought I'd remembered most of the book fairly accurately, but memories are strange—I was slightly off. But I guess that's to be expected since it's been 25 years since *Record of Lodoss War: The Grey Witch* was first published.

Record of Lodoss War: The Grey Witch was released in Japan on April 10, 1988, soon after Kadokawa Sneaker Books was founded. At the time, the "light novel" genre was new (only represented by Asahi Sonorama Books), so Sneaker Books was a sort-of pioneer.

Before then, I had been involved in the industry as a transla-tor of science fiction, but I had no way of knowing how a title in this brand new field would fare. The anxiety and accompany-ing anticipation practically kept me up at night. (Okay, I admit I was also under deadline to translate *Dragonlance*, which was published at around the same time.)

They say fear is often worse than the danger itself. Once pub-lished, *Record of Lodoss War: The Grey Witch* flew off the shelves, and the series came to its conclusion in seven books containing five story arcs. After that, the sequels came out smoothly, the genre expanded, and after a quarter century, what began with *Lodoss War* grew into light fantasy and the "light novel" genre we know today.

Before I go any further, since most people probably don't know, I wanted to explain the relationship between myself, Ryo Mizuno, *Lodoss War*, and this new genre.

First, the novel itself was the brainchild of Ryo Mizuno, the author. However, in the process of its creation, those of us who belonged to Group SNE (or its predecessor) along with Ryo Mizuno provided contributions through RPGs and "replays."

The RPGs (Role-Playing Games) I'm talking about here aren't the video games that are so popular in Japan. I'm talk-ing about their root form, the dice-throwing, talking-out-loud "tabletop RPGs." A TRPG is first and foremost a game, but ideally has a robust, ever-changing story at its center, and the players become the characters and take an active role in creating that story. People who enjoy computer RPGs are familiar with how fun they are. But, as they are the original form, TRPGs far surpass computer RPGs in their versatility and realism (though they take a lot more work). You understand if you've ever read an "RPG replay," which is basically a session report documenting the playthrough of a TRPG.

So *Lodoss War* was first played as a TRPG—Ryo Mizuno described this wonderful world, and we took that and expanded it humorously, and sometimes irreverently. It gained wider visibility through a new format called a replay RPG (adapted by Ryo Mizuno and myself), and it gained general recognition with the novel *Lodoss War* (that Ryo Mizuno rewrote entirely).

I think this makes the novel *Lodoss War* unique. A world that began in Ryo Mizuno's brain was honed through playing in it via TRPGs; sharing that story gave rise to the new format—replays. It then went through another round of rewrites by the original world creator, who transformed that adventure into a brand new novel.

For me, a TRPG is a game, but it's also a story advanced through group discussion. So I think it's a format where the collective unconscious comes through more easily. When it's adapted into a replay or a novel, the honing process doesn't simply discard the excess elements present in the game. The group summons all these interesting impurities, and these emergent odd and remarkable bits remain, while the unnecessary elements are pruned. I think this intensified as *Lodoss War* went through the adaptation process.

Every medium has its own charms, of course. It's fascinating to see this common world expressed in all those different ways.

After that, the subsequent novels further expanded Ryo Mizuno's world. The sequel, *Record of Lodoss War 2: Blazing Devil*, was a great lyric poem written without first going through a game iteration. The series then returned to its TRPG roots in part 3... *Lodoss* continued in this changing style all the way through.

I hope people will continue to enjoy this archetypal series beginning with this book: *Record of Lodoss War: The Grey Witch*.

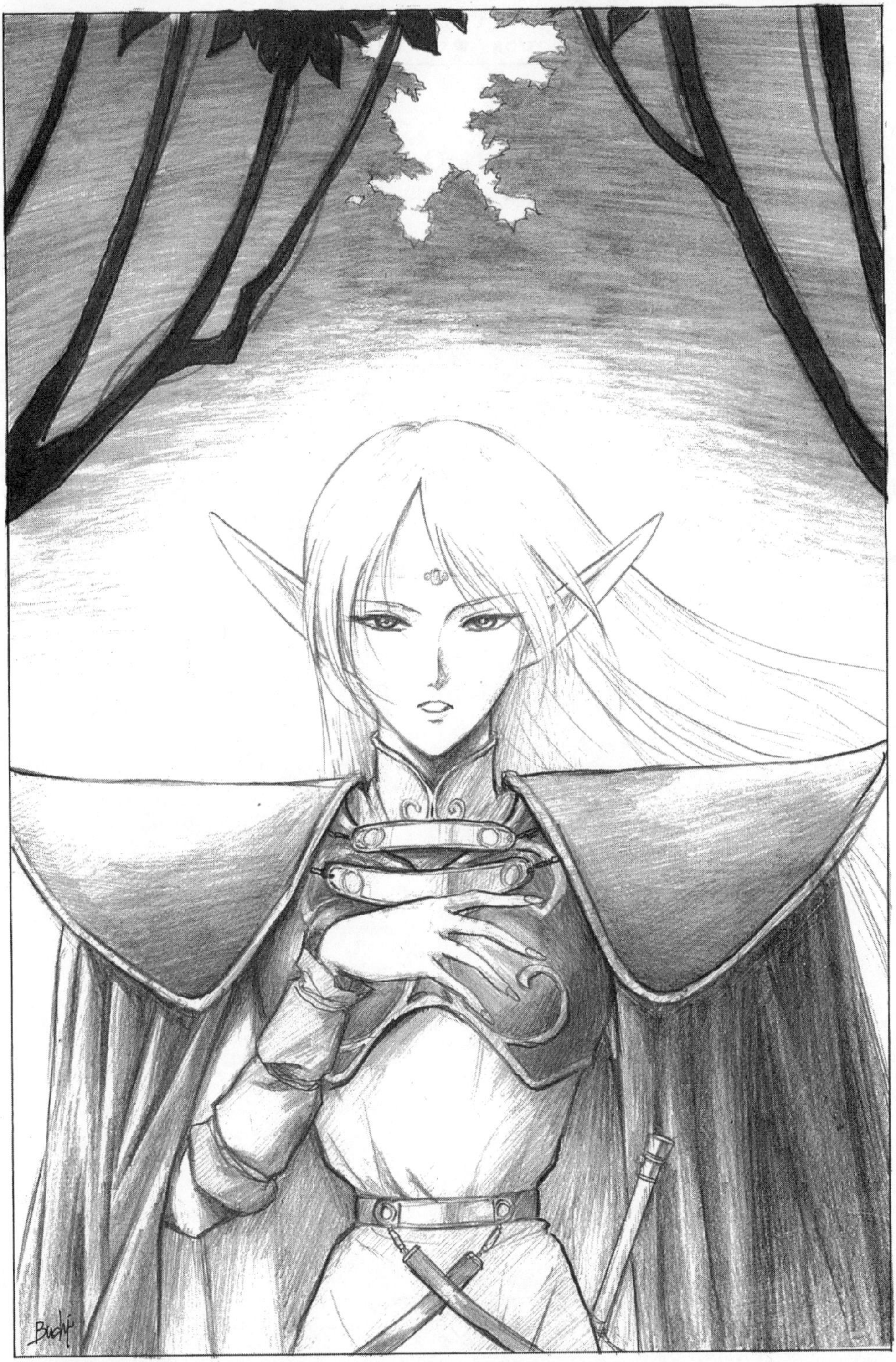

Ryo Mizuno was born in 1963 in Osaka. His first book, *Record of Lodoss War: The Grey Witch*, was published in 1988 by Kadokawa Sneaker Books. An author and game designer, he penned the *Lodoss* series, its sibling franchise *Rune Soldier*, the sci-fi series *Starship Operators*, and the fantasy series *Record of Grancrest War*.

GALLERY OF LODOSS

YUTAKA IZUBUCHI

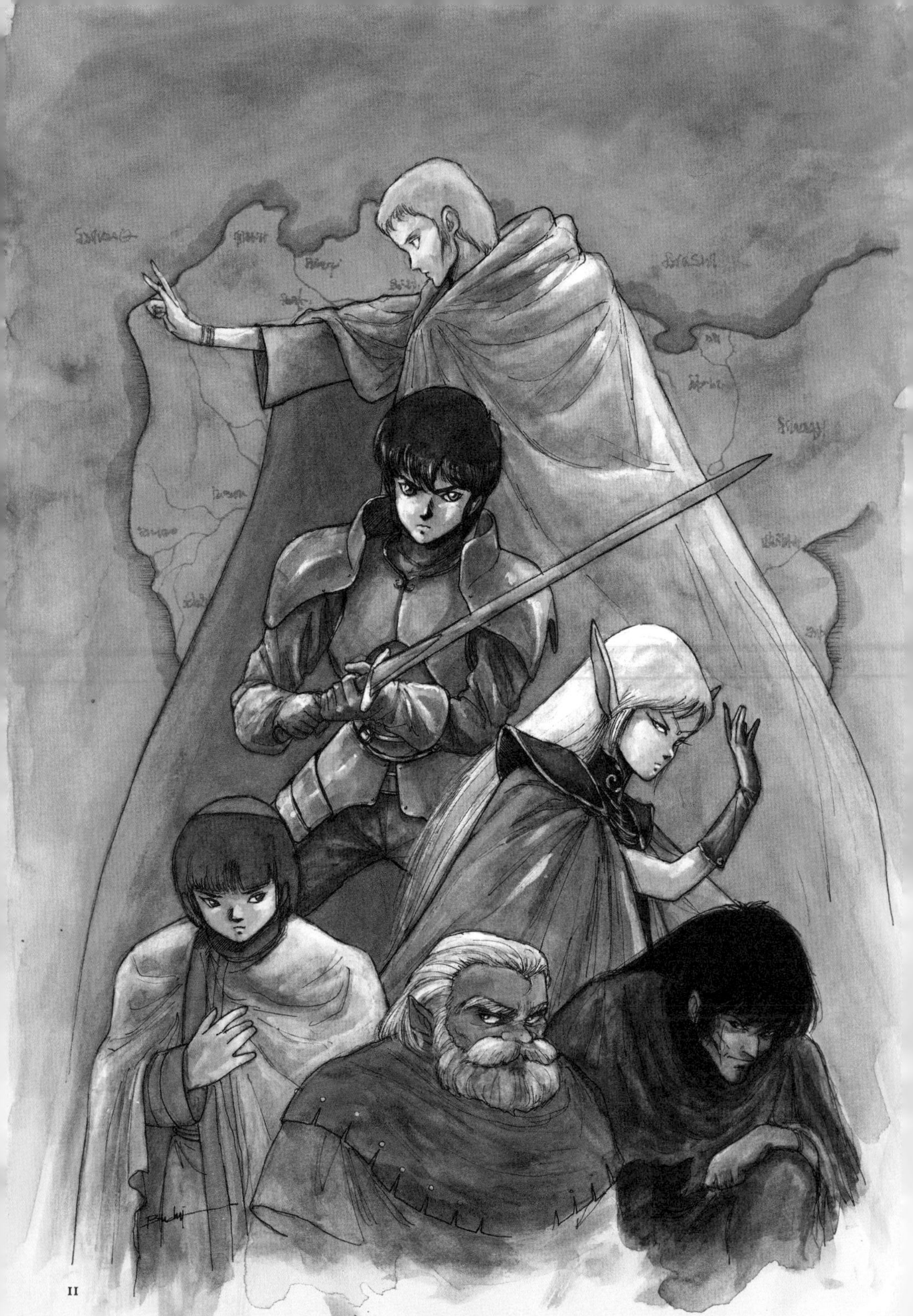

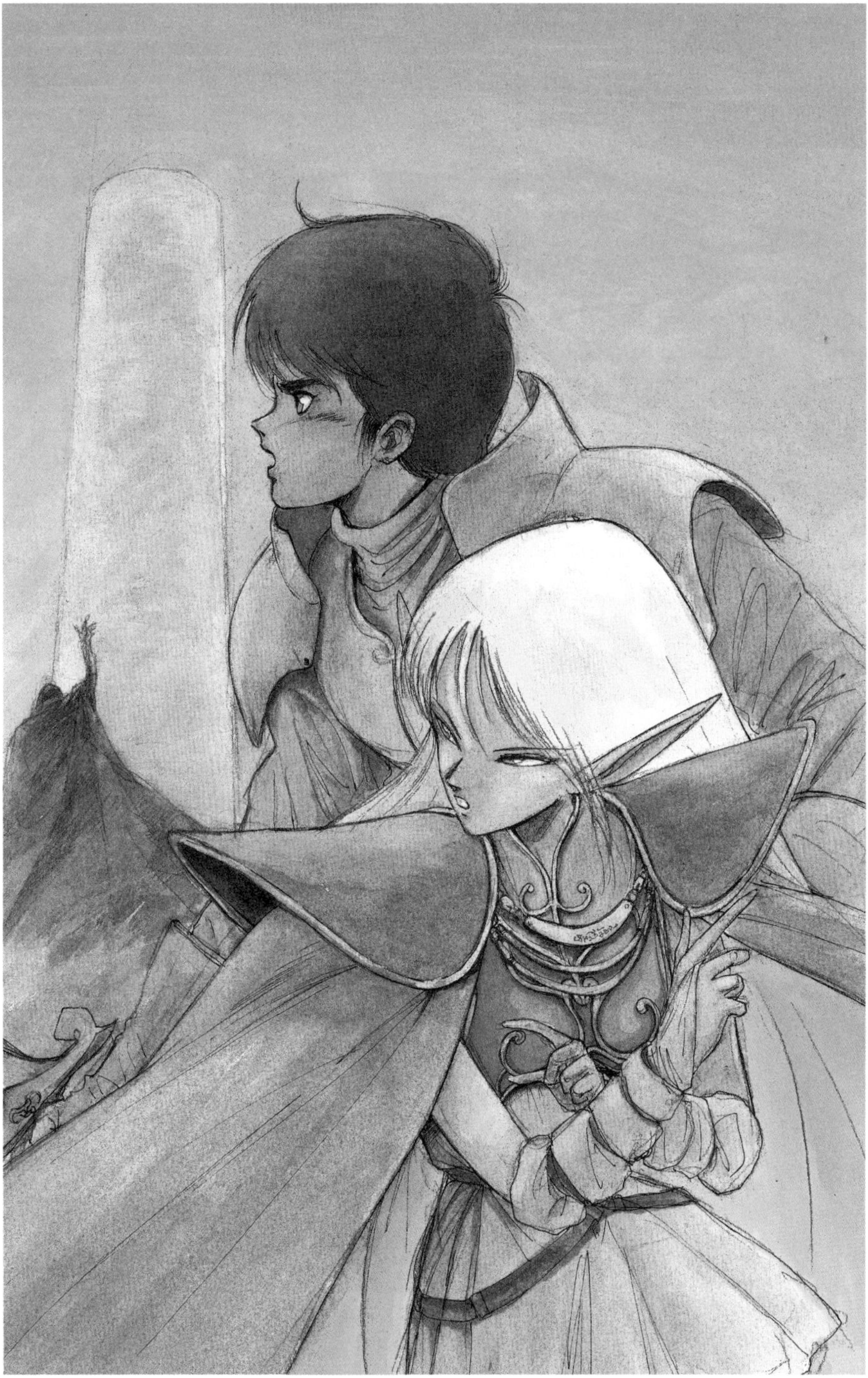

Record of Lodoss War III

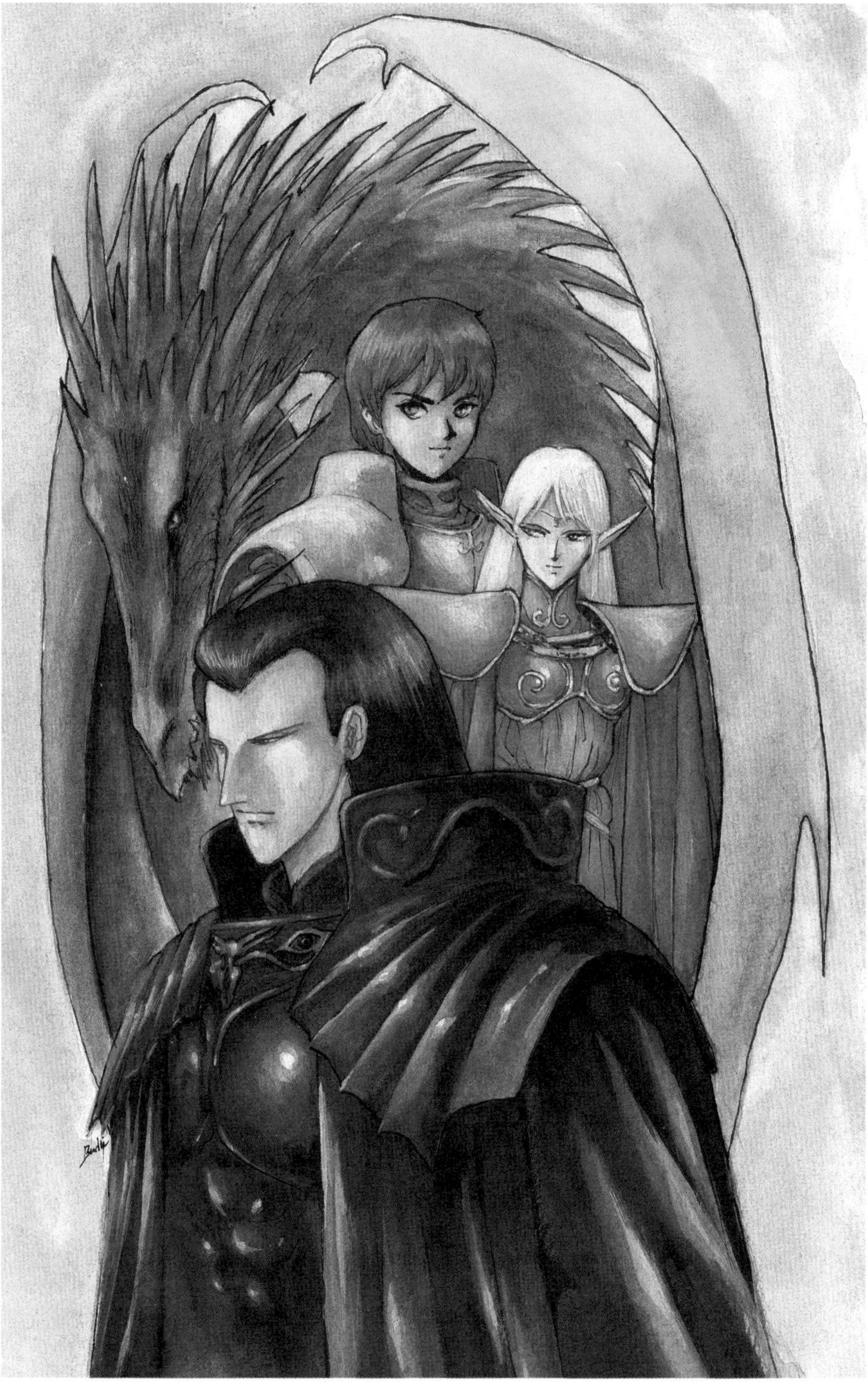

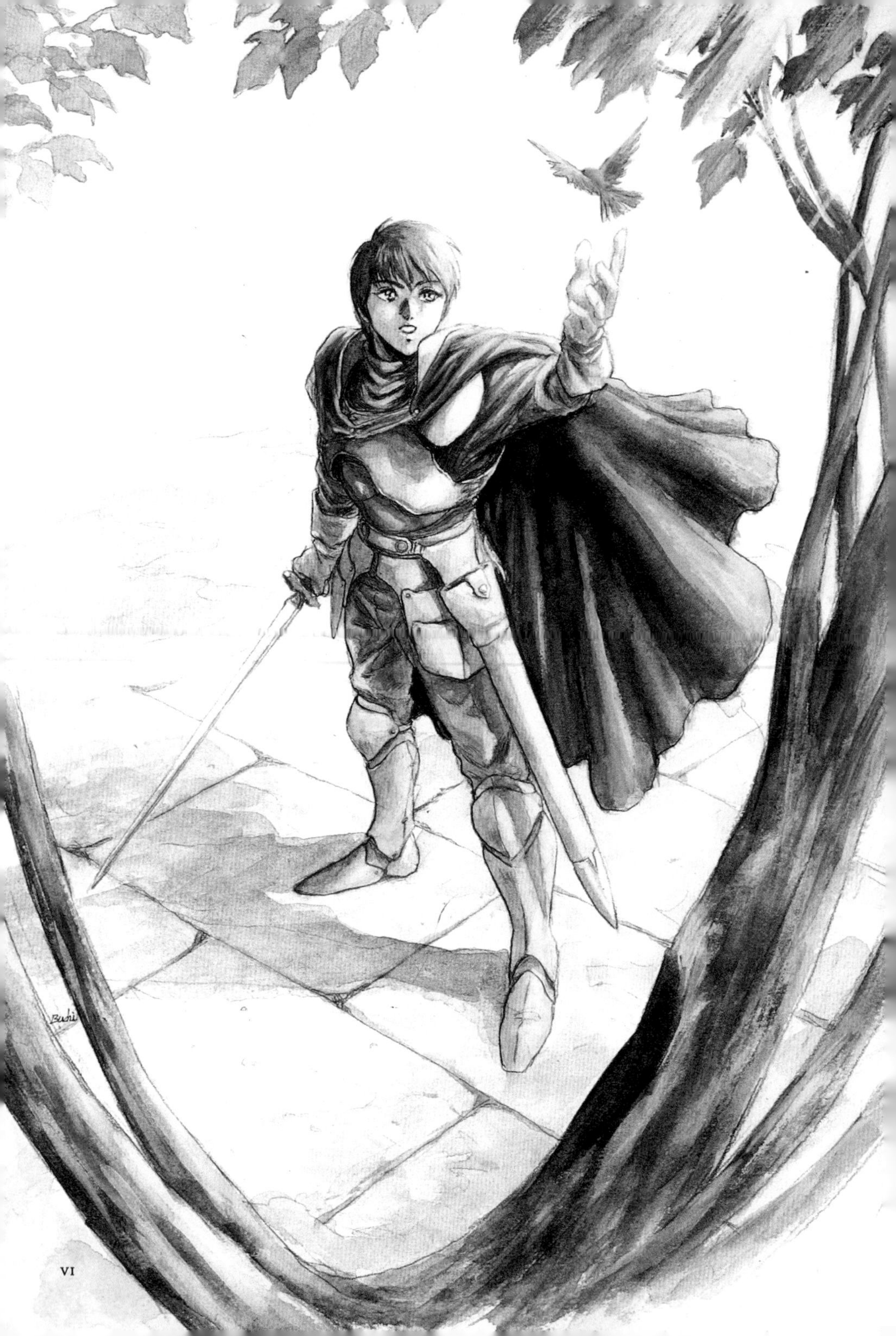

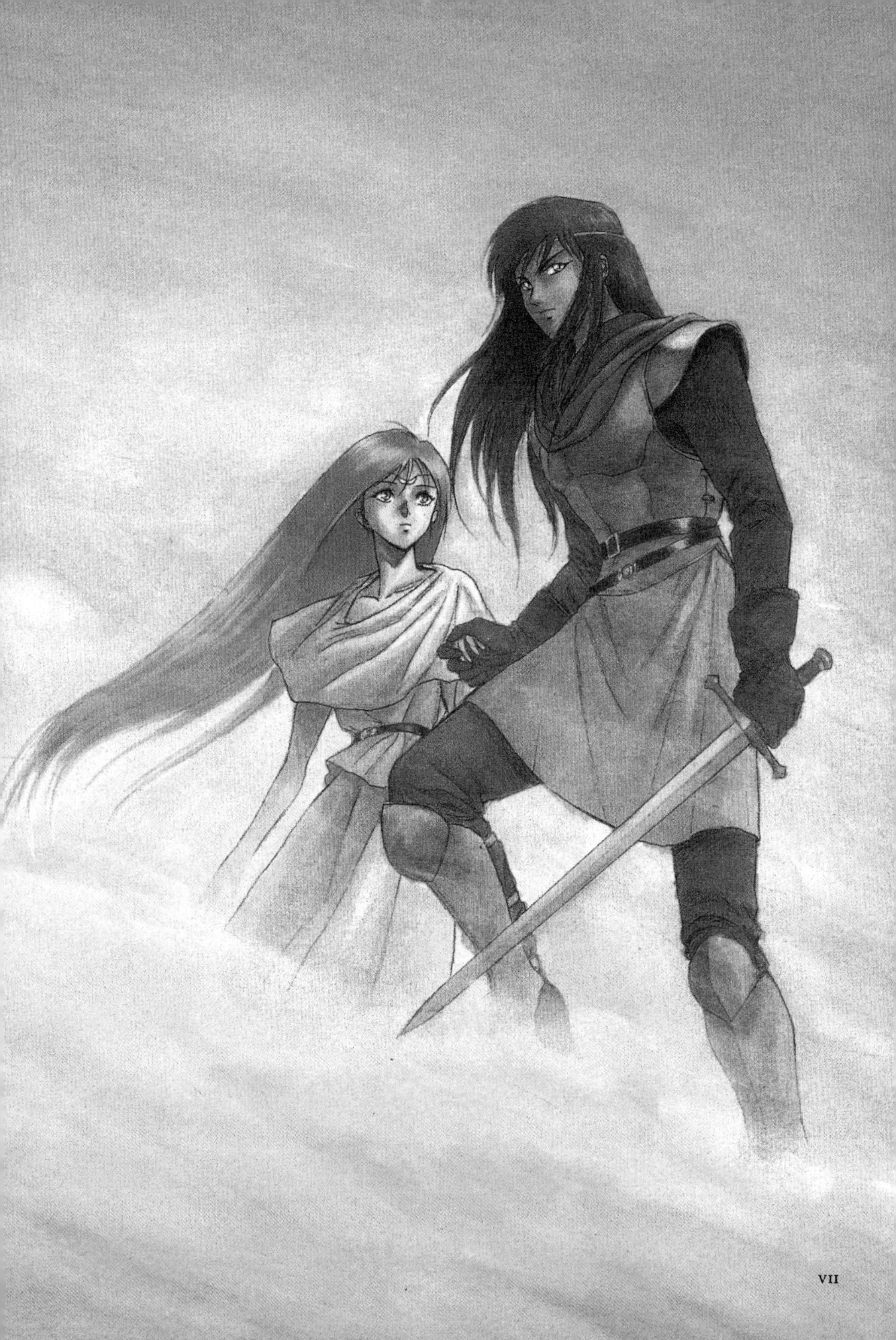

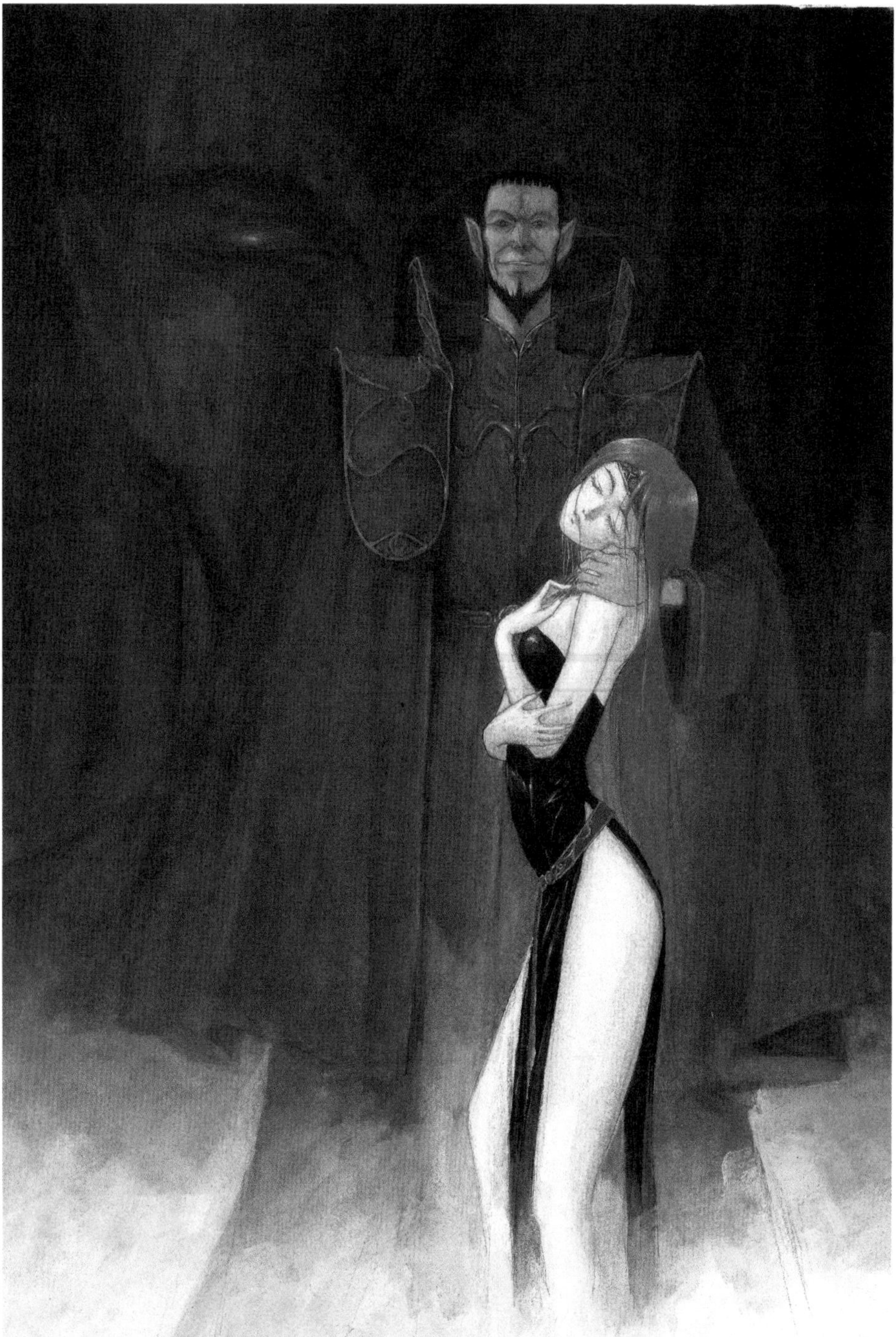

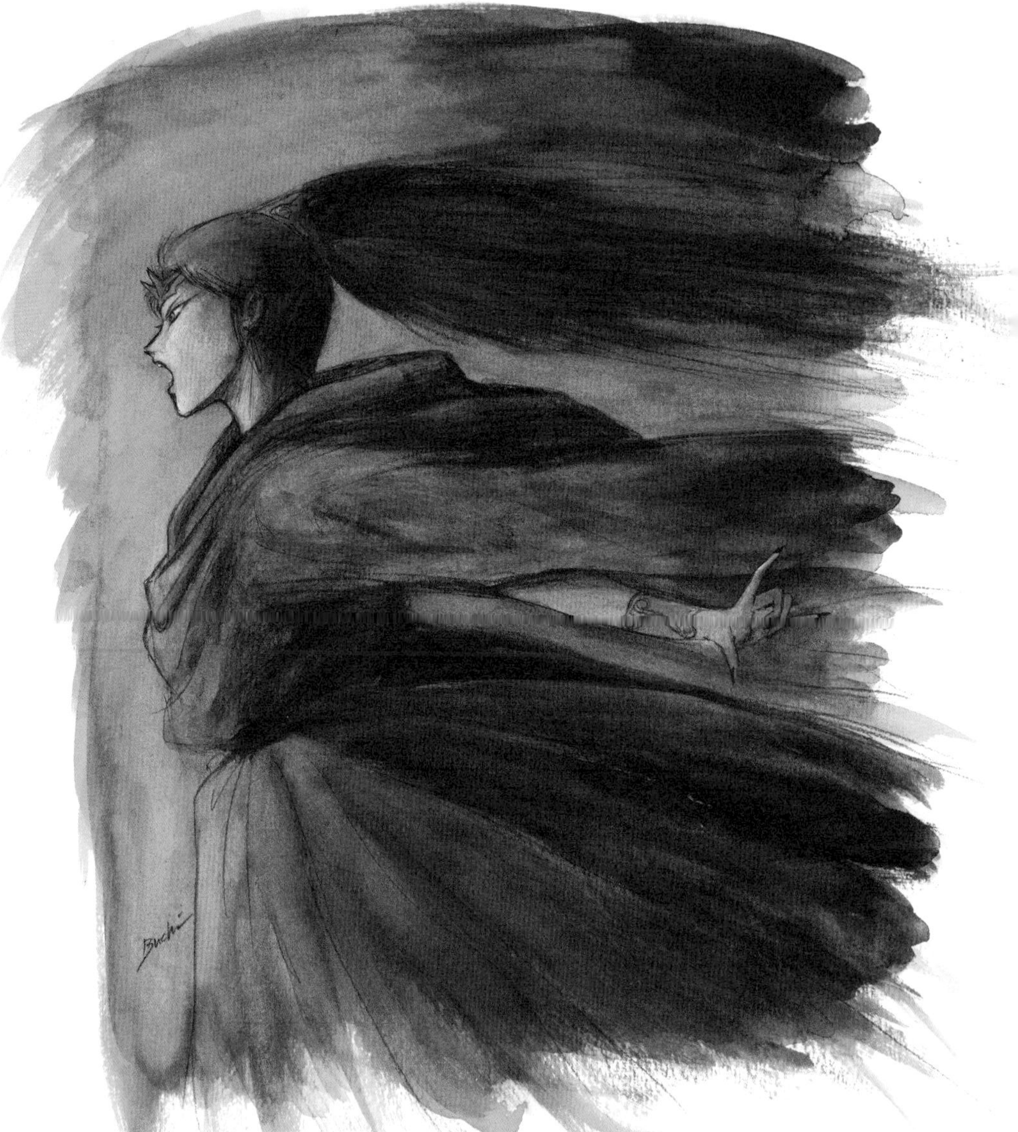
Buchi

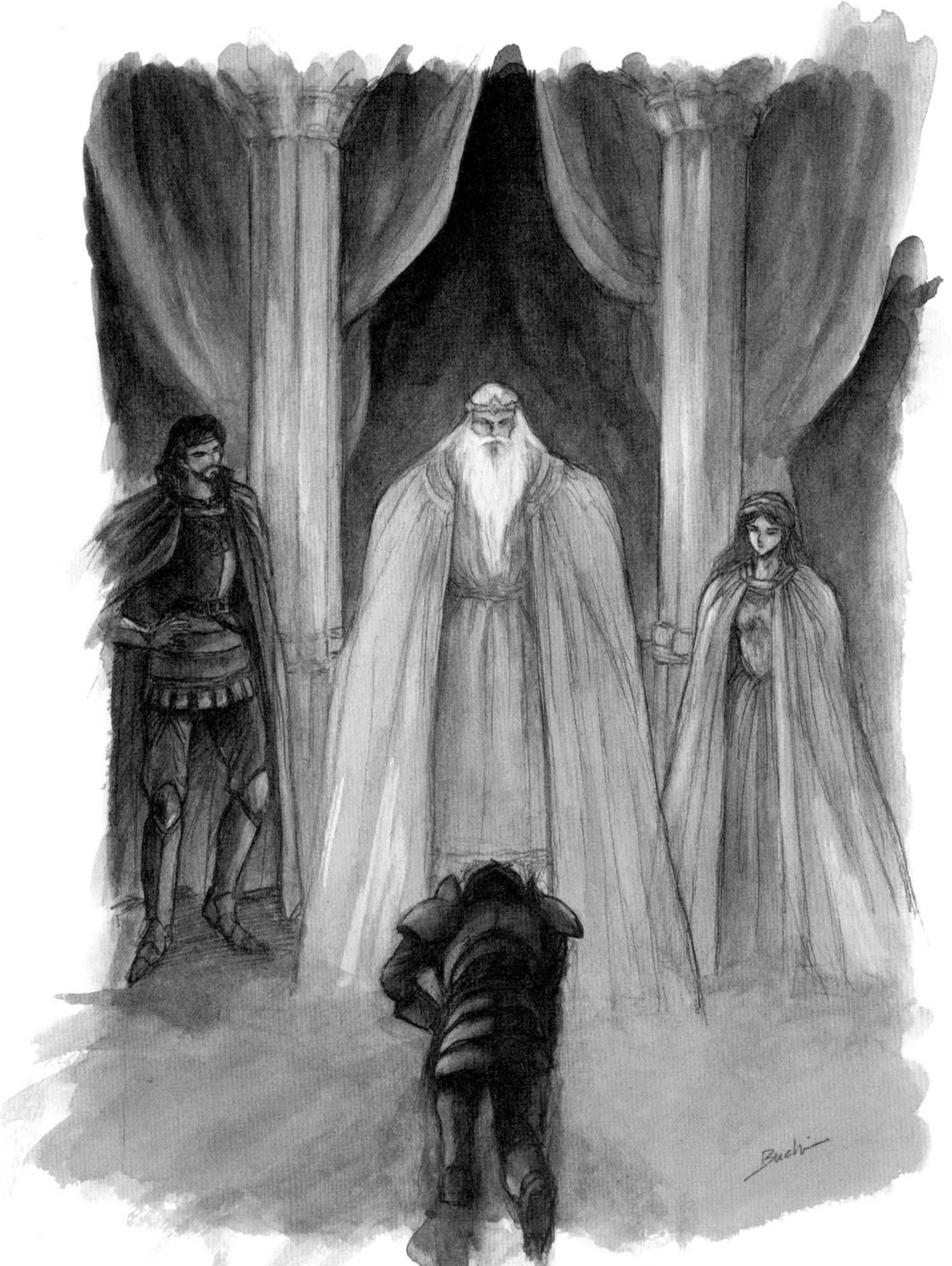
Buchi

Record of Lodoss War.
Buditi

KARLA

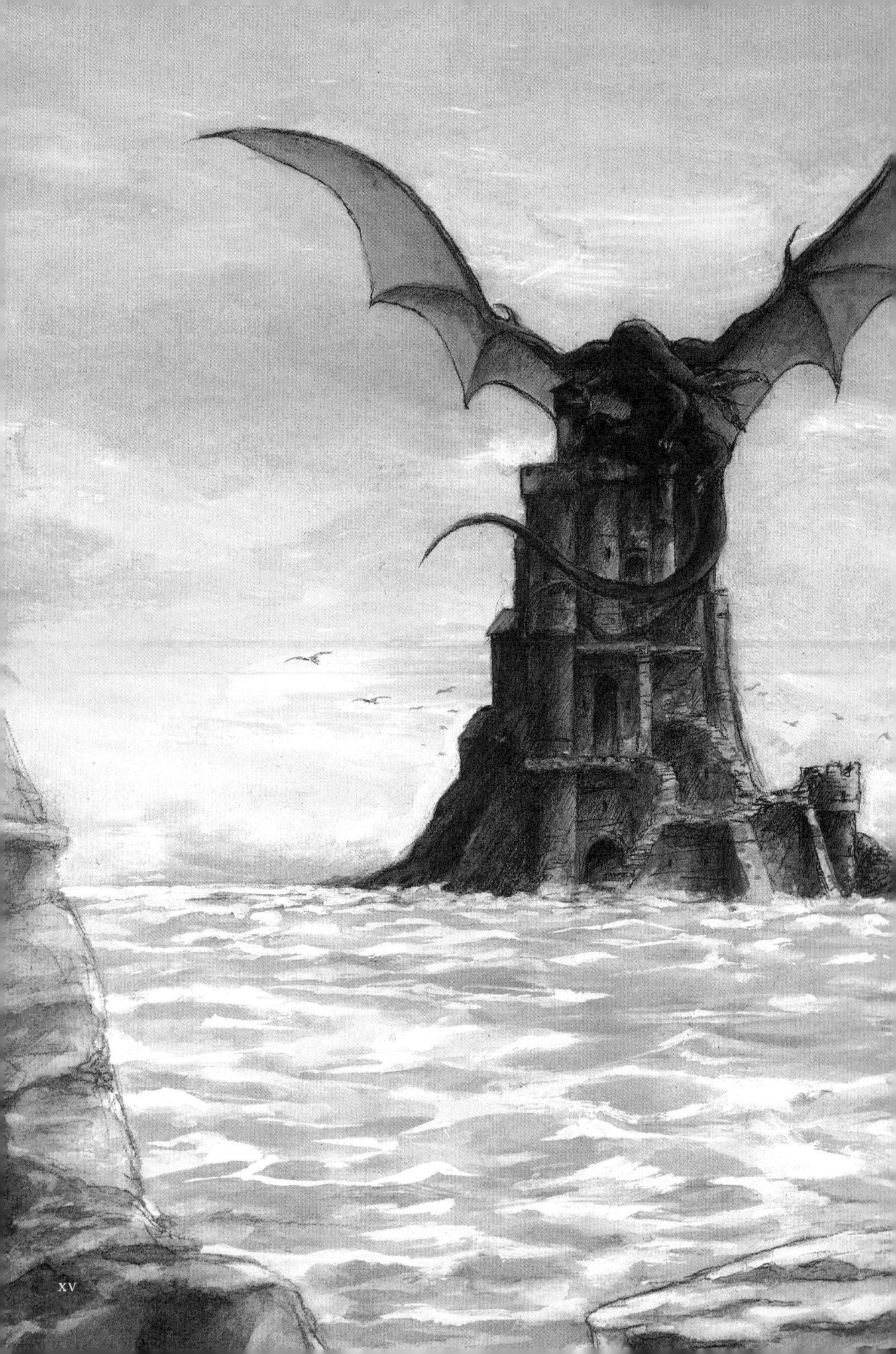

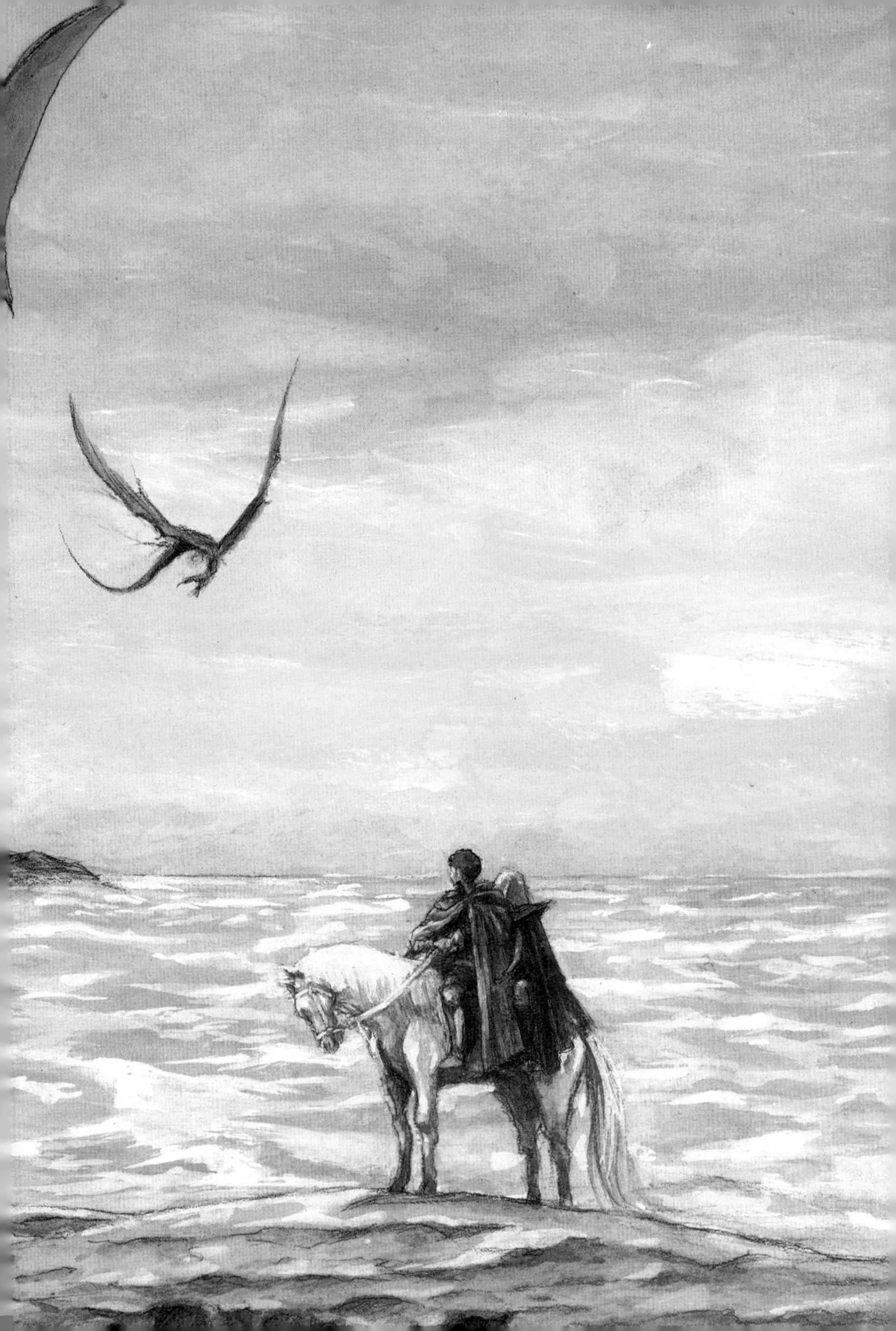

ILLUSTRATIONS BY YUTAKA IZUBUCHI